SLEEPING WITH RANDOM BEASTS

sleeping
with
random
beasts

karin goodwin

CHRONICLE BOOKS

SAN FRANCISCO

Library of Congress Cataloging-in-Publication Data:
Goodwin, Karin.
    Sleeping with random beasts / by Karin Goodwin.
        p.   cm.
    ISBN 0-8118-1989-2
    I. title.
    PS3557.06223S57   1997
    813'.54—dc21   97-22559
                                    CIP

Book and jacket design: Pamela Geismar
Composition: Candace Creasy, Blue Friday
Jacket photograph copyright © 1998 by Ann Giordano.

Printed in the United States of America.

Distributed in Canada by
Raincoast Books
8680 Cambie Street
Vancouver, B.C. V6P 6M9

10 9 8 7 6 5 4 3 2 1

Chronicle Books
85 Second Street
San Francisco, CA 94105

Web Site: www.chronbooks.com

1 It's Friday, October 30th, and I'm sitting on the Night Owl in South Station, Boston, pillow at the window and ticket in hand, willing my stomach to settle and trying to remember where I forwarded my mail. I'm hoping, vaguely, that these jeans look all right and that the heater works properly and that nothing terrible happens to me on this trip. On other levels I'm trying mentally to separate romantic love from marriage, humming the theme from *Midnight Cowboy* and wondering if Harrison Ford knows he's a replicant. I'm also wondering where in my pack I stashed the booze and if I had enough fiber today.

Behind me, and panting at my heels, are too many years at a boring bank, two and a half years with a boozer boyfriend, two years total under able analysis, and a little gray cat I rescued, then abandoned. I've left behind me also a couple of fine friends, about sixty pounds of fat and some heavy furniture I didn't want to deal with. Shannon has the furniture and Monica has my books. I'm more inclined to come back for the books than I am for the bed, and they both know it.

Sitting here, my hands cold with nerves, my brain on espresso speed, I'm watching the last stragglers running for the door and part of me is waiting for the slow, slow, almost imperceptible moment when the train begins to move out and I begin to calm down. I still can't believe I'm doing this, I can't believe these are my bags and my tickets and my Scotch. And my camera, a secondhand Canon AE-1 with three lenses and a flash that I haggled over a little bit and ended up buying for five hundred bucks at a pawn shop down by the Park Street T. Maybe five hundred dollars is a lot of money for a used camera, but the lenses are good, they threw in a camera bag, and one of the men asked me out. It's hard to get that model Canon anymore and he was cute, so even though I of course said no, I consider it money well spent.

When I told Travis I was going he said, "Good idea. Wasn't it mine? Do you need any money?" If Travis were a horse he'd be a high-stepping, mane-tossing, restless Palomino. He's my greatest friend and the kind of guy you can tell anything to and wish you could marry because then life would be easy and you would always have someone to watch movies with and your kids would be smart and good-looking and maybe even well adjusted as well as interesting. But that's not the way things go, not that easily, not for us tortured modern types.

Travis didn't like Patrick and was glad when we called the whole thing off. He called Pat the Coyote. Pat called him the Faggot from Farmington. Technically Trav isn't a faggot and he's not even from Farmington but for Pat the rhyme was always more important than the truth.

I didn't take any of his money. I told him to save it for when I was destitute and pregnant in Mexico and he told me that if I called him destitute and pregnant from Mexico he would give the money to the NRA.

Travis is this kind of friend: He knew me in Albuquerque when my hair was blond and I would have starved except for the meals he bought me. He knew about my herpes the same day I did and that afternoon gave me my first Valium, although he says now that if he'd known how much I came to rely on them he would have let me suffer. I called him from Cincinnati when Hank died and he drove five hours across state lines to meet me at the Amarillo airport and take me to the funeral. He flew to Boston one July and accompanied me to the Beacon Street Clinic when Stuart, who never put his foot down about anything, put his foot down about having a child. He knew me when I was fat and he knew me when I was thin and I think he loved me always, all the way through. In a perfect world we would have ended up together, married, with a whole mess of kids, seeing movies for money.

We were so unsuited to growing up out West. The difference is that I talk about New Mexico like the lost continent and he talks about it like a narrow escape from hell.

We just passed Route 128, the third and outermost Boston stop, and still no one's sitting next to me. Excellent. What I wish is that I had the guts to whip out my camera and take pictures of everyone, but you probably have to get permission or something. Anyway, I'm better at small groups and solo shots, so never mind.

I won a photography prize once, in twelfth grade. I won it for a picture I took of my sister Sarah standing smack in the path of an eighteen-wheeler that was barreling for her down a New Mexico state road. It's the road that leads to Tucumcari, after it drops off the edge of the caprock and unfolds across the desert like unrolled toilet paper. The photograph was black and white and it was early winter and she was naked. We had to stand there, like that, for fifteen minutes before a truck came up. Her nose was running from the wind but you couldn't see it in the picture because mostly you see the back of her, hair blowing the same color as the sand, shoulders accusing, hip cocked.

In the picture Sarah looks threatening and it's the driver you feel sorry for. My photography teacher loved it. Dad didn't. He said, "I wouldn't mind if it were at least a good photograph, but it isn't. This isn't art, Eleanor." Luckily the judges came from Albuquerque and didn't care that the naked girl in the road was my sister. One of them told me, "You need to do something with this."

I had no idea what she was talking about so I didn't say anything, but then she awarded me the two-hundred-dollar first prize. I wanted a scholarship to the photography equivalent of Julliard, whatever that may be, but the two hundred dollars came in pretty handy. It made me think to myself, I can leave, you know. I was talking to Mom, in my head, and I wasn't afraid of her. I can go places, I told her. I can do better than this dump.

Mom was living in Texas with Hank and Sarah, and I had moved back to Remie by then, but the next time I was up on a visit she said to me, before I even opened my mouth, "Don't start with me, Eleanor May. I don't know what you've done to think you're so high and mighty but keep that attitude for your father and your other house, do you hear me? One day when you're on your own you can come in here with your shoulders set and that look on your face but for now you can just settle down and get a start on your bathroom. And this time get behind the faucets."

Well, there went Providence, Rhode Island, and with it the last of the pasty white commuter types. Everyone on this train now is traveling somewhere more special than just home at the end of a working week. Commuting is such a waste of three hours a day, but it's precisely what people deserve for worshipping subdivisions and homogeneity. I see those suburban parents coming into Boston with their children on weekends, squawking at every pigeon and passerby as if we wanted nothing more than to kidnap and torture people with a 508 area code and I just want to walk up and slap the bovine looks off their faces. Instead I end up telling them where the Cheers bar is and a good place to find public bathrooms.

Frankly, Scarlet, I think it's time to pull out the Dewars.

"Excuse me, miss, is anyone sitting here?"

"No, go ahead." Fuck off, would you?

"You look so comfortable, I hate to . . ."

"No no, it's all right." Fuck fuck fuck. An aging Yankee with those long pelvic bones I hate so much. What's he doing on the train?

"A Scotch drinker, huh?"

Ah small talk, when will I learn to love it? "Looks like it." Oh, lighten up, Bean, the man is harmless. "Would you like some?"

"No no, not for me."

Of course not. He thinks sharing is for poor people.

"Is that a good book?"

"Yes."

"It looks complicated." He means he's surprised I'm not reading Danielle Steel.

"Oh."

"You're in school," he guesses.

"No."

"So, what are you hanging out on this late-night train for? I'm Walter, by the way." Walter looks like Mr. Ed and is trying hard to talk to me on my level, which is to say that verbally he's scrunching down on his arthritic knees. Pretty soon he's going to come out with, "Cool," or "Awesome."

"Hi Walter. I'm Eleanor. My parents live in Virginia, and I'm just going for a visit. It's my dad's birthday." Shut up, Bean. Three more words and he's going to think you want him.

"Virginia, huh. Richmond?"

"Uh-huh." Oh no. Don't say it.

"Neat. That's one of my favorite towns, Richmond. But I'm just going to Connecticut myself, unfortunately, ha-ha. Old Saybrook. Do you know Old Saybrook?"

"No." But goddammit, I'm trying to read *The Choiring of the Trees* and get drunk here, can't you see that?

"It's not a bad place. I'm only going down there because my grandmother died and left me her house. Well, it's more of a mansion, really." Of course it is, Walt.

"Hm." *Hm* doesn't count as a word. *Hm* the way I said it could be considered nearly rude, but not quite. He should get the point soon.

"Do you like mansions, Eleanor?" Oh Christ, here we go. I think I recognize this scenario from another life. He must have had a whiskey or two himself before boarding. He'll yak at me until my brain stops working, then the second he sees my eyes glaze over he'll put his hand on my leg and tell me to be careful now, the Scotch'll get to me. I'm thirty years old and not exactly one of those whispery, anemic, please-protect-me types. Why did I never learn to handle these situations easily? Well, I know why. Young I was a tomboy and clueless, and older I've always been attached. The scenes that never play out when you have a boyfriend, geez. Patrick would have given this guy one look and, small as Pat is, Walter would have sat in an entirely different car. I wish I could do that, but I'll have to try an attack of sudden deafness instead.

Oh Patrick. I hate that in my mind we're still together. I mean that I still see things and want to tell him about them, and my process of deciding what I think is to first figure out what he'd think, and then go the opposite way. I finally stopped missing him with my body and skin but I haven't stopped missing the piece of him in my brain, the piece that defined me.

When he visited Boston a few months ago Travis said to me, "So let me get this straight. You really loved him? Him? Like, true love?"

I said, "Why not him? He has beautiful feet." Travis snorted and everybody in line looked at him inquiringly. We dropped our voices. "What's wrong with him?" I asked. "I mean besides the alcoholism and infidelity?"

"He's too short."

"I like short men."

"He's too skinny." Pat only weighed a buck thirty-something saturated in 80 proof.

"I know," I said. "I was hoping our kids could be thinner than me."

"He substitute-teaches for a living, Bean. He spends every Tuesday telling stories to indigents in Porter Square and the rest of the week drinking."

"I like storytelling," I said.

"All right, I like it too, but it wouldn't be the high point of my life. Why does he only substitute? Why doesn't he settle down and teach properly?"

"He likes variety."

"Yeah, in partners if not in whiskey."

"What's the real problem, Trav?"

"Dammit, Bean, he looks like a gnome with rickets," Travis said. "How could you sleep with him? Think of your children, if you can't think of yourself. You would wish ugliness on your own offspring?"

"Travis, you asshole, when I met him he was reading *Dune* for the fourth time and had memorized the quotes. He's seen Tom Waits twice in concert. He scored fourteen something on his SATs, eighteen years old and FOB. He has the saddest eyes I've ever seen and that Irish accent is to fucking die for."

"Yes," Travis said. "All very impressive. But he's such a loser, Bean."

"Yeah, he is, but he's so smart. His intelligence radiates."

"Like a cracked ceramic heater."

"Well, it kept me warm for a long time." And at least he's heterosexual, goddammit, completely and totally heterosexual. The man lives for pussy and that's a nice thing in a boyfriend, OK?

Travis said, "His irritability radiates too and a bad-tempered man is hard to resist. I've fallen for it myself. But not for three years, Bean. One year should have been enough. Inside or out?"

"Out." We went out onto the terrace and shooed some greedy little birds off a table that we were lucky to get on such a fine summer weekend morning.

"And he must have been good in bed or you wouldn't have put up with the rest of it," he continued.

"Sad but true and I miss it I do." We were at Rebecca's having coffee and I took a long sip of mine, forgetting the fights for a minute and only remembering how much fun we had in the sack. "He's got a big nose," I said meaningfully, and Travis rolled his eyes.

"He's Irish," he said, "and we both know what that means."

"Just the accent," I replied. "And the poetic soul." Travis snorted again and made the international gesture for drinking. "Oh yeah, and the weakness for booze." Travis rolled his eyes. "And maybe those blue eyes as well. I think he's half something else, though, and his mom wouldn't admit it. His thumbs are huge. And actually his liver seems fine, in spite of the whiskey. Judging by performance, I mean."

"Believe it or not, I don't want to hear it. He got the stepping-out tendencies from that poetic soul, I suppose, one of those men whose creative genius is hampered by monogamy?"

"Mmh." We watched another trolley drop a gaggle of tourists off in the sun and both cringed as the recorded historical lesson crackled out at fifty decibels and overweight children from the middle of the country started whining to their sweating mothers about ice cream. "He's the only boyfriend I ever had who went with other women," I told Travis, swirling my coffee to cool it down and give me something to do with my hands. "I've had so much shit piled on my head in this lifetime that I really thought God was going to let me slide on experiencing infidelity. But no. And lie, sweet Jesus, the man could lie to the pope and not turn a hair. The more he looked like a choirboy, the more he was having me on. That's how I figured it out, eventually."

"So that's what finally broke you up?" Travis asked.

"Not really. I thought he was too artistic for monogamy too."

"Retract that, you sap, or I'll pour my coffee on you," said Travis, outraged, but I really did think it.

When Pat and I split up, everything I hung my personal Laws of the Natural World on just dissolved into puddles and evaporated. For two years I thought I was going to marry him and suddenly I saw that I wasn't. I can't tell you a thing that happened all spring except that I must have gotten up every working day and gone to the bank, I must have changed clothes and gone to the diner, I must have made my way to Monica's, and gone to the health club with Shannon as usual. Presumably I talked to people and they to me but I don't know who or when. It felt like I was walking around under nuclear fallout with my skin peeled off, and even strangers knew at a glance what had happened to me. I felt so abnormal, so leprous and ravenous and everyone else on the planet throwing a potluck dinner together.

Then, six weeks after the breakup, I slept with a Texan, a tender, gentle, sweetheart of a guy I served at the diner and recognized immediately as a safe port. He was in town on a three-month assignment and about as different from Pat as another white man in his mid-thirties could be. For one thing, you could see right off he had a small dick and a big heart instead of the other way round. Growing up in the semi-desert cultural wasteland of Remie, New Mexico, an ex–railroad town populated solely by rednecks, drunks, and Bible thumpers—a place I couldn't have fit into if I'd worn nothing but Wranglers and Justin Ropers and drunk nothing but black label Jack Daniels, which I didn't—you'd think Texans and I would have nothing in common but two-stepping and Merle Haggard. However, I heard his accent and saw his open, southwestern face, and I thought to myself, floppy-footed Labrador puppy, and without permission my heart cried out, Help me!

He was like Horton hearing the Who with that silent howling of mine. Shy by nature he put down his chicken soup, came right over to me and picked up my hand. "Darlin', why don't you come home with me and we'll set an' talk a while?" he said, and he said it gravely, in a low, sweet, east-Texas drawl. "You look like you could use a rest. I don't mean nothin' by it. Truly. We'll just talk."

There's not many men in the world who could have pulled that off, or maybe not many women who would have listened, but he stood with his sun-streaked hair and sun-beaten skin humbly before me, and he wouldn't look away, and I was so broken I would probably have gone off with the Reverend Moon if he asked me nice enough. So I went with him to his apartment after work that night and all the nights for a week and he rubbed my back and told me stories about his childhood and eventually we slept together just before his wife came up from Sweetwater to see him, and when that happened I fell off my little ledge and crashed properly onto the canyon floor below.

That was the end of April. I remember because when I called Sarah to wish her a happy birthday all I could do was cry and all she could say was, "You had sex with a Texan? Oh, honey." But the fact is, if you're going to use a man to short-circuit your death current then a Texan is a good choice. They're very full of life. We hated them growing up, though, because they were the only ones skiing Taos with any money. New Mexico is, unfortunately, a poor state.

Where I was mostly raised, five hours east of Albuquerque, there was nothing to look at but the land and cows and a whole lot of sky. All of Remie looked temporary; even the fancy houses seemed only as durable as doublewide trailers in hurricane country. The old adobes on the Mexican side of town seemed to belong best, but we never lived there and weren't supposed to have friends from there either. I remember our house and I remember the people, but for the most part what I remember about New Mexico is the light. Even on the high plains, where there's no shortage of it, I was grateful for the sun. But I always knew I'd leave.

"When I was growing up I could hardly wait to live in a real city like this and be an artist," I said to Travis last summer. It was late at night and we were on the T after a Jackie Chan double feature, heading over to the Boston side of the river for one last beer before bed. He gave me one of the annoying you're-such-a-hick looks that he's specialized in since work started sending him all over the globe.

"This isn't a real city," he said about Boston and didn't care, plainly, who on the train might be listening in. "This is a backwater. And last time I checked you were still a bank teller."

"Accounts representative. And don't pick on me. I'm one of the brokenhearted, don't forget."

"Yeah, yeah. You hate your life here; you should leave. Now is the time. You're eaten up by misery and the place is nothing to you. Look around, Bean. Boston is a pleasant enough, somewhat provincial town with a large population of uptight white people and even more uptight homosexuals, along with some very good restaurants. That is not what you need. Now, London is a city. Moscow is a city, New York of course, Paris my favorite, even Chicago qualifies. But not Boston."

"Oh, OK World Traveler," I said. "I guess you bought some dehydrated sophistication on your last visit to Canal Street. Just add water and voilà, the backwoods country fuck is gone? Where did you say you grew up? Nowhereville, New Mexico?"

"Exactly," he said. "I know my backwaters."

"Fine," I said. "How's this? What I want now is to live in a small village, big city, medium town, backwater, or the middle of fucking nowhere in a trailer park. I don't care where I go, as long as I can live cheap, do photography and get some decent coffee. I want to be an artist, not a bank teller. Photography counts as art, right?"

"It can," said Travis. "Anything can but most things don't, and since you know what you want and that's more than most people know, why the hell aren't you doing it?"

Mom, by the way, doesn't think women make good artists. She doesn't think women are good at much of anything and art is only one of those things. She thinks women are boring, except for herself, and she's not boring because she's so charming when she drinks. She's the only person I know outside a country song who glamorizes alcoholism. In her book it's far better to be an alcoholic than to be a bore. It's better to be a psychotic than to be a bore. It's better to be anything rather than be a bore.

Apparently I'm a bore because, she says, I take after my father. He, of course, says I take after her. "Eleanor May"—she always calls me Eleanor May and not B or Bean like other people do—"your father is a Bore with a capital B. He's all the boring things of this world rolled up in one. Baseball games and golf and church and PTA meetings and khaki pants and sensible food and never spending more than you have. I can't imagine why he was with me, except to bore me to tears." Mom has a mean streak, but it's better to be mean than boring. I grew up in a house that should have had this embroidered on a wall plaque: *Nice Is Boring*. Or maybe, *Better A Whore Than A Bore*. Either one would have worked.

My mom is half Mexican. Latina. Chicana. Hispanic. Whatever you're supposed to say. I didn't know that for a long time. She used to tell us she was an orphan, everyone dead but Marisol, her aunt. She used to say Marisol was an Italian name but my dad finally spilled the beans when he left, by screaming in the middle of the fight that broke the camel's straining back, "This doesn't have one goddamn thing to do with your goddamn Mexican mother, goddammit!" But Mom didn't believe him and after that it made much more sense to me, why she used to think that anyone born blond and blue-eyed was better than us and why she hated my atavistic, black and kinky hair and brought home every straightener you could buy back then in Remie, New Mexico.

My poor mom. If you squeak "WASP" when someone pulls your string, she loves you. I'll tell you right now that the only reason she married Dad, besides the advent of me (and to get out of student teaching), was because he had honey-colored hair and dark green eyes. But what the hell. There are plenty of other marriages that are based on more important things and they don't last either.

"Well, good-bye Eleanor. Enjoy your stay in Virginia. Maybe we'll run into each other again, out on the silver track, ha-ha."

"Ha-ha. Bye Walter. Enjoy your mansion. Don't let ice build up in the gutters." And good riddance, you bore. Nice eyes, though. Oh God, now I do sound like Mom.

Ahh. I've got the seat to myself again. Let me just fill my all-purpose, well-traveled, most-favorite Coffee Connection travel mug with water so I don't dry out, and then maybe I'll pull out my journal and start my travel log with this question: I wonder why a fifty-year-old man and a fifty-year-old woman are two such different beings? At fifty women get suddenly older, not dating material anymore, not really sexy except for the few lucky ones. It's as if they say good-bye to the younger world and don't even mind, but men aren't like that; they hang on for longer. Then at sixty it changes again and suddenly the men are old and tentative and the women have new energy. Why is that? Walter must have been about fifty and he thought nothing of tossing me a line. And why not? I dated a forty-eight-year-old over the summer and hardly felt weird. Well, actually it was after the summer, and we only sort of dated. I was desperate for company and just stayed at his place all of October until he had it out with me over the issue of my "distance" three days ago. Poor Sal. Distance is not the half of it. I spent my last three nights at Monica's and never even told him I was leaving town.

I'm a perfect example of why you should never get involved with a brokenhearted woman. After a bad break-up a man will cling to the first woman he dates like an orangutan baby, but a woman keeps things strictly transitional for at least two or three men more. I told him that, but it never does any good to warn someone. It never did any good for a man to warn me. Even Patrick tried to tell me about the depth and storminess of his drinking but I sailed blithely on, confident that I could navigate anything.

Connecticut always depresses me. Is there anyone in the state with a big nose or a bad haircut? I'd settle for a few zits, for God's sake. There must be massive imperfection here, like everywhere except California, but I've never seen evidence of it get on the train. It's all identical-looking nonethnic student types with wide faces, good teeth, and blondish hair, talking languidly about TV and who was at the party and what's the next thing to buy. They're so skinny, these kids, so word-limited, so mall-socialized suburban, and so goddamn bored. Ick. Don't kids have fun anymore? Don't they rebel? I don't understand how twenty-year-olds can be so blasé. They never giggle, they never argue, they discuss nothing. They're indifferent. I grew up in cow shit and we still talked and shouted and laughed and enjoyed ourselves, but only shopping interests these kids, and that only marginally. Ennui oozes from their tiny, well-scrubbed pores. They're in a subtle competition for the title of Most Passive. All they do is shop and watch TV. It's all their parents do either but you'd think the children could throw that off in some kind of rebellious fever. What else is adolescence for?

This is the reason I'm probably not going to be raising well-adjusted children, even if I could. I would hate any offshoot of mine to consider a Connecticut suburb, an upscale mall, and a ninety-word vocabulary the apex of life. Sure, they're ultracool, this MTV spawn, and they look pretty good, but I'd rather raise someone interesting. Kids like this might be taught to appreciate art, but they'll never create it. Nobody that bored turns out Picassos.

I guess I subscribe to the belief that you can't be happy and, in the same life, be an artist. I once told Travis that I stood a very good chance of succeeding with photography because I've been so thoroughly haunted by various kinds of depressions and compulsions for most of my conscious life. Travis said, "Artists may all be unhappy people, but not all unhappy people are artists. Look at your dad. He's an accountant." Actually, was an accountant. He got the pink slip two weeks ago, in perfect time for his fifty-fifth birthday, the birthday that got me a time frame for my train trip and, in a way, made the whole pilgrimage coalesce.

A few months ago, when the bountiful August sunshine made me brave enough, I returned a call to Richmond from maybe six weeks previous and with no questions asked was invited out for Dad's birthday party—now "retirement" celebration—on Friday night, November 6th, an affair that promises to be worth attending if only for the chance to see my dad without a job. Travis calls my dad the Ram and it fits. He's a ram with a bad temper and routines bordering on the obsessive. He has routines for taking out the trash, ordering the tool shed, and cleaning bathrooms, routines for running, for showering, for washing cars, making coffee, grilling steaks, and for all I know there's a routine for fucking but no one's gotten into the details of that with me. When Mom is sober she's a clean freak with a ramrod demeanor but she's got nothing on him.

To make up for the two of them, Sarah and I turned out absolute slobs, like preachers' kids who are always wild. Look at Joe Bloch, my one-time best friend and later sworn enemy. His father, the Reverend Bloch, was a locally famous Baptist minister, one of the real hellfire types who sermonized against the showing of belly skin, couples dancing, and the New Math. Joe's three older brothers went from fighting and drinking to bull-riding and heartbreaking, and then Joe turned out gay, which didn't surprise Sarah but came as an absolute shock to me.

Sarah isn't coming to the party. She said she couldn't make it in from Tucson and provided some stupid alibi which translated into "busy having big fights with Samson." Auntie Buzz made feeble excuses as well, but Bernard, the uncle I haven't seen since I was seven and he and Mom were caught necking at a Christmas party, has already RSVP'd yes. He's supposed to be a maverick type and good looking. Dad can't stand him and he's bringing his new wife and altogether it sounds like possibly an interesting time to show up.

Consequently, at the invite I said, "Count me in. I'm so glad I'm not fat. I'll bring the Scotch. And oh, by the way, I'm leaving work for a year. Do you mind if I ship some clothes and things down there to store in the attic?"

I was talking to my stepmother at the time, with whom I have a relatively smooth relationship, unfraught with the issues that cloud and bind my genuine blood ties. Cindy reminds me of my favorite teacher in elementary school, the first adult who found me charming. She's always been easier to deal with than either dad or mom, so I wanted her to break the news of my downsizing to the old man rather than do it myself.

"No problem," she said, after a second or two. "We've got all kinds of room in the attic. When did you decide this? What are you going to do? Do you want to come down here and live with us for a while?"

"Oh, about as much as I'd like another hole in my head, thanks anyway. Nothing personal, of course, I just think it's time I did a little sorting out of stuff, stuff inside me mostly, stuff from my past. You know. And I want to try my hand at photography. I think it's where my talent lies."

"Hm. Does this have anything to do with Patrick?"

"Maybe."

"Are you pregnant?" Anytime I do something drastic they want to know if I'm pregnant.

"No, I'm not pregnant, and I'm not suicidal, and I'm not in trouble with the police. I'm not taking drugs, I have money in the bank, and I'm not fat again."

"I didn't mean it like that, Beanie Bean. Don't get all riled up."

"OK. I know you didn't." I sighed, wondered how straightforward to be, and decided to go for 80 percent. "I just don't like the way my life is going, that's all, and I want to step back from it and figure out a different way. If I don't do it now, before kids and a husband and a mortgage, I'll never do it, don't you think?"

"I suppose."

"Besides, I'm dying of heartache here, and I feel like I've got nothing to lose."

"Ah." She knew the truth when she heard it and was satisfied. "Are you sure you don't want to just stay here a while and sort it out? We'd be happy to have you. Your daddy too, you know." Uh-huh.

"No thanks. And you don't need to speak for him. I'm sure we know what he really thinks. Anyway, I already bought my train tickets and I've got friends expecting me all over."

"It does sound like you have it planned. Are you going to see Sarah?"

"Of course. And Mom. Lily too. I've been promising a visit to Chicago for years. And Jessica. Remember she went for some graduate courses in Kansas? Now she's wrecking herself on some married guy and says she'll never go back to Boston. It should be educational. Then I'll take turns staying with Sarah and Mom so I can be in Tucson for the whole winter. Then San Diego maybe, and San Francisco possibly, and Portland in April or May. I don't know where else. Colorado. I've always wanted to spend time in Colorado."

"B, are you planning on coming back?" My dad's family is stuck on the letter B but Sarah named me BB for Big Butt when we were kids and I've been called B and Bean and variations thereof ever since. I don't mind it, actually, despite the origin. Eleanor never did suit me. It's too prissy.

"I think I'm coming back but I'm trying not to lock myself in. You know."

"Kid," she said throatily, putting on the Lauren Bacall, "you've never locked yourself in to anything but the shitter."

I laughed, but cautiously, wary of letting my guard down. "I always felt like I did. Maybe after this trip I'll stop being so claustrophobic."

"Hm." Cindy's not the kind of person to jam her views down your throat. She's pretty different from the rest of the family, who all own crowbars for that very purpose, and I knew she'd break the news of my new instability tactfully to Dad.

Well, finally we're leaving New London. They switch engines there and let us sit for an hour while the crew changes over and the snack car gets filled and people in the sleepers sleep on. I guess I'm suffering a little insomnia. I dread seeing Dad. He's such an agitated depressive and now he's an agitated depressive without a job whose oldest daughter is also without a job. Great. I don't even want to think about the cars, Jesus. They're probably clean enough to perform hysterectomies in. Cindy's going to go back to work, apparently, which has given both me and Trav endless material for speculation.

My prediction was, "Now he'll see what it's like to be financially dependent and have to ask for an allowance every week and keep the laundry done and bills paid and dinner cooked and homework kept up with and feelings noticed and animals filled and emptied. That should be fun."

Travis pointed out, "What'll really happen is that Cindy will still do all that and just add forty-hour work weeks to her schedule."

I said that no doubt he'd get irritable and unshaved and watch too much television.

Travis said, "What would really make you happy is if he had to start selling insurance or something, door-to-door. Telephone sales. Used cars. Cold calls. And maybe he'd have to go to counseling to help him deal with it. If you're really lucky he'll get fat and depressed and then you can gross out on him for once." What can I say? It's pretty satisfying to me that we're both having a life crisis at the same time.

I can't believe they're still having his birthday party. He gets sacked and we get wasted, isn't there something a little warped in that? But it's a warped family. I think the B fixation stands for Bizarre. Dad loves the tradition but my mother resisted wholeheartedly. His real name is Bookman but she always called him by his middle name, Nelson. If he had had his way, I would have been named Bianca and Sarah would have been Blaire. "How about Biltmore and Bangladesh?" my mom would say. "Then we could just call them Built to Bang for short."

I don't know if he ever thought she was funny. Certainly by the time I was old enough to notice their relationship she wasn't amusing him much. But I don't know if anything did. Nothing I ever figured out. I can pretty well sum up Dad by repeating one of his favorite statements: "If you were fucked up after Vietnam, it's because you were fucked up before Vietnam." End of story.

Beatrice is considerably gentler. She's the middle child and the only relative I know at all. She hates to fly but has an adventurous streak for a Republican. Four years ago at Thanksgiving was the last time I saw her. Sarah and I were both there; I'd come down by train, Sarah had flown up, and Buzz had driven cross-country on a ride-share. It was on that trip that Buzz released the news bulletin of her switch from male partners to female. She did it on video and prepared us by saying, "You know, I've been in San Francisco a very long time." We were having mock interviews in the living room and when I asked her about important events in her life recently she came up with that one. Sarah nearly dropped the camera.

Then it was my turn but we had to wait for Dad to recover. He said, "But what about Charlie?" She said, "Charlie's dead." He said, "Well, I hardly think we need to hear the details of your personal life, Beatrice," and Auntie Buzz said, very pompously and mocking him, "But perhaps I needed to reveal them, Bookman." He wanted to know why it had to be on Thanksgiving but then Cindy kicked him and he shut up.

I wanted mostly to change my eating, which was out of control, but I was too ashamed to say this on tape so instead I got the focus off my weight and said I wanted to change my relationship with him. He said, "What the hell is wrong with our relationship?"

I said, "Well, it isn't one, is it? I mean, as long as I fold my underwear into perfect cubes and keep my ears cleaned out and my mouth shut then you think you've done your job, right? Your whole motivation is to get me to act a certain way and once I act it you can relax and ignore me. Job done, boot camp over. I mean, do you know anything about me at all? Do you know my birthday, the books I read, my boyfriend's name, a color that I like, anything?"

"I know you're a bleeding-heart liberal," he said. "And it wouldn't hurt you to go on a diet."

Things got ugly after that, with accusations and shouting and me bringing up favorite injustices from childhood and him not remembering them and then telling me to get over it anyway, and Sarah taped the whole shooting match. I was swinging into my low, sweet chariot, the worst point of my life. I weighed over two hundred pounds and my hair was clipped as short as a poodle's. I was crying and my skin was blotchy and I was wearing an expensive, sanded silk shirt exactly the color of a seasick person. It strained at my shoulders and gaped at my boobs. I wouldn't be surprised if Sarah, an artist of sorts herself, zoomed in and out at my bust to capture occasional flashes of my black camisole to break up the monotony of that shimmering chartreuse ocean.

What I remember thinking about, as my mouth went on and on regarding Dad's lifelong nagging and irritability, was how much I'd like to eat the entire white chocolate cheesecake cooling beckoningly in the fridge. At the same time I remember a sharp longing for Stuart, who hated my family and would have summed up the entire situation as, "Nuts, just like I warned you," and then gotten me a piece of cheesecake without my having to ask. He would have been my unshakable ally but I didn't want him as an ally anymore. We had met in Virginia Beach three years before, during one of my traveling summers, waiting tables at the same cheesy restaurant. He had Nice Guy written all over him and I'd pass out routinely on his sofa at four in the morning, after partying hard with other people all through the wee hours. In August he told me to just move in, and a month later we were having sex. By that video Thanksgiving we'd been together for Hank's death, several cities, and a sixty-pound weight gain, but I wouldn't let him come to Virginia for the holiday because he'd made me get an abortion in July, and he was smart enough to know the end was looming.

After I went, Sarah said she wished she could be honest, like me, and let people get close to her. Then we both cried, her from relief, me because she had no idea how wrong she was, and Cindy taped us scrupulously. I don't think any of us learned a thing from that little exercise in video, although Sarah went back to Tucson and got involved with Elliot, a.k.a. Samson, Ivers immediately afterwards, and the fact that she's still with him should say something, although I'm not sure what. Beatrice was calm as a mountain lake during the entire procedure and asked us when it was over if it was too early in the day for cognac and chocolate. It was 2:00 P.M. and we decided that it wasn't.

They didn't see me again until summer's end of the next year. I was down to one-sixty, many moons, one boyfriend, lots of therapy, and all the Geneen Roth books later. It was Labor Day and they were up at the Cape for two weeks' vacation.

I stayed with them for the last few days of trinket shopping and icy water and then went with all the traffic back to Boston. Dad hugged me on that vacation but I didn't hug him back. Six weeks later I met Patrick.

We're pulling into Penn Station, New York. I can't believe I'm still awake. Now I have to sit here while the lights turn on and off and they service the train again. I hope no one sits next to me. I swear to God I'm going to finish this last bit of Scotch, one more page of my journal, and then I'm going to sleep. I have no job, no man, no worries, and all I can do with my time is remember stuff from when I had those things and wished that I didn't.

I keep thinking I'm going to end up with money one day. Does everyone think the same thing, that the future will take care of itself? Put like that I can see why Dad thinks I'm hopeless. God, I dread Richmond. I can't believe I agreed to fourteen days of lousy coffee, lopsided conversation, and the suburbs, all without Sarah or a boyfriend to buffer me. I must be secretly masochistic. But at least I remembered my pillow. Little things like your own pillow and a bit of morning sun can make all the difference when you travel. A few hours from now we'll be clicking past government buildings in D.C. My legs will be stiff and the train will smell of breakfast and bad coffee. If my stomach holds out, I might try having some.

In the magical beginning of one summer I kissed Ricky Serrano. It was late at night. Dad had left us and we hadn't yet moved to Texas. The rules at home changed with Dad's desertion and we came and went as we pleased if we weren't blatant about it. Mom was a heavy sleeper. I was fourteen that summer. High school lurked like Mordor. Ricky was younger than me, even younger than Sarah, probably still twelve, the age Ralph was in *Lord of the Flies*, and just as beautiful. Sarah hated him, or hated that I liked him, so I only told Lily about the walk and the kiss.

It wasn't unusual for us to crawl out of our bedroom windows at night to explore a new house they might be building up the street. These houses, cropping up all over as people in the west got rich on oil, were really compelling. We liked best the ones that were already carpeted and were awaiting final things like the right sink or extra large bathtub special-ordered from Mexico. There were twenty thousand people in Remie and none of them seemed to worry about thievery, so the new houses were never locked up. Sometimes we took plasterboard and broke off pieces and used it like chalk and marked the places with graffiti, but mostly we just went and hung out. We didn't smoke, and none of us had started drinking yet. It was just a way to be alone and rebellious, even more alone and rebellious than we were already.

This night was unusual because it was only me and Ricky making our way across the dark streets, and we were oddly silent together. Purposely, I hadn't asked Sarah to come, had even waited until she was asleep to sneak out, and Lillian wasn't staying over because her parents had grounded her for skipping church the week before. Joe Bloch had been sentenced to a religion camp for most of the summer, and for some reason Ricky hadn't gone by Frank's place. It occurred to me that I'd never been alone with Rick before, and it felt odd, not like being with Joe. Joe and I were always going off together to do things the others didn't want to do, borrowing books from the library or swimming at the city pool. My sister hated the city pool. She said it gave her athlete's foot.

"Where's Sarah?" Ricky asked me, first thing.

I said, "She didn't want to come." She was making me nervous by then, the way she would watch me, silently, and never just have fun with the group, hanging out. We still shared a room but we didn't talk much. I didn't tell her my secrets anymore. I hated school and everyone there, and I knew high school was just going to be worse. The only good things anymore were summer vacation and friends. We hadn't seen Dad in weeks.

"Too bad," he said. "I thought I was going to have the both of you to myself for once."

I just shrugged. If Frank weren't there, Sarah wouldn't have come anyway.

Ricky and I wandered around the empty, half-built house. It was two in the morning and we weren't sleepy and neither of us felt much like chalk writing. There was no glass to break, not even light bulbs. Ricky was disappointed. The bathtub was in. It was a sunken kind, big and square, and I would call it ugly now, the kind that can also be a whirlpool. We thought the tub was neat and we wanted to get the water to come on. It wouldn't, of course, so we sat with our legs hanging over the side and tried to talk.

It wasn't as easy as when the others were around. He stared at me and I was getting sweaty. I was afraid he'd feel my hands and think they were clammy, so I sat with them under my legs. It made me even taller. I was towering over him. To me he suddenly looked fine and precious, like the kind of bone china you can see the shadows of your fingers through. I felt around his small, neat darkness like I felt around Sarah and Mom, clumsy and uncertain. He had long-fingered, mobile hands and muscular, smooth brown legs. Next to him I was large and pale, and my tongue was dry and sticking to the roof of my mouth, but he kept on looking at me and smiling a little and the sweat was trickling down under my T-shirt.

After he hadn't answered three stupid questions in a row I jumped up and said, "Let's go home."

"You sure you really want to?" I don't know what made him so different that night. He was always the one we laughed at, if we weren't laughing at Lily, but he was more confident than me now. I just looked at him, actually waiting for permission to go. He waited too, posing like a cat on a roof beam, enjoying himself and his natural balance. I don't know how he knew, or even how I knew, but he was the leader. It was understood. My heart was pounding. There seemed to be something I was supposed to do, but I didn't know what it was and I didn't want to do the wrong thing. So I stood, frozen, waiting for some kind of clue. It wasn't forthcoming. I distinctly remember thinking, This would never happen to Sarah.

He was still smiling at me when he shrugged and said, "OK, let's go back to your house for a while. Mom's out of town and Santos has a date tonight." Santos was the uncle who looked after Ricky and Ricky's little sister when Mrs. Serrano needed help, which was relatively often. Ricky hated his guts. Santos was loose with his fists and we always knew when he had been babysitting because Ricky showed up with bruises that he wouldn't talk about. Mom hit us, too, but Dad was more likely to call you a stupid pain in the ass and take you out on the highway, make you clean up the trash next to it, come back for you in two hours and you'd better have made some progress. Lily never ever got smacked, but Frank's dad was mean as a snake and big as a barn, and Joe's dad was a preacher, so of course he was constantly catching beatings. The boys all thought we had it good at our house. And maybe we did, in between the shitty times.

Ricky and I didn't talk on the way home. I tried to say a few things, making conversation, feeling like an idiot. He didn't bother answering. For a second I wished Joe was around, but then I realized I wouldn't have traded the comfort of him for the excitement of this any day of the week. Back at my house I started to open the kitchen door and go in, wondering what was going to happen next. Ricky stood a few feet away, in the grass of the backyard, watching me. I closed the door, quietly, and sat down on the porch instead. I wasn't really surprised when he sat down next to me, then put his arm around me and pulled me down to lie beside him on the grass. It was nothing we had done before, but what I felt was wonder that it had taken us so long to do something so logical. We lay like that, looking at each other, and then he started talking to me like I used to talk to my cat Angie, soothing and sort of stroking me with his voice, only it wasn't his voice anymore, it was someone else's, an older voice, scratchier and purposeful, someone with a plan that I couldn't help but follow.

We were both lying on our elbows, heads propped on our hands. I had my arm down between us so my breasts wouldn't touch him. He kept talking nonsense with that magic voice and at some point I put away the knowledge that Sarah Jane wouldn't be caught dead on the ground with Ricky Serrano at three o'clock on a summer morning, melting in her underwear.

"It's OK," Ricky was still quietly hypnotizing me. "You know I always have liked you. Have you ever kissed anyone? You're looking real good this summer, Eleanor May." When he called me that instead of Bean my mouth got dry again. "Frank and me have been noticing that you're growing up here," and he brushed my chest, lightly, with his free hand. I was mortified, and thrilled. I thought Mom would be able to take one look at me in the morning and know, immediately, that I had been up to no good. But even as I pictured her suspicious face, my stomach dropped with weakness, and a sucking, hollow feeling started in me that I hoped would never go away.

When he finally kissed me it was like magic, like warm water or toffee was pouring through my body from his mouth and making me loose and fluid and beautiful. I could even breathe, with his tongue in my mouth, and I felt I could stay forever like that, with our lips moving together and my whole soul open to him.

I don't know how long we kissed. We didn't do anything else, and didn't talk. After a while he went home and I went inside. Sarah was awake. "Enjoy yourself?" she asked.

"Oh yeah, we had fun, just walked around." She knew I was lying, and in the darkness I flushed but refused to elaborate. I lay silent in my bed and she lay silent in hers. I don't know what she was thinking, and I don't know if she remembers the night, but for once I fell asleep before her.

2

The visit started out so well. For the first four minutes I almost believed that everything was going to be different this time. "How's my Elephant?" That was Dad's old nickname for Eleanor, but he stopped using it when I got fat so hearing it out of him a month ago in Union Station told me he was pleased with my appearance. I put down my things and gave him the big smile and brief hug that he prefers over suspect female clinging and tried not to touch him with my tits. Not touching someone with your tits is not that easy when your tits are any size at all. He ruffled my head and I wasted my millionth second wishing that I had long, silky straight hair and nicely polished nails. He loves long, silky straight hair and nicely polished nails, and girls who are quiet and well behaved and don't have problems finding themselves or bodies that stick out all over the place. Instead, he got me.

"I'm doing good, Dad. Really good. It's good to see you. It'll be, uh, good to be home. Yeah. Everything's good." He never wants to hear about the bad stuff, or the way you're struggling with something, or how you think your heart is broken and you wonder if you'll ever laugh again. He thinks that kind of subject, if you're weak enough to even acknowledge it, should be dealt with quietly, on your own, and that conversation should be about ideas and events, not feelings. He's a man's man, my dad. He likes politics, loves the Cowboys, hates welfare. When I was younger I used to argue leftist bullshit at him but I haven't the energy anymore. Besides, I'm not sure I have the right. He enlisted in the Marines knowing full well he would get sent to Vietnam. Mom tried to talk him out of signing up but he wouldn't hear of it, and you've got to give the old goat credit for putting his money where his mouth is, or at least that's what I think now. He came out of the service when I was four as a staff sergeant with college money, but he didn't sign up for that only. He signed up because he believed in the cause. He actually wanted to stop the spread of Communism. "Thanks for coming to get me, by the way, Dad. I would have been fine waiting for the next train down."

"Oh no, I like a good drive, you know that. Gives me time to clear the noggin." And he tapped himself on the forehead in the old, familiar gesture.

"Yeah. I remember the long drives." Like the one to Florida when you left us, for example. "You look good." He did look good. He's built on the short side and getting stocky, but he's tanner than the average Bostonian and his hair is graying nicely, the same way Sarah's will except that she'll dye hers. He still cuts it very short, not a man who regrets his service time, time I hardly remember and Mom refers to as "those hell years around those snot-nosed families." Sarah had been born while he was overseas on a second tour being a hero, and she could not stand Carolina. Still, those years at Camp Lejeune were their happy ones.

"You too, honey. Here, I'll take that. How was the trip?" We set off towards the car his favorite way, on the double.

"Oh, the usual. I didn't sleep much but I had a lot to think about." Not, of course, that he'd ever ask what, in case I actually told him. We trotted on in silence and he led the way to the spotless Buick.

"Hm," he finally said. "So what are your plans?" He was packing the luggage carefully into the pristine trunk according to some personal system of efficient space usage and I was watching from a safe distance.

Now, my dad is a definite kind of guy, an orderly, perhaps even ritualized personality, and I was tempted to lie so he wouldn't have to know how nebulous my next year was really going to be, but I didn't. I told him the truth like an adult should. Mostly. "Oh, I'm going to travel around and explore the country a little. You know. Everyone goes off to Europe but I couldn't afford that, and besides, there's a lot to see here. I'm not stopping in places where I don't know people, I'm just going to cities where my friends are and staying with them. And Sarah of course. Mostly I'm staying with her. A winter in Tucson can't be bad."

"Hm," he said, and sniffed. Oh God, the meaningful sniff. I'm like Pavlov's dogs with that sniffing of his. He sniffs and I sweat.

"They don't mind, Dad. They want me to come."

"Hm."

I am not a loser, not a loser, not a loser, and I will not ask for his approval, won't won't won't, goddammit. "You don't like that idea, Dad?"

"Why now? That's all I want to know. Why couldn't you do this when you were twenty?" He broke off to pay the parking and chat with the attendant, and I wanted to yell at her, "Save me! I've been kidnapped!" But I didn't. She wouldn't have been sympathetic anyway; she liked him, I could tell by the eye contact. He pulled out into heavy traffic and resumed with the Reid Technique of Interrogation. "Don't you think it's time you settled down? Got married? Had some children? Life is hard! You can't be irresponsible forever. Can't you handle growing up?" That's it, right there. Putting his knuckly finger right on the sore spot of my whole development.

Keep it together, Bean, think *Dance of Anger*. Think Deborah Tannen. Think Zen thoughts, whatever the hell that means. Get a grip on the situation right now and keep it short, don't explain, don't apologize. "No, apparently I can't." But on the other hand, you old coot, I wouldn't be so far behind developmentally if my parents had done a better job parenting me, all right? So get off my back.

"Elephant, you can't have everything. Why do this now?"

Because I'm scarred and wrecked and my whole life is washed up on the goddamn reef, that's why. I've got nothing to live for anymore and this is my way of finding something in the wreckage, OK? Can't you see the blood-tinged foam, the savaged flotsam, my ravaged soul? "Oh," I said, "I wanted to get it done before I have kids and all that. Had a little money saved, they wanted to get rid of one of the tellers anyway. You know."

"No, I don't know."

Answering was beyond me. I think I gave a helpless waggle of my right hand. My lower lip was starting to do that trembling thing and I made myself think away from the car and the conversation and I wondered, briefly, about normal people and what they talked to their parents about. I turned the radio on to Dave Brubeck doing "Take Five."

He turned the radio off and said, "What are you now, thirty? Thirty-one?"

"Thirty. My birthday's in February." In case you don't remember.

"Thirty. I had two children and a house when I was thirty."

Yeah, and an alcoholic wife and stress-induced eczema, and the two children you had you hardly knew, don't forget. "Things are different now, Dad."

He brushed that off and went on in his sensitive way. "Aren't you a little old to be living out of a suitcase?" What a guy.

"Maybe."

"Then what are you doing? Honey, I just want an explanation."

"Look Dad, I couldn't find any meaning in my life."

"There *is* no meaning to life, for Christ Jesus sake! You work, you have a family, you retire, you die. What's the mystery?"

"That's enough for you, but not for me, OK? I couldn't face another day at that bank, staring at wads of other people's money and then afterwards, at the diner three nights a week, staring at chicken soup. I couldn't do it. I was losing my mind." I stopped talking and waited for him to interrupt me with a pertinent war story, but he didn't so I went on. "There was this one beautiful day in June. The sky was so blue and the air so clean that I stopped on my way to work and walked down to the river instead. I sat on the cement wall looking out over the water and I couldn't believe that this struggle was my life. The sun was shining on me and the grass was green and I breathed the summer smell in and I realized that I was absolutely miserable." And I saw that Travis was right. Why stay? "That's when I realized, Hey, wait a minute, there's no prize here. If I do everything I'm supposed to for the rest of my life you know what I get? A bigger house in a better neighborhood. That's all. That's what I spent the last decade on? What a waste."

"Not a waste. Good jobs don't fall off trees."

"A waste for me, Dad. I don't consider spending nine hours a day miserable for the rest of my life a good job, just a long lesson for a slow learner. It finally occurred to me that the sky wouldn't fall on me if I quit. I should never have been a bank teller to begin with. And as for accounts representative, what a joke! The classic job for women: customer service and no advancement. Well, I'm done with it, I'm sorry."

"Sorry is right. Sorry is exactly what you'll be when you're sixty-five and Medicare's gone bust and you don't have two dimes to rub together."

"Dad, just listen to me. I'm sick of pretending that I care about these things. If I'm very good at this role I get to play it forever. Do you have any idea how the idea horrifies me?"

"Don't be ridiculous. You're talking about being poor and believe me you don't want to be poor."

"You know what, Dad? You don't know a single goddamn thing about me." But that was harsher than I intended so I softened up the rest. "Look. I'm going to take a year to sort out what I want to do, what I'm willing to do for rent money, and if I'm ready to pursue photography. And then I'm going to come back and do it. It's OK that I'm thirty. I'm a late bloomer. Emotionally, I mean. Ha-ha. Not the other way." Oh God, why do I say things like that?

"Honey." He paused. "Eleanor May." He paused again and shook his bony goat's head sorrowfully and then decided, I guess, to try and teach me something one last time. "Eleanor, do you play pool?"

"Uh, yeah. I played more when Stuart was around, though. Why?" I meant Why, at this age, did I still feel the nervous bladder clutching of a little girl about to get into trouble? There's only so much trouble you can get a five-foot-nine, hundred-and-fifty-pound grown woman into. But then he wouldn't have to do much. My own guilt would do most of the work since I was disappointing him and hurting his feelings. When you're a proper girl it's not OK to disappoint people and hurt their feelings. It isn't nice. I have demerits already for my frizzy hair and dubious past, but to willfully let down my dad is like having a dog pee on a rug right in front of you. Bad girl!

"I'll explain. You think you should play pool because you love the game, and you think that loving the game is enough, but actually that has nothing to do with it."

"Nothing?"

"Very little."

"I never knew you played pool, Dad." It was hard to imagine him in a pool hall, bullshitting over a pitcher of beer with a bunch of hairy bikers.

"Well, I gave it up when you were a little tyke but I used to be quite a shark." A shark? A tuna maybe. "And of course I played in the service. So did your mother." My mother? No way. "We all did. Those were fun days, I'll say that for them, before we moved to Remie and her drinking got so bad." He trailed off just when I thought his unusually revealing mood was about to get interesting and instead turned to give me the professional look he uses occasionally to make up for the years in between of vacancy. "You're not starting on the pills again and all that crap, are you?"

No Sir, Sergeant Sir! Name, rank, and serial number, Sir! "No, I'm not." But give me a week or two in your company and then ask me that question.

"That's my girl." Yeah right. You wouldn't claim me at a swap meet. "Let me tell you one or two things I've learned." No, really, please don't. "Honey, it's the little things you hate to do that make the game worthwhile in the end. You have to practice. Line up the shot. Bend your knees and get down and dirty into the thick of things. Pool isn't something you can understand in your head. It isn't something you can get good at by dabbling in here and there and then farting off to do something else. Pool is like life. You have to stick with it even during the boring parts of learning it. You can't keep shucking it off and think you're going to master it."

Wow. That's deep. "It's hard to exactly shuck life off, Dad." Although, believe me, I've contemplated it once or twice.

"Don't split hairs like your mother always did, Eleanor. You know I hate that."

I do indeed. Why do you think I did it? "You're worried that I won't settle down, aren't you?"

"Damn right, and more than that! How much money do you have saved?"

"Four thousand dollars and I'm debt-free." That was a lie and we hadn't even gotten to Dale City. I had three thousand two hundred and another maybe five hundred coming from my last couple of paychecks and that wasn't counting return fare to Boston from wherever I'd be a year from now or my two remaining school loans. But I'd worry about that later. Maybe even try to defer the big one from U-Mass. I was going to work some coffee-shop job in Tucson anyway for spending money. A couple months of that and I would have closer to four thousand, so it wasn't a total lie.

"Four thousand dollars is wonderful. Put it in the bank."

"It's in the bank."

"Leave it in the bank. Or, better yet, invest it. Go back to work and add to it. Work for me!"

"You don't have a job anymore." Misdirection. I meant that I wouldn't work for him if my only other choice was flipping burgers in a polyester negligee for rent money.

"I'm going into business for myself. Didn't we tell you?"

"No." I'm the one you never talk to, remember? "Accounting?"

"No. We're thinking about a franchise. Dunkin' Donuts or Subway. Or maybe a Chesapeake Bagel. Cindy wants to do a gourmet pretzel place but I don't know. It'll be something along those lines."

"Well, shut my mouth. Isn't that risky?"

"Now's the time. You know that Cindy'll be working at Nabisco starting in the new year, right? Well, they're paying her extremely well for her trouble."

"I see. So while you have that safety net, you think this is a good time to . . ." torture your oldest daughter?

"Right. This is a good time to branch out."

"How much money do *you* have saved?" As if he would ever tell me.

"More than a peck, less than a bushel." The standard evasion. "There's always something you didn't count on. I gave Bernard the down payment on their house last year, and just recently we paid off the loan for Sarah's master's degree.

There's college for the twins, too. And retirement. But we've got a chunk of useable funds."

I had no idea they'd given Sarah money for that degree. The little sneak never told me, just let me think it was Samson paying for her all along, but I'm not surprised. I knew Dad liked her better than me. She says he doesn't but he does. She says I don't read him very well. She's always telling me, "Deep down he really loves us, BB, and he's proud of us. He just doesn't know how to show it."

Doesn't that tickle you pink? I can't tell you what it does to me when women say, "Deep down, on the inside, I know he loves me." You always want to say back to them, Sure, lady, but outside he's beating the shit out of you, or maybe ignoring you for years at a stretch, and he does nothing all day long but watch TV and drink beer so I'm just wondering what the fuck good all that inner love is doing you. Maybe you should find someone who loves you a little less on the inside but shows it more on the outside.

Damn him. She gets money for college and there's no way he'd give me money for what I'm doing now. No way. But I guess maverick photography isn't the same thing as a master's in economics. He's in love with higher education. He's always saying things like, "It's why this country is still the greatest goddamn country on the planet, goddammit!"

"I thought it was our right to bear arms that made it so great," I said once, in response to this.

He said, "There's a lot of reasons for America's greatness," at which I cracked up, so he then of course said, "Hey, Missy, if you don't like the place you can always move to Colombia, you know. Or maybe China, where they encourage people to speak out against the government."

"Yeah, but Dad, the whole point of being able to speak out is that we *should* speak out, don't you see? You shouldn't shut me up, I'm exercising my rights."

"You're exercising shit," he said, irritably. "You just want to get me going." Which was about the long and short of it, actually.

Dad looked my way, suddenly, and I realized I had let the conversation lag. I half smiled, no teeth, and tried to make my eyes wide and nonthreatening, with not too much of the whites showing. See? No hostility here. I'm on your side, Dad. To my surprise he leaned over suddenly and gave me a quick kiss on the cheek.

"It's great to have you here, Elephant, even under these circumstances."

"These circumstances?"

"Mutual unemployment and staring at the crossroads of life, of course."

"You sure are acting different, Dad." Has he been getting high on the sly? "Maybe it's good, your seeing Bernard after all this time." Or maybe, since he never could stand his little brother, he's secretly started on a serotonin re-uptake inhibitor.

"Well. Maybe that's it." What? Is Dad agreeing with me on something? "It's amazing how important family connections are when you get old. I never thought I'd say this but it's good to see him again. And Chankah is fantastic."

"So I guess we can't escape our biology after all."

"What does that mean?"

"Well, you know, we're a social species and we need to stay in touch with our roots. We try not to, by living more and more apart the richer we get, but the isolation starts working on us eventually. We have this need to weave ourselves in with the other threads in the quilt."

In response he shrugged, the older person's equivalent to *Whatever*. As he's said so many times, he doesn't buy that "touchy-feely self-help bleeding-heart New Age crap." He's afraid it'll lead me to the current equivalent of full-fledged communal living and free love. Free love is bad enough, but communes don't even have 401Ks. "The situation with being laid off is that I saw it coming," he went on. "Or Cindy did, actually, and we've been planning around it for a few months now, so the change is really a godsend."

Uh-huh. "But psychologically it must be hard."

"No, I wouldn't say so. Hasn't troubled me much, but I could see where it might some people."

Yeah, some lesser, mortal types. "Not to get mushy or anything, Dad, but aren't you going to miss the people at work? That's what I miss."

"Not particularly. I don't get as close to people as you do." You noticed that? "And anyway, I was never happy doing accounting. Do you know what I wanted to be when I grew up?"

"I honestly have no idea." A prison warden?

"I always wanted to be a history professor at the University of Texas in Austin."

Excuse me, pardon me, uh, Mr. President? Do you have an emergency fund for people whose fathers have been abducted by aliens? "But, Dad, that's such a cool thing to do." UT-Austin is where he met Mom and it's where he finished his accounting degree after Vietnam, but I don't remember Austin anymore. "Why didn't you do it?"

"Life doesn't necessarily turn out like you think it will, Elephant." He meant that I came along and ruined everything.

"So I came along and changed all your plans."

"Oh, I don't think it was exactly like that. I was already getting discouraged and I was slacking off at college. Then I met your mother and that whole, uh, business . . ." He fell silent and I watched him struggle for a minute and didn't help him out. He went on. "A relationship was more important to me than school, and later it was clear that accounting was going to be much more of a sure thing than being some kind of second-rate history professor."

"So you just gave up the professor thing and joined the Marines."

"Yes. And I wanted to do the right thing for the country, of course."

"Of course. And you never looked back?"

"Exactly."

So let me get this straight. You spent twenty-five years at a job you hated and that's the kind of sacrifice you think I should make. Hm. I can see that we're never going to be eye to eye on this. Never. Your soul would have been eaten up, old man, except that you packed it away in mothballs so long ago. "Gosh, Dad, I don't know what to say." Could I have a Valium? A Xanax maybe? Just an old-fashioned Quaalude? Anything? "You look good in spite of it all. Happy. I guess it wasn't so bad, getting fired, if you never liked the job in the first place."

"Laid off."

"Laid off. Sorry."

"That's all right." And we sat in silence for a while, watching the exits go by. Then he looked over at me several times. I could see him out of the corner of my eye but I wouldn't look back. "You know, Eleanor," he started. We were thirty miles down from D.C. on 95-South and the traffic was bad. It had been a while since I'd been carbound and I was wishing he'd keep his eyes on the road but instead he leaned over like he was about to reveal Truth itself and paused. I tensed automatically but all he said was, "Chankah."

"Chankah?" I didn't say it like he did. The way he said it was slowly and meaningfully and as if he were sucking on the syllables like nipples. Chankah. Uh-oh.

"Bernie and Chankah think we should come and visit them in Ohio and I think maybe we should."

"We?"

"The family."

"Ohio?"

"Sure. Why not? One last vacation together before the two J's go off to college and you and Sarah settle down with kids of your own. What do you think?" I think that the drugs you're clearly on are very high quality. When was the last time you wanted a family vacation that included Problem Child and PC Junior? I can't wait to tell Sarah.

"It sounds great to me, Dad." Of course, it'll never happen, but hey. "So Chankah's nice?"

"Nice? She's incredible. And damn good-looking, if you don't mind me saying it." Which I do. Incredible. Good-looking. I don't believe it. He's got a crush, and on his brother's wife. Is this revenge?

"Um, Dad?"

"Mmh?" He said it absentmindedly, no doubt deeply involved in a complex fantasy that I was keen to shake him free from, perhaps a midfifties threesome that included Chankah, Cindy, and various mirrors, or just the videocam running from a tripod. I felt mildly sick. Doesn't the covetousness ever stop? Why do we even torture ourselves with monogamy? It's so unfair, the innate incompatibility of men and women.

"It's not supposed to be fair," Mom used to say, to justify her many reversed decisions, or during those months, when she was newly sober and exceptionally irritable, of denying our every request, no matter how reasonable. "Wipe those tears away. Life is cruel. Be glad you're not a rabbit." To give proper credit, it's what she said when Hank died too, and she said it unflinchingly, the way she always said it to us, unmoved by our tears and unmoved, apparently, even by her own. "We have to move on." The truth is, things were sometimes easier with Mom when she was drinking, at least in the first stages of it, and we would heave temporary sighs of relief when we came home to the unmistakable smell of gin again. Life was kinder for a while and I was always looking for that. I guess I still am.

I turned the radio back on. Chuck Mangione's "Feels So Good." I was grooving on it. "Dad, were your parents happily married?"

He turned the radio off. "You know what bothers me about your generation? That you think it's so important to be happy all the time." I guess that means they weren't. "My folks had their problems, sure. My dad had a bad temper. He wasn't the steadiest worker. But they never thought about divorce. They relied on each other and that counts for a lot more than having a good time and being 'happy.' OK? Got it?"

"Got it."

I napped desperately the rest of the way home and when I woke the car was slowing to exit the interstate. There was a crease on my cheek and drool on my chin and, perhaps less visibly, dread in my heart. I wiped my mouth, fluffed my hair, and freshened my lipstick. Nothing helped discernibly. He drove slowly to accommodate me and warned me of approaching bumps and said I was pretty enough without prettying myself up any more and I understood that it was his way of trying to patch things up.

The first person I greeted was my stepmother. "Cindy! You look so good, how are you?" She looked the way she always looks, fat and sassy and satin-haired, the kind of person who's little but feels good to hug because she's so solid and warm. Cindy is a pampered Persian cat, curvy and very feminine in a Dallas–Fort Worth tinted-blonde well-manicured expensive-handbag regular-facial kind of way that I'll never be able to emulate in all my whole life and couldn't even if I were born with a Gucci in one hand and keys to the horse farm in the other. She says she's nothing but white trash, and she's given to country dancing and tight jeans, but her Baylor College–Nieman-Marcus education shows often enough.

"Oh Beanie Bean," Cindy had her soft little hands on my face and her silky brown eyes two inches from mine, examining me for wrinkles and minute signs of stress. "Why do you always wait so long to come home? What are you using on your face? Where's all your crap? Is this the only luggage you have?

Where are your clothes?" Cindy has three closets in the house that are just for her and she still has to switch summer and winter clothes out of storage.

"These are my clothes, Imelda. It's too hard to lug around eighteen suitcases so I gave my stuff away. I don't want to work in a bank ever again anyway. Adiós, control-top hose. Oh God, you animals, you're going to break my neck!" It was Jacob and Jasmine, nuzzling and warm and giggling like little tots again, except that Jake smelled good for the first time like a grown man and Jazz smelled like Clinique. It made me uncomfortable. Why is it so much easier with kids? I don't want the two of them growing up. They're going to realize how uncool I am and it's going to break my heart. Cindy is good-looking and the twins' father must have been drop-dead before he dropped dead because both the kids were blessed in their bone structure. Lucky shits. And their family life was even good.

A wave of self-pity slammed over me. They'd go to private college and finish in the normal amount of time or less, then either turn into urban professionals or go to art school, and never have to run mad for seven years to escape their first seventeen. Spoiled little cubs. They're more at home with prosperity than I could ever be, and such smooth skin! Such white teeth! Such perfect manes of hair! The property looked good, too. To think of the effort that goes into keeping a big house looking nice, ugh. Just to hire a gardener at the correct time of year is too much work for me.

Just then I saw Bernard and decided it was time to mosey on over and say hello to my long-lost uncle. "Well hey there," I said, laying on a pretty bad southern accent. "I'm your niece Eleanor and you must be my Uncle Bernard."

"Hey there yourself," he said. "I thought you'd introduce yourself as Bean. I've seen some of your photographs, did you know that? Your dad sent them to me years ago. You have quite an eye. I'm impressed that you've decided to go for it. Hang tough, don't let the money thing get in your way."

"Really?" Well, it never got in his way. "So you think I have talent? Do you think photography is art?" I was still talking like someone named Bobbie Sue and each question took about two minutes to enunciate so I could have more of his time.

"Sure I do. Oh, let me help your stepmother in the kitchen. She's a wonderful woman. You must feel very lucky to have her in your life."

"Yes. Definitely. Uh-huh. Bye now. Nice to see you again." And then, to his back, "Thank you for your encouragement." So that's my Uncle Bernard. Yikes. I'd say a long-horn steer, same big shoulders as Dad, same knuckly hands, but nearly six feet tall and rust-colored hair. Rangy. Nice hips, obviously a good ballplayer, but the same pale blue eyes as Buzz and on a man that's trouble.

"He's nice looking, hm?"

"Oh, hi Chankah. Yeah. Reminds me of Dad, but looser." Chankah was nice looking herself, medium short, slim, strong and dark, with string-straight black hair, a big nose, and an athletic, sure-footed way of standing. A black panther, but not cruel. Very compact, very supple, nobody's idiot. Middle Eastern but I didn't know what country. She looked very much like Mom except for the muscles. And Mom would have been in heels and a short skirt. And drunk. Her accent was heavy and attractive, her voice whiskey-deep.

"Your father is like a grown-up version of Bernard, who should have had fewer adventures and more children."

"So he's still wild?"

"When we were dating I called it wild and exciting. Now that we're married it's infantile and annoying. But I suppose I picked him for a reason. Don't give me that look; this isn't serious, just the first-year blues, I think you would say. Your aunt Beatrice warned me but I didn't want to listen. Now I look at a man like your father and I think, 'Ah. That's it. There goes a real man.'"

"My dad?"

"Your dad."

"But Bernie seems like so much fun."

"Fun." She said it like other people say "toenail fungus." "There is more to life than fun. Your father does not go . . . carousing, am I right? And the bills are paid, yes?"

"Yes. Yes to both."

"Yes." Chankah sighed. "A real family man." Then she shrugged and smiled at me. "Ah well. There is always something to be unhappy about. Of course," and again the shrug, "also the opposite is true. Now, let us get some coffee and coerce your stepmother into being less energetic. And perhaps you can pay more attention to your photography and not as much to my husband, who doesn't need encouraging?"

"Sorry," I said, but she waved me off. I guess she's used to the downside of having a babester mate.

We went inside then and she made us all drink Turkish coffee you could walk a dog on. Dad said it was the best coffee he'd ever had. Bernard said Cindy's coffee cake was the best coffee cake he'd ever had. Cindy said the two of them must have a wonderful, free life together. Chankah said she envied anyone with such a beautiful house and lovely, stable family. I ate macaroons until my teeth hurt, then set up a tripod and took intermittent pictures with a long cable so I could sit with the group. Every time the flash went off there was consternation and protest but I ignored it. I drank a lot of coffee.

Too bad Bernard and Chankah had to leave as soon as they did after Dad's party because they were effectively distracting. And the event itself turned out quite reasonable. Lots of dancing, lots of drinking, lots of flirting. Cindy had found a mariachi band from God knows where and for some reason that Mexican music had us all into the tequila up to our shoulders. But two

days afterwards the equal and opposite low hit me hard. I was
the only guest remaining and leaving bed became a struggle.
Dad was finishing out the year with the company and returned
home every evening in a blacker mood. My presence was only
adding to that misery. I spent so much time on the couch that
within two weeks seven extra pounds were ensconced on my
ass. If Patrick were still in the picture—which I have to keep
reminding myself that he isn't—he would have had a seizure.
He wasn't one of those little men who likes his women big. Still,
just because he's gone doesn't mean it's all right to lose control
utterly and I did. Pork out, zone out, chunk out and fight with
Dad. That's home life.

Suburban living is an utter mystery. I can't believe intelligent people set themselves up for a lifetime of that kind of
inertia. I got to Richmond already longing for my books and
movies and favorite coffee shops, and the next thing you know
I was functionally catatonic. Good coffee and meaningful conversation don't exist there. No one reads. The movies suck.
Nothing is walking distance and there aren't any sidewalks
anyway. How do those people live without getting unbelievably
fat? If I stayed with my parents for six months you couldn't get
me through the front door. There's something soporific about
the manicured lawns and pots of skunk cabbage. Sweet williams
around the mailbox posts do to me what the poppy fields did to
Dorothy. In the suburbs it's so easy to live easily, and so hard
to live interestingly.

Nonetheless, I did practically have to get kicked out in order
to leave. I'm the one who planned this train trip, I wanted to go
on it, I knew it was right for me, and still when it came time to
begin the journey in earnest I said, "Um, I think I'll go next
week." I postponed three times. The last time was early this
morning and Dad just lost it. He slammed down his coffee,
which he takes black and bitter, of course, and narrowed his
algae-colored eyes at me. "Look, are you going on this little

jaunt or aren't you?" I hated him for that. You never know when he's going to suddenly notice what's happening around him and demand explanations. Out of old habit my tongue froze. "Goddammit," he snapped, barking his chair on the linoleum as he stood up. "Eleanor May Shank, I'm taking you to the train station tomorrow morning whether you're ready to go or not. I was against this trip at first, but if you say it's important to you and you say you need to do it, then by God that's what's going to happen! You're staying on because you're yellow and I won't have that. So you had another lousy relationship go bad. What else is new? If you think you can use that as an excuse to sit around on one of my sofas like a nesting hen for the rest of your life, think again! Pull yourself together, for Chrissakes!"

"Bookman," said Cindy, warningly, but he ignored her.

"You're putting on weight and overstaying your welcome, Eleanor." Pow. He was saving up for that one and it hurt. "When is tomorrow's train?" he asked, feeling in his pockets for something to write on. "I'll get you out of bed plenty early and take you to the station myself."

"Don't bother," I said, thickly. "Cindy said she'd take me today if I changed my mind." A lie, but I knew she'd stand by me. "I'm catching the 11:00 A.M. to D.C. and the 4:00 P.M. to Chicago. I just need to call Lily and Amtrak to finalize." I ran out of the room like a teenager then, pounding upstairs to panic and pack and phone my friends.

Now, just another passenger waiting for departure on another westbound train, the real me has returned. True, I'm afraid of what I've set out to do here, but it's that tingly, impatient fear, the kind that energizes you, not the paralyzing, numb kind you despise yourself for. I can't wait to see Chicago. And I'm thrilled to be *sin mi familia* again. In past generations it was probably all right, but in the last decade of the twentieth century a month is too long to spend with your parents once you've left home for good. It's disconcerting to watch yourself regress and I'm not sure I want to know why I stayed there as long as I did. My itinerary only allowed me two weeks in Richmond, not the four I ended up staying. I got on everyone's nerves, including my own, got fatter instead of thinner, and we resolved no issues at all. It was the other way around, in fact. The issues multiplied like so many meteors and even so I couldn't fight the gravitational pull hard enough to yank the satellite of myself to a safer orbiting distance. Thank God that's over. Now all I need is a good burp.

I broke down in Union Station and went shopping. Ended up with two shirts I don't need, a pint of Dewars that I paid too much for, and to top it off had a giant calzone with anchovies, feta, and black olives so I could retain plenty of fluid later. I probably shouldn't have planted myself over by the food court, but the nice side was dangerous too, so close to the shops. I'm on a budget. Nothing makes me want to spend money faster than telling myself I'm on a budget. And I'm on a diet. Nothing makes me want to eat more than telling myself I'm on a diet. Oh why couldn't I have been born rich, ectomorphic, and happy-familied instead of chunky, addictive, and doomed?

I should have spent November in the Bahamas instead. Or maybe the Fiji islands. Or really any sunny place in the world, just not home with Dad, decompensating in the suburbs, scrounging pills and ice cream to help me cope. If Auntie Buzz had only flown up I wouldn't have become so desperate. She would have been good company and gotten me stoned and that would have been helpful, but no, she blew us off for romance. I had to push my Zovirax to four a day because someone in the house has stopped taking Valium since my last trip home. All I need is to start a year's sabbatical with a stress-induced herpes outbreak.

I feel better now, but not quite good. I actually felt improved the moment I sat down on the Silver Star this morning, or whatever the train is that creeps up the continent from Florida and takes you with a lot of senior citizens to Union Station, D.C. That's how it is when you travel, though; you get all worked up beforehand, you wonder how you can leave, you didn't finish this or that, you didn't settle something else, what's going to happen in the place you're going, what if you run out of money, what if there's an earthquake, et cetera. And then the moment the train starts moving or the plane taxis back, all your worries drop away. It's magical, it's out of your hands. I'm only ninety-six miles north of where I was at 7:00 A.M. but it might as well be a thousand and ninety-six, that's how detached I suddenly am from that old life. Everything that happens from here on out is unknown. From this point on I'm the one who sets the rules, not Dad, not the bank, not Patrick. When the Capitol, Ltd. pulls back at 4:05, I'm totally on my own.

Yuck. That thought has got me suddenly blue and full of resentment for my new seatmate. It's bad timing for company. I want to sit alone and brood; I don't want to chat about late-breaking news topics with this guy. He's too good-looking for me, too friendly, too well-adjusted, and he probably liked high school. I hate him. Looking at him makes me lonely. The early dark and crispy cold has got me missing Patrick, and it's hard to go into winter without a boyfriend. I'm afraid that if I saw him out this window, standing on the platform and begging me to come home, I'd go. I miss him, I miss Bootsie, I miss working on the house and doing the crossword together.

I hope Chicago helps me out with this. I hope the architecture grabs me and Lily's friends like me and I get over the ache in my chest. I hope it's so interesting there that in two weeks when someone says Patrick to me I can say back genuinely, "Patrick who?" And if that doesn't happen, then God, at least let me get some decent photographs.

☆ ☆ ☆ ☆

Lily and I agreed that fifteen was an age where interesting things should happen. At fifteen you could drive. You could date, if someone asked. You were having your period, getting a body, wearing makeup to school, flirting with boys you didn't know, catching the eye sometimes of grown men. Fifteen was high school, parties with drinking, kissing boys who touched your breasts. Fourteen was small potatoes but fifteen was the big time, and I was there and looking around.

It was Valentine's Day. I didn't have a valentine but I wanted one. Some girls had carnations sent to them in homeroom and the rest of us had to sit around looking stupid and pretending we didn't care. Sarah was still in junior high and didn't have to suffer this yet and I envied her for a while. We weren't getting along, though, and I was mad at her for it. I resolved to do something grown up and by myself so I told Lily that she and I were going to go driving around with Joe Bloch and one of Joe's cousins that night, the four of us in a truck and no room for Sarah. Lily gave me a comprehensive look but agreed. Joe's cousin, Thomas, who the guys called Tomahawk, was good-looking and older and Lily knew she'd be matched with him. She didn't like Joe and Joe didn't like her, but we both considered that secondary to hooking up.

Joe and I were good friends and had been for years, but there was a growing tension between us which I usually seemed to feel more than he did. Earlier, when he had checked the night's plans with me, he had put his hand nonchalantly on my belt, his thumb hooked inside the waistband of my jeans. That was unusual. Thinking about it made me nervous. I stopped thinking about it.

At exactly 8:00 P.M. the doorbell rang and I said, "That's Joe. I'm going to go riding around with him but I'll be home by twelve." I couldn't look at Sarah as I left without her and I wouldn't let Joe come in and say hi.

As we pulled out of the driveway he said, "Your hair looks good." I had spent an hour on it and I said, "Thank you," as if he were a stranger and not my buddy Joe and then I scooted a little closer to him and he patted my leg, then left his hand on my thigh. Once we collected Lily and Tom, I was pressed right against him, with Lily on my other side, and after an hour of driving up and down the main drag Tom said, "Well, put your arm around the girl, for Pete's sake," and Joe did it. Tom had put his around Lily from the beginning.

Next Thomas suggested that we go to his older brother's house, out in the country, and Lily and I kicked our ankles together but didn't say anything. There was no one home and Thomas put the television on to HBO and pulled Lily down on the sofa with him. Joe and I watched the movie with our arms around each other until Thomas said to Lily, "Come on, Valentine. I want to show you something in the back room." On his way out he put Elvis on the stereo and my whole mood changed. When we were young, Mom playing Elvis Presley signaled trouble of a certain variety. It signaled a weekend with Dad out of town, strangers in the house, different smells, different voices from the bedroom, then terrible fights and days of silence, when Sarah and I communicated with one another by sign language only.

I said to Joe, "Uh-oh," and he said, "She'll be fine. Tomahawk won't do anything she doesn't want to do." He was stroking my back and looking at me and then he said, "Maybe we should do more than just sit around."

"Like what?"

"Have you ever touched a guy?"

I looked at him and again he seemed to be no one I knew. I thought, Maybe you're not really supposed to say the word penis. Mom didn't want us growing up talking street trash like she thought the Mexican girls did, so penis is what we called it at my house. We also had to say vagina and rectum. Or maybe anus, I was always confused about which was which. I said, "You know I haven't."

"Do you want to?"

"Do you want me to?"

"Yeah," he said. I looked at him. "I do want you to. Here. Touch me here," and he took my hand and put it over the front of his jeans. I didn't know what to do so I gripped, a little bit, and he said, "Wait a minute." Then he undid his pants and I was looking right at his penis, which was half hard in its dark blond curlings and didn't look eager and scary the way I thought it would. His stomach was flat and pale, with horizontal rows of muscles from the weight-lifting. The way he was sitting, with his shirt pulled up and his jeans pulled down to just above his knees, reminded me of walking in on my dad having a bowel movement. Dad called it having a bowel movement but we said number two. Two for pooping, one for peeing, and we never settled the issue of three. Was it diarrhea or was it vomit? Zero, of course, was farting, which my parents called passing gas. We were definitely not allowed to say the word fart.

Joe said, "Hold onto it like this. Put your other hand here. Now move up and down. Do your fingers tighter. No, looser." I did what he wanted but nothing happened and I got sweaty and embarrassed and after a while he said, "I guess it's the beer." I didn't know what to do. I sat back against the sofa and he said, "Don't worry about it," but I was. He tucked himself into his pants and zipped up and then he said he had to go to the bathroom. He was gone a long time.

Lily and Tom came back into the living room and Lily was very quiet. Tom put some other music on and got himself a beer from the refrigerator. He asked if we wanted one but we both said no. We hadn't started drinking yet. "Where's Joe?" he asked.

"Bathroom."

"Yeah? Did you guys have a little hanky-panky going on out here? I bet you did, I can tell by the look on your face. I hope he didn't take you further than you wanted to go." Thomas laughed. "He's pretty hard to turn down when he wants something, that ol' Joe is." I didn't say anything. Lily didn't say anything. "So are you all boyfriend and girlfriend now?" Thomas wouldn't shut up. "You spend enough time together, you might as well make it official, especially if you're going to start fooling around. And hey, it's Valentine's Day, after all."

"Shut up, Tomahawk," said Joe, coming out of the bathroom and not looking that good. "These girls have to be home by midnight and it's nearly that now. We'd better get going."

We piled into the truck and Joe put on Foreigner and Tom drank and none of us said anything. Joe didn't put his arm around me and I sat, huddled next to him, feeling miserable and hating my hair. Thomas was playing with Lily's fingers and when we were close to my house he lifted her into his lap and said, "You can just snuggle right here 'til we get you to your place safe and sound, Valentine." She laid her head meekly on his shoulder and I moved so no part of me was touching Joe and for the first time I was glad about Dad being gone. I was hungry and my stomach hurt and I couldn't wait to get home.

3 I'm in Chicago with Lillian Chase in a huge, drafty house off North Ashland. I've been here nine or ten days and have never been so cold indoors. The sun is shining but this makes no difference to the temperature in the house since, I guess, the builders forgot to insulate. It's cold in the kitchen, it's cold in the attic where we sleep, and it's fucking freezing in the bathroom, which is my primary concern. I'm beginning to understand why people in the olden days didn't bathe all winter. It's hard enough to relax and get a routine going in any strange house but in this house, where the toilet forms icicles and the bathroom is strategically located right between the kitchen and the main staircase, showering is death-defying and a satisfying bowel movement is out of the question.

Too bad I'm not more like Sarah, who like a guy can shit anywhere and doesn't know the meaning of the word irregular. I guess Lily's like that too because she doesn't care about the fact that all household traffic gets funneled past the toilet. I'm more inhibited and have begun the old dreams of purgatives and high colonics.

"Hey you. Warm yet?" Lillian Chase is dancing around happily to *Little Creatures* with a coffee cup in one hand and a joint in the other, apparently unaware that most of the civilized world spends its weekday afternoons working.

"Oh yeah, toasty." Right. I'm dressed in everything wool that I own, she's dressed in black velvet vintage, and I'm the one shivering and stiff-jointed and longing for the Caribbean.

"Want a hit?"

"Yeah, thanks." Oh why not? It's got to be healthier than the fast-acting, rather addictive anti-anxiety agents she's storing in the medicine chest, and maybe it'll put my cold nerve to sleep. "The only drawback is that if I get the munchies from this I'm liable to starve to death."

"Why?" Lillian looks genuinely surprised. It's too much work to expound on the whole mechanics of calorie intake so I roll my eyes and take another toke before bothering to explain myself.

"Food, Lily."

"Chase." She doesn't go by Lillian anymore; she says it's nothing but cow shit and train tracks to her and she hates it.

"Food, Chase. Are you familiar with it?" Those little anorectics are really something, aren't they?

"I eat," she says, defensively. Uh-huh. And I do tantric yoga. "I eat when I go out on dates. I just haven't gone on any lately. Do you think it's because I'm getting old?"

"Yeah, that's probably it."

"No, Bean, I'm serious, it's my skin. I have the skin of an old woman, don't I? This goddamn Midwestern weather. It's doing me in. What am I going to do? I have wrinkles. Wrinkles! I shouldn't be living here. Do you think I should start saving up for laser treatments?"

"Definitely. I can't believe you've waited this long."

"Ugh, I shouldn't do this. It's bad for my lungs." She shakes her head sorrowfully, takes in a huge hit, and hands me the bone.

"Yeah. Maybe another cigarette will help."

"Shut up. We're not all as together as you."

"You're funny."

"I mean it," she says, changing the music to P.J. Harvey. "You're doing great."

Sure, but you haven't had protein in three years. Who knows what that does to brain functioning? I go and get more coffee and bring it back to the living room. No more cream. I can't stand coffee without cream.

"You look like your mother," she says suddenly, and I cringe. "What?" she asks. "You don't like that?"

"I'm petrified of turning out like her."

"She's beautiful, though." She is. "And she was fun sometimes." She was? "And oh boy could she party."

"Exactly. Who wants a mother like that? She has the maternal instinct of obsidian. And Jesus, all those men. I never knew if I wanted to be nothing like her or if I'd give my right arm to be just like her."

"Yeah." Chase raises her wispy eyebrows and nods, slowly. "Your mom could score the guys, no question about it. She could even score our guys."

"And did."

"And did," she says, and the next thing you know we're laughing helplessly, rolling back on the couch and holding our stomachs because that old bitch mother of mine could score anyone back then and probably still could today.

Half an hour later we're solidly stoned. In the meantime we've scavenged bagels, put on Hank Williams, had more coffee, found the portable heater, and persuaded the cat to cuddle in my lap. I'm actually warm, sprawled back against the sofa with Lily leaning up against me and singing along to "Lonesome Blues" or whatever it is and she doesn't, apparently, care that we never used to lean up against each other like this. She hands me the last of the joint and then, when I toss it in the general direction of the ashtray, leans up very casually and kisses me, right on the mouth. Not with her tongue or anything, but firmly, like I can't pretend she doesn't mean it. And I'm high and it feels good and so I don't move, and then it's over and the cat's still purring and she goes back to singing Hank and after a minute or two lights another cigarette.

I can't help it. I have to ask. "Lily, what was that all about?"

She shrugs. "Oh, I don't know. The usual, I guess. I always wanted to and then I figured, why not? I'm not as afraid as I used to be. You don't have to freak out though. You aren't, are you?"

"No. Not very." Yes, totally, yikes.

"So what are you thinking?" she asks from behind her cigarette smoke.

"I don't know. Boston is very far away right now."

Chase says, "And it's a good thing. You've been there too long." She stretches her legs out and puts her boots on the coffee table and she's so damn skinny that I either want to shoot her or shoot myself.

"What does that mean?"

"Nothing." But I know what it means. It means I've gotten dull and she's right, I have. When did it happen? I'm thirty years old and dull dull dull. She's thirty years old and interesting. I'm never having a thin friend again. Nothing is going right. Something tangible should be happening, something visible, something impressive. Even coming from a broken home and public schools I should be moving in a definite direction by now, making my mark, leaving behind me a tail like a comet. Instead I'm traveling the country aimlessly, leeching off everyone I know with an apartment, and all I've got to justify my behavior is a second-hand camera and the sketchy pipe dreams of a photography book. I have no real experience, no money, no coherent plan, not a darkroom to work in, not a lover to my name.

And sitting on the sofa next to me is the skinniest person on the planet with boobs and you know what else she has? Shiny straight hair and clear blue eyes and a career on stage and sex whenever she wants it and she's even sold paintings for real money. Yes. She's going somewhere with her life and

I'm spinning my wheels in perpetual neutral. What a sucky day and I can't even blame it on PMS.

I should call Travis for a pep talk and comic relief but I've vowed to make this trip on letters alone. He would just tell me to stop whining and go for a run, but I can't face the first mile. He would say that at least I dressed like a normal person and could afford to have my apartment heated in winter, but who cares about heat? Who cares about tailored pants and Bar Harbor weekends and the perfect system for paying bills? My greatest accomplishments to date are losing sixty pounds and never getting red-lined on a gas bill. So I'm no longer fat and the utility companies like me. Wow. That's impressive. That's really something. What have I been doing for the past ten years but wasting my inner light poring over somebody else's ledger books? Oh God, I'm boring!

Great. Chase has put on Cowboy Junkies to lighten things up a little. I'll just commit suicide right now and get this over with. She's crooning soulfully and sounding lovely and it pisses me off. When did she become beautiful and self-confident and why isn't it happening to me? I wish I had her boobs. I wish she'd go off somewhere and eat fifty doughnuts.

Damn, I hate when I get like this. There's only one thing that will help. The opposite sex. One flirtatious man could make all the difference and it wouldn't matter if he were old, ugly, adolescent, inappropriate, in the middle of a bank robbery, or a father of four. He would just have to be male and appreciative and single me out. That's not asking so much, is it?

"What are you thinking now, Bean?"

"I love the Cowboy Junkies. They may be the most perfect group ever for depression. How did we get by without them?"

"Leonard Cohen."

"Oh yeah. Christ. Don't put him on—you'll find me hanging from the rafters."

"Come on, you."

"Come on me what?"

She's jumped up off the couch and is grinding out her ciga-rette purposefully. "There are beautiful men everywhere, and especially at the theater, so that's where we're going. I believe what you need is a pick-me-up, something along the lines of a heterosexual artist or two with photogenic bones."

"Uh-oh. Beware of men with long hair and repartee, for truly do they tempt me."

"What about their bodies, B?"

"Oh yeah. Nice hair, nice bodies, and high IQs. But what if they don't like me?"

Chase goes in to the bathroom to fix her hair and start mak-ing up and says, "Like I said, you've been in Boston too long." I go in behind her to brush my teeth and put on lipstick and realize, glancing quickly into the mirror, that I look all right. Maybe even good. My hair does better when I let it be.

Well, the playhouse is humming, as always, and full of photo opportunities. Chase disappears to probably have sex with someone and I've taken a dozen pictures when the guy they call Plain Blane walks over and starts talking me up. This is how he does it.

"Hi Bean. Remember me?" I nod and take another picture. Plain or not the boy is sexy and I've had more rational days. "Do you like Chicago, Bean?" I nod again and then he says, "So, how long has it been since you've had a one-night stand?"

I put my camera down for that one. "Not long enough." I hate one-night stands. Is there a person alive who doesn't hate one-night stands? I've never had a single one that was any good. You're expected to take care of yourself, that's the problem, and when you're young you don't know how. Then, when you're older and you do, you aren't interested anymore in one-night stands. Ironic, huh.

"Are you broke?" he asks next.

"Yes, O subtle one."

"Want to get some coffee to suppress our appetites? I can afford coffee."

"Will you sit for me?"

"Only if you'll let me do it naked."

It's hard to imagine Blane naked. He's one of the stand-up improvisational comics I met the other night through Chase's favorite roommate and I must say I'm glad to see him here again, stocky, hirsute, and sweaty, standing close enough to smell me and vice versa. He smells good. Clean but musky. Not a cologne wearer. You can picture the guy bowling but you can't really picture him posing nude for art.

"You may not have noticed this but you're pausing at a very awkward place in our conversation."

"Oh. Sorry. I had to stop and think about you naked and it waylaid me."

"If it helps to make the decision, you can be the naked one. Are you ovulating?"

"Excuse me?"

"Well, when women ovulate they send out fuck-me-now vibes, and you're sending them out."

"Perhaps it's your feverish imagination."

"Nope. When you're not handsome, you learn other things."

"What else have you learned?"

"I give a mean foot rub, I make superb pesto, and I clean toilets. Not my own, of course, other people's."

"OK, enough, let's get the coffee now," I tell him, no-nonsense because what we had at Chase's place was either terrible or ruined by marijuana and suddenly I want nothing more than an hour of talking to this guy alone over a steaming cup of Chicago's best java.

"You're tho forthful," he says, lisping, but takes me by the arm and steers me first to the stack of coats and then out the door. But we don't get coffee after all. It turns out that he lives just around the corner and none of his roommates are home.

He's a slob but I don't mind because for one thing so am I and for another Patrick was the neat freak from hell and anything different is nice. Patrick washed the sheets three times a week and would reuse neither towel nor glass. He wouldn't even drink after me, can you believe that shit?

Blane puts on some country music and says, "I consider Lefty Frizzel the perfect makeout artist, don't you agree?"

"Well, in my mind he runs a close second to Marty Robbins."

"Marty's a little raucous for me. Oh, you're pulling my leg. Here, chunky butt, shut your mouth and dance with me, would you?"

"You can dance?"

"What, you think you have to be tall to be coordinated? Haven't you noticed it's always the short guys who accomplish things in this world?"

"Why is the world so obsessed with six footers, then? And why are people getting so tall so fast? Good food isn't enough to explain it."

"The world is a crazy place, my dear. Now, stop that inquiring mind for a moment and dance with me."

He really can dance, beautifully, as beautifully as Joe Bloch used to and Joe Bloch was the John Travolta of my high school. If men had any idea how vividly erotic the waltz can be, how easy it is to seduce a woman you've danced with, how dancing is a perfectly satisfactory foreplay replacement, would they do more of it? If I found out that 93 percent of men were really and truly turned on by spike-heeled shoes, bleached-blonde hair, and playing dumb, would I do it? Not.

Oh God I like a man in no hurry. He's taken off my two top layers and we're waltzing around the hardwood living room to some romantic as hell song about Lefty's mother and father, with me dressed only in my socks and underclothes. He's still got all his clothes on. I like that. Maybe Patrick's right and I'm a secret exhibitionist. Hey, where did that thought come from? This is Blane's hour and nothing to do with that old Irish agony, goddammit.

When I called Travis crying last spring to say that I was leaving Pat, Travis said to me, "Why Bean, why him? Why is he the one breaking your heart?" And I said to him, "You know what? I don't know," and the fact is I still don't.

Blane and I have gotten to that point of dancing where we're really just swaying to the music and I'm now wearing socks alone. He keeps adjusting my breasts so they squash against his chest and rub against his sweater. I tell him I'm going to get a rash and he says, "Superchunk, this is just the start of it. I haven't shaved in days."

By the time he leads me to the bed, which is unmade but very sturdy, I've got that sharp ache that says it's been too long without sex. Still holding on to the belt loop of his jeans I say, "This bed reminds me of you. Messy but solid."

"It's a very good bed."

"And you're a very good guy?"

"You're a very fast learner. Now lay down and spread your legs, babe, and let me look at you. Hold yourself apart. Mmh. You're wet, aren't you?"

"Uh, as a long-ago boyfriend used to say, FBP."

"Fucking beautiful pussy?"

"Flood of biblical proportions, darly-doo. Do you think you could hurry up and fuck me and we'll go slow next time around?"

"I can live with that, but ask me again, and ask me nice."

I do, and he does, and I come twice and he comes the requisite once, looking right into my eyes and telling me I'm beautiful, and later on we get a tiny little bit stoned and he goes down on me, wonderfully, to of all things Nine Inch Nails.

Now he's sitting naked on my naked bum and rubbing my feet with almond oil as I lie on the bed, looking at the soft pine floor and wondering, idly, how I'm going to describe this scene to Chase, in what detail. And then I wonder how well she knows him. It's unlikely that she's slept with him since she only dates lookers. She's going to shake her head about ol' Blane, but I myself am suspicious of good-looking men. I can't take them seriously. On the other hand, being seen in public with them is such a balm for the ego, and I'm not sure I'd really want to be seen at, say, my twenty-year high school reunion with Plain Blane from Chicago.

That could change, though, after enough good sex and stimulating conversation. A month of his mouth and I'd probably follow the guy to Nome, Alaska. Two months of it and I'd be telling my friends how gorgeous he is and believe every word. I love his body already, I love the fit of him against me, I like his hairiness. And he smells good. He has the kind of scent that makes you want to bury your nose in his armpit. He kisses my toes, each one separately, and then says, "Give me a minute, I need the shitter."

Sarah says no woman needs a good-looking man, just a rich one, and if you're lucky he might even be interesting. If you're damn lucky, he'll also be tall. Blane is one for four and actually that seems like plenty. I wonder if she'd appreciate the poetry I can hear him reading to me from the sanctity of the bathroom. Half-assedly educated as I am I have no idea who he's reciting, Yeats or Keats or who knows who. I'm still lying on the bed but on my back now, still naked, still sticky and wet, still vaguely stoned. Screaming Trees is playing low on the CD, making me rowdy and blue at the same time, the way they do. I can't see him from here but Blane is I guess taking a shit with the door open and chanting quietly about an old man in front of a fire remembering the woman he loved best and the curve of her neck or something and before I know it tears are seeping down my temples and into my hair and my nose is all runny but I don't want to sniff in case he hears. Then the phone rings. He swears and wipes and flushes and runs past me to the kitchen, balls flopping, toilet ring imprinted red on his ass. I take the opportunity to sniff hard and wipe my face on the sheet.

"Hey baby," he says happily to someone on the phone. "Oh yeah? Fantastic! No, nothing much, working tonight on some new stuff. OK, sure. Love you too. See you there. Bye." Then I hear him running the tap, filling a glass, and taking a long drink. "Ah," he says, and calls out to me, "Want some water?"

Wow. In all my life this has never happened to me. I mean, I've been with otherwise engaged men a couple of times, but I always knew about it beforehand and went into the encounter suitably armored, emotionally removed, inwardly contemptuous. Not so this time. I actually admired this asshole. And I thought it was mutual. I thought it was special. I have a stupid idea left over from my Barbara Cartland education that good sex means something much more than good sex. Time and time again this proves to be not so, and time and time again I'm surprised. Holy romantic panic, Batman. What an ignoramus I am! I was lying on this bed actually liking a man I've known for less than five hours, not even intending to, intending, in fact, to put the whole thing down to hormones and timing but the quality of the sex making it different afterwards than before and now I'm devastated.

This must be what drives men crazy about women. God knows, it drives me crazy too. Ugh, now I have to act all cool and nonchalant and the next time I see him, which will probably be tomorrow, I'll see him with his honey and have to act even more cool and nonchalant and I hate hate hate that shit.

"No thanks," I say, struggling for a neutral tone.

"Come on," he says, "you need to drink water and pee after sex or you'll get a bladder infection. You know the rules." He walks into the room with a big glass of water and I take it obediently. He gives me a hard look and then sits down on the bed next to me. "You look pretty bummed, Bean. I take it you didn't know that Mimi is my girlfriend." Mimi is one of the actors at the playhouse, about the only woman there who was nice to me. Better and better.

"Mimi. Great. I like Mimi." And his face is so sympathetic that I go on. "Oh Blane. I feel really stupid and really horrible and I don't even know why." Although I do.

"I'm sorry, sticky bun, I should have told you. Then I thought, either you know because Chase knows and she and Mimi have been together before, or you'd laugh at me for thinking you'd care. Or maybe I thought that telling you would ruin my chances and I wanted so badly to be with you. Do you hate me?"

"Kind of. Mostly I just feel like an idiot because it's bothering me so much."

"Here. Come here." He leans against the wall, puts my glass down on the floor, and pulls me back against his chest. He cradles his arms around me and just holds me with the blankets pulled up and then, when he feels me relax, says, "It was nice, wasn't it? The way we were together, I mean. You don't find that kind of chemistry every day, don't you think?"

"I guess."

"Do you regret doing it?"

"I guess not."

"If it had to happen all over again, would you do something different?"

Yeah, I wouldn't cry because you quoted me poetry. "I'd step on your toes while we were dancing," I say, sniffing. He laughs and I feel his penis stirring against my backside, so I get up, quick.

"Felt that, did you?"

"Aye, laddie, I did."

"Not up for another round?"

"You're right, I'm not."

"You up for that coffee we blew off earlier?"

Jesus, this guy is so nervy. He should be in sales. "You should sell vacuum cleaners," I tell him over my shoulder, walking around the apartment and gathering my clothes together.

"Why, because I suck? Or because I'm the quintessential salesman?"

"The latter. And the former."

"I love Mimi, I honestly do, but what you and I had together was one of those rare physical things and I for one am glad I didn't let it go. Now, will you have coffee with me and be my buddy?"

"Do you care if I'm not too talkative?"

"Nope."

"Then it's a done deal. Where are my panties?"

"I can't keep them?"

"They're just cotton," I tell him, "and not too new."

"Mm. Experienced. So I can have them?"

"Yes, you persistent son of a bitch. Now chatter to me about movies or something so I can get my mind off our illicit affair, would you?"

"Sure. And weren't you going to take some pictures?"

All I can do is stare at him. And then I get my camera and balance it on a book shelf, set the auto timer and we take pictures, the two of us, naked except for socks, dancing.

On Friday, three days later, I'm still in Chicago, battling the cold with late nights and booze and struggling to keep up with Lily, who's struggling to keep up with herself. She's going through her Camel Lights in record time, easily two packs a day, plus coffee by the pot, Scotch and pool until late every night, and only occasional bagels and Guinness to fortify her. If Kansas and Jessica aren't much slower than this, Tucson is going to see a very wrecked me.

By early afternoon on this bitter cold, pale gray day, we've been in the living room for hours already, huddled around the heater with the cat and our coffee and quilts around our shoulders like the shawls of old women. So far we've discussed Tucson, Blane, and Ricky Serrano, Joe Bloch, old times, and of course sex, sex, and sex, but now we're both tired out and quiet and she's sunk, suddenly, so deep in the blues she can barely keep her nostrils clear to breathe. I don't know the reason why and I don't know how I know this, but I know that she's mad at me and I know that she's probably right to be because without doubt it's something shitty I did when we were kids and if she's going to start checking off those incidents in her mind and wanting some sort of retribution then I'm afraid my last couple of days here are going to be long and hairy.

It's not helping that we're both done in, physically. I didn't think it could happen without bringing on hospitalization but she looks as if she's lost weight since my arrival. Her pallor and hollows have increased to the tubercular point and I myself am feeling peaked and headachy and almost frail. There seems to be a faint echo in the room. I've either got the flu or my herpes is acting up again but I can't feel the tell-tale tingling that portends an outbreak. Still, better safe than sorry. I need to drink more water and lay off the Joe but, in the meantime, prescription drugs please.

"Where are you going?" she asks me listlessly, the shadows under her eyes nearly as blue as the eyes themselves.

"I need to load up on my Zovies."

"Your what?"

"My herpes medicine, remember? I usually take one a day, or sometimes none, but when I feel something coming on I take more. I think I feel something coming on." Years ago, when I first told her about the herps, she thought I meant a fever blister, and I had to act like a free clinic film and tell her about virus transmission and STDs. She hasn't changed. Herpes, PID, warts, chlamydia, gonorrhea, crabs, trick, whatever, it's all the same to her. She's one of those women who sleeps with a thousand men, uses a condom twice a year and has never even had a yeast infection. It's enough to make you puke.

I'm not so fortunate. I got zapped in Albuquerque by a guy with a cold sore going down on me. At first, when I was panicked and crazed and completely grossed out, the blisters were everywhere and I felt like Typhoid Mary, but now I only get a little one every now and then when I'm sick or stressed or eat peanuts and chocolate. The hilarious thing is that we never had real sex, I mean with penetration. We were roommates and he could dance his ass off and we were together occasionally until I left the state, but I wouldn't fuck him because I didn't trust him. Pretty funny, huh. Chase told me that she didn't have oral sex for months after I told her my story. She had regular sex, though, unprotected; such is the logic of the human mind.

Just to see if she'll keep talking I say, "I need to cut down on the coffee, too."

"Oh." She flicks her ash, head nodding, eyes not meeting mine. She doesn't seem to be shaking her blues and I'm getting nervouser and nervouser. For one uncourageous moment I toy with the idea of hopping the Southwest Chief two days early.

"Should we play something else?" I ask, but she just shrugs. I try again. "Do you guys have a thermometer?" She's so forbiddingly silent that I nearly retreat upstairs to read more of *Zen Inklings* and freeze in the attic. I've been in Chicago long enough to get on her nerves, long enough that our conversation has graduated from mostly polite to mostly real. It might help if I could disappear for a few hours, but I'm on such a tight budget, and there are no coffee shops around here, and it's three degrees above zero outside not counting the wind chill, and besides, maybe we should talk it out. Gulp.

"A thermometer. Uh, I don't know." She rouses herself slightly. "I doubt it. Are you feeling feverish?"

"Yeah."

"Me too. And it feels like my head is one of the Carlsbad Caverns."

"Hey, me too." I'm thrilled to get complete sentences out of her. "We must have caught something. Maybe I don't have to take all those pills, then."

"Maybe not." Once again she isn't looking at me. She's staring into space and listening hard to Tom Waits. We've got *Rain Dogs* on the stereo, one of the best albums ever made, but today we should opt for lightness. I can feel the weight of his sorrow and the threat of her emotions and the rawness of my own heart and that, along with my fuzzy head and general fatigue and the numbing cold outside, is pushing me to the limit.

I look at the cat and the cat looks back, purring expectantly. "Yeah, I've been thinking of giving up coffee for a while now and switching to more healthy things instead." Lillian's white-blonde eyelashes don't even twitch. "Do you have herbal tea?"

"No."

I hate herbal tea anyway. She flicks her ash, sips her coffee, bends her head to the lyrics. I reach out to rub the cat's nose and it lifts its face to my hand, purring louder and looking at me with that temporary feline love. I try again. "Back in Richmond, Lily, there were these pictures of us that I found in a box in the basement, you would die if you saw them."

"Chase and don't remind me, OK?" She sounds serious, and I turn to see that old, haunted, miserable look on her face.

"They're not that bad. Chase. What's the matter?"

"Bean, those days sucked. It was always you and Sarah against me, or me feeling stupid and poor, or me being made fun of, or me being the ugly one, or whatever. I never told you this before, but if I ever had to go back there I'd kill myself."

"Are you crazy? It wasn't that terrible." And you're beautiful now and skinny. Doesn't that make up for everything?

"Don't minimize me, OK?"

"Sorry." I'm not opening my mouth again. Geez. What's with her? And what's with that "minimize" stuff? Her past analysis is showing. "Really, the pictures were cute. We just looked like rednecks, that's all."

"Yeah. OK." She sucks on her cigarette like it's not OK. Tom Waits gravels on. His pain is my pain. "What I can't forgive about those days, Bean, is that I never once stood up to you."

"But you did!"

"No, I didn't. Did you know that Ricky Serrano and I had an on-again off-again thing for years when we were kids? No, you didn't know. When he left for Cruces I was brokenhearted, did you know that? No, you didn't. You asked me why I dumped you in high school? That's one of the reasons. I couldn't tell you about him and do you want to know why?" I don't think so. "Because you couldn't conceive of the possibility of someone you liked, liking me better. Am I right?" She doesn't wait for an answer, which is a good thing. Ricky Serrano and Lillian Chase, I can't fucking believe it. Except that I do. Lots of little things are now making lots more sense. "And what about all those times you and Sarah used to laugh at me? You acted like you were in your own private world and I was some alien who couldn't speak your language. You treated me like shit. You didn't call me once my first year of college. And then Tucson!"

Tucson. Ay, Diós mío. Tucson after Hank died, when Sarah and Lily and I tried to recreate old times and succeeded all too well thanks to the enhancement capabilities of liquor and cocaine. At the time, even I thought I had gone insane. I did so much coke. We all did. Sarah and I came to blows that weekend over Hank, but that wasn't even the worst event of the vacation. We hadn't slept in two nights when I got possessed by the feeling that Sarah had been fucking Hank as well as Jimmy, and that they used to sit together up at the farm and talk about me and what a loser I was, and they would laugh at me for being ugly and pathetic. I just knew, suddenly, that that was the reason Hank used to write to me every Thursday. I could see him clearly in my mind showing the letters to Mom and Sarah before he sent them to me in Remie. I could see them all laughing. I could hear them all whispering, "She's so pathetic. She's so pathetic."

I was wired, jumpy as hell, and wouldn't listen to reason, but Sarah was wired too and wasn't offering much. In the middle of the fight Lily tried to intervene and, inexplicably, we both turned on her. If there is a hell and I end up in it, one of the items used to torture me will be the look on her face in that moment. She went home to Chicago the next morning and none of us spoke for two more years.

I haven't answered her accusations when the telephone rings. Few times in my life have I been this happy to be interrupted. Chase snatches up the phone like she's relieved as well and then says, "It's for you. Your dad," and hands it to me without looking at me or even exchanging pleasantries with him, an opportunity she would ordinarily jump at.

"Hey," I say to her, "I'm sorry for all that. You're right, we were shitty. We would never have made it without you, though, and I guess we always thought you felt the same."

She shrugs. "I should have told you before." And then she goes into the frigid bathroom to start the lengthy process of making up for the day.

"Dad?"

"Elephant?"

"Yes?" Uh-oh. He sounds emotional and quiet and unlike himself, and even though I'm always asking for exactly that, now that he's done it I can't help wishing he'd go back to his usual thing. Is the fifth decade going to be squishy even for the Iron Man? It's hard to believe. "How are you?" I ask him, and even to me I sound remote and cold. "Is everything all right?"

"It's fine," he says, registering my tone of voice. There's a long pause. "How's Lillian?"

"Oh good, very good. Yeah."

"And Chicago?"

"Just great. Everyone is so nice, even at bars and restaurants. I forgot that people in the rest of the country are friendly.

But they dress like lunatics, even the normal ones. I can't believe how conservative Boston is by comparison. Whenever I tell people where I'm from they say, 'Oh, Boston. It's pretty there but really uptight.' Chicago's not uptight like that, do you know what I mean?" He doesn't answer so I speak on, quickly. "There's not that rigid differentiation between the classes. Everybody in this part of town goes to the same coffee shops, no matter where they went to school and no matter what jobs they have now. I really like that. It's cold though, bitter cold. Windy like New Mexico but much colder, and darker, and sort of intimidating, weather-wise. I guess that's why the rest of the country doesn't live here."

"Uh-huh." Pause.

I realize he's got something he wants to say to me. Great. I wish we had screened the call. Today seems to be another day for revelations and I'm not in the mood. I'm not going to help him out. I'm not going to give him an opening. He's a grown-up, he can reach out on his own. He never makes it easy on me, why should I make it easy on him? "What's up, Dad? You sound like you've got something on your mind."

"I do." There's another long pause. "I've been thinking about some of the things you said to me when you were here, and some of the things I said to you. And I just want you to know that, uh, that, well, that I love you, and I think that what you're doing is terrific. That's all." And I hear him gasp, the way you do when you're crying silently. "Do you need anything, honey?" His nose is stuffy.

"No." I can barely choke it out through the lump of tears that's about to burst in the back of my own throat, but still my voice sounds cool. He waits, and waits some more, but my jaw is clenched and I can't unclench it.

"Well," he says, with some finality, and waits for me again. Then, giving up, he says, "OK. Good-bye, Eleanor May. Have a great trip and take a lot of pictures. Call us if you need money."

And he hangs up. I can hear in his voice that he thinks he failed again.

When Patrick and I used to fight, sometimes he would say, "Hey, I'm not your dad. I'm not the one who abandoned you." And I would want to deck him one because my dad didn't abandon me and I don't have hang-ups about that. I should have said to him, "Yeah? Well I'm not your mom. I'm not the one who starved you when you were a toddler, remember?" Maybe I did say that, come to think of it. We pretty much said it all, me and Pat, and anyway, he did sort of abandon me, Dad I mean.

"Chase?" I know she can't hear me through the hair dryer, though, so I sit and weep and rock back and forth until I feel better, and then I go join her in the bathroom with the cat under one arm and the heater under the other, to blot my face and tell her I'm sorry and tell her another episode in the saga of me and my father. Then we gravitate back to the living room and guiltily brew another pot of coffee. We also toast a couple bagels but take off the Tom Waits. He makes us both too weird and blue, at least on the days that are weird and blue already.

"So tell me about Patrick," she says. "I thought you were going to marry him and settle down and now you're in Chicago, sleeping with comedians. What happened?"

"What didn't happen? I'll tell you how I knew we'd break up. One day we were standing in the laundry room fighting about whether the whites should get washed in hot or not and I called him a fucking compulsive and he said to me, 'Bean, if I never changed would you stay with me?' And I froze, right there, with my arms full of sheets and I just stared at him. It was an unbelievable question, exactly the right question to ask, the question that put our core issue onto the table. We looked at each other and I could feel my heart beat and then I rolled my eyes and pretended I didn't have to answer but the truth is that I knew, right then, that the answer was no.

If he never changed, would I be with him? Hell no, I'd as soon murder him as stay with him. That's when I knew I had to leave."

"So you packed your bags and moved out?"

"Not exactly. Before Pat and his drinking I was always the fuck-up, but with him, no matter how bad I let things get, he was worse. That made it hard to go. Before him I was with men who wanted to rescue me and they're easier to ditch."

"Yeah? I could use me one right about now and I wouldn't leave for years." She's smiling a little, the first of the day.

The other thing is that Patrick had had an American aunt on his mother's side who got him into the country when he was eighteen and then died, five years later, leaving him her house in Quincy and a little bit of money. I'm ashamed to admit this but I probably wouldn't have given him three years if it weren't for that real estate.

"What was it like, thinking you were going to marry someone? Nice? Cozy?"

"It sucked. All of a sudden it wasn't fun being irresponsible. One day we're getting stoned together and having a blast, the next day I'm telling him, 'How am I supposed to explain your marijuana habit to the children?'"

"That reminds me," she says. "Should we smoke that joint now or wait for later?"

"Now." And then, inexplicably, I start crying for the second time today. "God, Lily, am I ever going to be in love again?"

"Yes," she says, handing me someone's T-shirt to wipe off my face with. "But not for a little while yet. And it's Chase. And I think you could use a Midol but we don't have any." She lets minutes pass with me sobbing and the Pogues singing and then she says, "So you found someone just like your mother but with different plumbing and you said to yourself, Honey, you're the man for me."

"Yeah?"

"Yeah. Only this time you had the upper hand, which you never had with her."

She's right. With all his screwing around it didn't feel like the upper hand, but it was. It was because we both knew he'd never leave and we both knew that I would. The day I did the sun was shining. It was a cold morning in early March and I phoned in sick to the bank. Everyone I worked with knew what I was doing. Patrick was teaching in Lynn and there was snow on the ground. I figured he'd be home late. He figured I'd be leaving. When I walked out the door with the last of my things Bootsie was sitting on the windowsill, one paw up on the glass. I had found her half-drowned in the gutter and talked Pat into keeping her at his house. A lot of times when the two of us couldn't manage a civil sentence we would end up crouched around her, murmuring little love words that we wouldn't let ourselves say to one another. I put my hand up to the window and she butted the glass with her head. I thought I heard her meowing. Then I got in the car and Monica drove me away.

"Want more coffee?" Chase asks when my sniffling dies down.

"God no. I've got palpitations as it is."

"I've never had them."

"Well, no. You thrive on bad habits. I'll bet your lungs clear up with high-tar cigarettes."

"Speaking of which, I need more. Let's go out for a while and get some air."

"But it's daylight out there. Doesn't that shrivel you up and melt your flesh?"

She flips me off professionally and we start layering up for the journey outside, a long process. I hope Kansas is warmer, but I can't count on it. Arizona, however, will be a small piece of heaven. It's hard to imagine Tucson though; hard to believe in dry, sunny days, being warm without effort, hiking and biking and walking the desert, and all of it in less than a week.

As we head into subzero degrees I stop at the door to do a quick mental check. Chase asks me what I'm doing and I say, "I'm not sure but I think I'm changing."

She knows what I mean. She says, "Cool. Let's celebrate with double mochas. Can you buy?"

My mother met Henry Hawthorne at the grocery store in late September or early October the year my dad left us. Dad left the day before my fourteenth birthday. It was the beginning of February. He took a leave of absence from work and went down to Florida for the rest of the winter. He needed time to think and one of his good clients was out of the country for an entire year. He offered Dad his condo in Palm Beach and Dad went. We didn't see him until the end of April, after Sarah turned thirteen, when he came back with presents and a tan.

That was my first camera. I remember being surprised that he picked something so good. He got Sarah a guitar. Of course both of these turned out to have been Cindy's idea. I guess she went down to Florida too. Years later she told me she had meant for me to get the guitar and Sarah the camera but he mixed up the presents.

When Hank saw my mom knocking on squashes to find the ripe ones he turned to her in the fresh vegetable section and said, "I think what you're looking for you're more liable to find in me, ma'am." She went to the Holiday Inn with him that afternoon and when school ended the next May we all moved from the edge of fucking nowhere, New Mexico, to the middle of fucking nowhere, West Texas. I was fifteen. I didn't want to go but didn't exactly have options. Sarah didn't care about anything that year, Mom was an unstoppable force of antinature, and Dad was too busy playing house with Cindy to worry about me.

I caved in under pressure and sulked my ass across the indifferent high plains to settle into country life.

I was miserable then, but when I look back now all the memories are good ones. Quiet. I remember the new things I learned, the time I spent with my stepfather, the hours and hours of peaceful summer, reading under the giant oak or walking with Horatio, Hank's German shepherd, off the section roads and into the middle of a sighing green ocean. It's so flat out there, so much horizontal sameness. You learn to mark your course by the silos and the little clusters of poplars around farm houses. Our house was visible from a long way because of the giant oak.

Out in the country you know every truck, every car, and most of the horses. Everybody waves. Even to strangers you wave but it's not elaborate, just lifting the index finger of your driving hand. That summer we painted the farmhouse canary yellow with a dark, green-blue trim. The house was made all of cinder blocks and had a porch running around three sides. There were only three bedrooms, but they were big, with old-fashioned windows that you wound open. You could look out into the dark, cool stone courtyard, out onto the back section and the corn, or out onto the front section and the highway. There were three bathrooms as well, one attached to each room, so the place seemed huge because of that, and private, or full of places in which to be private. Sarah hardly spoke to me that summer but we shared a room. We even shared a bed, king-sized and rock hard and fortifying. Usually the wind blew, sometimes dangerously.

I remember lots of desks and lamps and books and packed shelves and built-in cabinets. There was a baby grand in one of the living rooms, old and slightly warped. Every now and then Hank would play on it and sing hymns and Mom would join him. She cooked a lot and painted the woodwork and they went antiquing together. Even though a maid came regularly we dusted every day and vacuumed constantly, Sarah and

I, because the fine prairie dust filtered in under the doors and through the closed windows and between the blades of the swamp cooler and coated everything with a heavy, reddish powder, the coal dust of the high plains. Mom was convinced it would eat our lungs, and I had begun to cough a little. But I was also smoking. Sarah was too.

I shared cigarettes with her sometimes, standing on the shady side of the long porch, alone at the house. We were like boys then, her still skinny and small, me already big but not soft, leaning against the pillars in our jeans and work shirts, squinting out over the acreage, half cotton on that side of the house and half corn, not talking to one another, not looking at one another, just sharing experience. There was no television. You have no idea how quiet a house is with no television, or how fast you get used to it.

The place had a name. Most of the houses around there had names. Ours was Oak Grove, and the guest house a half mile off where Henry's coyote-ass brother, Jimmy, lived with his wife and kids was Little Oaks, although the trees around it were actually pines and poplar. Oak Grove was the most solid, comforting place I'd ever been, but I didn't know that I was happy. I just wanted to be back in my own town, hanging at the pool with Joe, shooting the shit with friends, and sneaking out at night. The thing is, when we did go back to Remie to stay occasional weekends with Cindy and Dad, nothing was the same there anymore. I was a ball of loneliness and Sarah was no help. After Jimmy gave her a part-time job and a lot of attention, things for me were even worse.

Then, one day in midsummer, I went out walking with Horatio. I was feeling sorry for myself, as usual, and maybe was even crying when suddenly the dog took off like a bat out of hell across a cotton field.

"Ray! Come back here! Ray! Come! Come! Goddammit!" And I took off after him, terrified that Mr. Asshole Otterman, of the

very large farm behind us, would shoot him like he said he was
going to if he found that "goddamned wolf-looking piece of shit"
near his sheep again. Not very many people had sheep and he
was crazy about his. He had three guard dogs for them and electric wire and still he laid down poison and threats. Henry hated
him. I wasn't crazy yet about Henry, but if he hated someone,
I was pretty sure that was a person worth hating.

"Ray!" I tried to make my voice deep. Dogs listen better
to deep voices. Horatio had disappeared into the maize, and
I'd already run through two fields after him, tripping over
the mounds and furrows. I stumbled on, cursing but my tears
forgotten, and then I heard a whistle, short, sharp, and author-
itative. I stopped where I was, on another dirt road, this one
very narrow and curved, a tractor road, and a minute later
I heard Horatio crashing through the fields. He panted up to me
happily and then turned to wait for his whistler, who appeared
through the head-high greenery a moment later. It turned out to
be an irritated-looking Mexican boy about my age, with a very
unapologetic air about him.

"Here's your dog. You shouldn't scream after a dog. Always
keep your voice low. And it's better to train them so they
don't run off. It's hard to get them back when they head for the
hills. Not that they'd find any around here." And he made a
contemptuous gesture that included the flatness for a hundred-
mile radius.

I said, "I like it flat."

He shrugged. "Some people do." He turned to go and
I stepped forward, involuntarily, towards him. I think I reached
out my hand.

"Wait," I said. "Thanks for bringing him back." We stood
bareheaded in the sun, looking at each other. Ray foraged
in the corn for rabbits and when we heard him panting we
smiled at one another. "So," I said, "who are you?" I was brave.
I was brave because he was Mexican and looked poor, and

I was essentially white and not poor, and that's the way it was there.

"I'm Esteban Dominguez. You look like you've been crying." I looked away and wondered how messy my face was. "Are you one of the girls who's living with Henry Hawthorne now?" He went on without waiting for me to answer. "You must be the older one, right?" His eyes were intent on me. He had very black eyes with very black lashes and his teeth were white against his darkness. I didn't answer him and he made an impatient, clicking sound with his tongue, waiting for me. "My mother cleans your house, that's how I know who you are."

"Oh, Esther."

"Mrs. Dominguez, you mean."

"Mrs. Dominguez. Yeah." Esther Dominguez was mean as hell. She was afraid of no one, not even Mom. The two of them would do the house together, top to bottom, Pine-Sol everywhere, and sometimes I heard them laughing. I think Mom liked her, even though Esther would only talk Spanish to her the second Henry left the house. I almost said to Esteban, She does a great job, but I stopped myself in time. "She's nice," I said instead.

He raised his eyebrows. "Then it must be a different Esther Dominguez." We both smiled, again. He was attractive and my stomach was fluttering. I pretended to look around for Ray.

"Well," I said, "Mom likes her and my mom doesn't like anyone." Anyone in skirts, that is. "But you're right. She isn't exactly nice. She yelled at me once for laying a book over on its face. She made me go get a bookmark."

"That sounds like Mom." I could tell he admired her and I was jealous.

"Are you the one who keeps the family going? The one who wanted to go to college?"

"That would be me, yeah. But not for a while I guess." He didn't even look bitter about it. "Anyway, what's your name?

Don't you know you're supposed to introduce yourself after someone else does?"

"You sure do like to lecture, and I thought you knew it all anyway. I'm Eleanor May Shank, but everybody calls me Bean."

"Bean? For being Mexican?"

"For having a big butt. I mean, I used to have one. It's a long story."

"You're no twig now."

"Hey," I said, offended. "That's rude."

"Oh, I never meant nothing by it." His tone of voice had changed a little, to something warmer and younger-sounding, or maybe just unguarded. "I like the way you look. Do you believe me?"

I looked at him and I said, "I believe you." We were quiet. Ray came back over and thrust his head under Esteban's hand for a pat. We both rubbed his ears and crooned at him and he gave us that huge German shepherd grin and then bounded off again on big, padded feet, his tail like a banner behind him. We began walking after him, slowly making our way down the tractor path.

"How old are you?" I asked.

"I'm seventeen but I know I don't look that old."

"It's true, you don't. Seventeen is pretty old." I meant for a Mexican male, to be unattached. "Are you, uh, do you have a girlfriend or something?"

"Not all wetbacks get someone pregnant at fifteen, if that's what you mean."

"It's just that you have a ring on your finger, stupid."

"Oh." He looked down at his hand and then smiled at me and I felt that Ricky Serrano melting feeling starting all over again. "It was my father's, before he passed away. So my mom gave it to me because I'm the oldest boy and this is the finger it fits."

"Shouldn't you be working?"

"I do, at the packing plant, but this is my day off."

"The packing plant? Then let me see your scars." Indeed, he had them, up and down his arms. Everyone at the packing plant got scars sooner or later, and lots of them lost fingers too. So far he'd only needed to be stitched twice, from fighting gooks, he said, not carving meat.

Our flat and barren corner of the world had become a big center for Vietnamese refugees and those kids could fight like nobody's business. They were fearless and knew karate kinds of things and you could never tell what they were going to do by looking at their faces. They went about their affairs in efficient packs that apparently operated telepathically and were too dangerous for wetbacks and white boys alike. No one messed with them if possible, but it wasn't always possible, especially at places like the meat packing plants. I kept looking from his face to his arms and shaking my head. He seemed far too sweet to be spending his life bathed in blood and cow guts and fighting Asians.

We walked on for a long time that day, talking. I got to know his schedule and we met when we could, but I never told anyone about it and I don't think he did either. Right from the start we knew that we'd never survive public scrutiny.

So I never invited him over, and he never invited me, and when I was a junior he got stabbed in one of the race riots between the Vietnamese and the Hispanics at work. I had known him a year and a half. My mother said to me and Sarah in the living room, "Esther Dominguez isn't coming to clean this week so you two had better not make plans. Her oldest son, Esteban, got killed in a fight at work yesterday." Then she looked my way and said, "I assume you won't be taking those long Sunday morning walks anymore."

Sarah gripped my arm hard enough to leave marks. I didn't say anything and I didn't cry but the room began to echo and then big black patches appeared at the sides of my vision and the next thing I knew I was lying on the floor and Mom had her arm under my head. She sent Sarah to mix up some orange juice and sugar for me and she said, stroking my forehead, "I'm sorry." I still didn't say anything and I still didn't cry and I realized years later that the touch of her hand on my forehead was the only tender motion she had shown me since we moved to Remie when I was five. I also know that when she first reached up to smooth my hair back I flinched. I couldn't help it. She pretended not to notice.

My Sunday morning walks, when I was out at the farm, didn't stop. It was back to just me and Ray and the wind, and that pale blue, high plains winter sky. I was lonely again but this time it suited me more. I thought a lot about leaving New Mexico for good. Photography kept me going. Math sucked, my dad was nowhere, Cindy tried to teach me to sew. On weekends I partied professionally. Joe Bloch and I were inseparable and I discovered pot and astronomy with him and sex with other people. My loneliness showed mostly on the inside, where I did something strange. I stopped having my period and I got really, really constipated. I was only going number two like every week or longer and eventually I got sick and had to tell someone, so I told Cindy and she took me to the Walgreens. That's how I discovered the laxative section of the drugstore and entered the next, secret, phase of my life.

4 I'm sleepless on the Southwest Chief at just after two in the morning. The train was held up by a sudden snowstorm that dropped down from Canada like a great wet blanket, and after waiting for hours on the station floor with all the luggage and fretful children, we left Kansas City only minutes ago. My plan is to stay on the Chief through the whole of Kansas, the corner of Colorado, and the top of New Mexico, then detrain in Albuquerque late tomorrow afternoon. This isn't the most efficient use of Amtrak's services for someone ending up in Tucson, but I'm not a fast food chain and efficiency doesn't rule my life. I need to see Albuquerque again. I've been feeling the urge to snoop around my old digs with Colette, have a croissant and coffee at the Hippo and eat green chile cheeseburgers at the Fat Chance. Travis says I should get some skiing done while I'm in the neighborhood, but skiing isn't the best hobby for the unemployed photographer who wants to spend an introspective year. I think I'll pass. Colette has never skied anyway, not even cross-country. She's allergic to sports.

After a day in Albuquerque we'll drive to El Paso, where she's been living since college and where I'm getting a massage from some funky friend of her cousin's and meeting up with Sarah. Full-body massage isn't the best hobby for the unemployed either but it is a good aid to mental well-being. I realized in Richmond that I'd need stoking-up for Tucson, and sitting on the train now, only days away from Mom, I'm getting nervous already.

I packed up my things in Kansas City today—yesterday really—after an early dinner of pizza and beer with Jessica, and we proceeded to spend the entire evening in a bar. I still haven't settled down. Not long into the night we ran into some friends of hers and I hit it off entirely too well with one of them, a grad student named Zeke with clearly a girlfriend somewhere but I didn't care because I'd be gone in three hours. At this rate of exposure Patrick will fade like a bad tattoo. We were behind the bar talking and necking when Jess came running out with the news that my train was due to leave in twelve minutes. We would have just made it, maybe, but the damn thing was delayed by the storm anyway. I got her to leave me at the station and go back to the bar. I didn't care about having to wait. You get used to it with trains. When you're looking at the kind of journey where one leg takes two days, an hour in a depot is nothing. Jess had been flirting with a basketball player who shouted after her as we drove off to hurry up and come back and I wanted her to do it. Anything to distract her from Ralph and that inevitable married-man catastrophe.

When they finally boarded us at 2:00 A.M. I got sat down in the semidark next to a coastbound squid in uniform who had fallen asleep with his book still open on his lap. It's a book about building your own log cabin and I want quite badly to take it out of his hands and page through it. For some stupid reason I find this wishbook of his touching. I always find it too intimate, seeing what people's fantasies really are, like going barefoot for the first time in spring. It's so exposed. You look at someone else's feet after months of leather and steel, and the heartrending little things just kill you, the shape of the nail beds, the length and slope of the metatarsals, the degree an ankle bone sticks out or doesn't. I mean really, homemade log cabins that you order by item number, assembly required. You've got to be kidding.

Pretty soon I'll shift around, I think, wake him up and start talking. I can tell by his catalogue and build that he won't mind the interruption. I'll bet ten bucks this guy wrestled in high school. Those short, thick thumbs and packed shoulders are a dead giveaway. He would have had to battle to keep his weight under limit but I guess that's half of wrestling right there. He's pleasant looking, actually. Young, but sturdy, and there's something beckoning about that innocent ridge of bone above his ear. The most unfortunate thing about him is that he's pear-shaped, and heavy thighs are a hard thing for a man. He's probably a good athlete, with lots of endurance, but he's not mean enough. This is a guy born to be used by women. It's so sad. Personally I'm not going to use him for anything but conversation but there you are. I want to talk so in a minute or two I'm going to wake him up and talk. Other women? They want drinks, then dresses, then trips to Hawaii. And all he wants is someone sweet to build a log cabin in the wilderness with. Like, right.

I should pull out Annie Dillard instead and lose myself in insect life but I'm too wired to read. I'm in the kind of mood where a few beers and three Scotch-and-waters are hardly putting a dent in me, and susceptible men are lighting beacons in the dark and they don't even know it. I wonder if this mood could be technically considered hypomania. A few days of junk food and drinking and sorely needed working out, and then the whole make out session with Jessica's little Civil War specialist friend, Zeke, and yikes. I am up up up and I'd just about kill for a cappuccino to get me through this blizzard, although, God knows, Kansas has nothing on Illinois in terms of weather. I've discovered why they grow Russian wheat in the Midwest; one winter here and you're ready for Siberia.

But the train is warm and we're making steady progress. The Southwest Chief is doing good holiday business, packed with a motley assortment of the not-quite-middle class, some with Christmas presents and some with food. I would have brought at least good cheese and olives myself if the visit with Jess hadn't been so frantic that a domestic excursion to a grocery store seemed out of the question. I ran myself ragged in Chicago and did the same in Kansas City, just with more food and less pot. Now I'll have to live for two days on pretzels, pea soup, and peanuts from the cafe car, but at least I feel like I'm really traveling. There are cowboys with Stetsons on this train, New Yorkers who've never seen the desert, and real live foreigners more used to trains than we are, patient in a way no American can be. Of course, there's your usual assortment of insomniac old people too, some of them adventure-seeking and bright-eyed even at this hour and some of them whining habitually, unable to sleep in the middle of the night because a train is not an East Florida suburb. I hope I don't turn into one of them one day. A lot of the guys are wearing boots and jeans and still heading in and out of the bar car. If I were braver I'd head in there myself but I think that's too much testosterone in one place for l'il ol' me.

I don't know why, but as you go west the men begin to look better and the women start to look worse. Then you get to the other coast and the reverse is true again. Hunksters are a dime a dozen in Chicago, all varieties, and more straight than on the seaboard. It's a mecca after Boston. I keep trying to tell Sarah how good she's got it but she's been in Tucson from eighteen on and has nothing to compare it to. I've lived in more places than she's worked, that's how different we've made our lives.

I called her while I was still at Chase's to tell her about Dad crying on the phone. I did it to diminish my guilt but instead, of course, it accrued. If guilt drew interest I'd have an account that gets compounded daily. I don't know why I phoned her in the first place, since she blames me roughly 90 percent for my strained relationship with the father unit. This time was no exception.

"Dad called me," I said, to start things off.

"When?"

"It was here. We were fighting in Virginia, big surprise, and he called to say sorry. He was crying."

"Crying?" Sarah sounded horrified.

"Yeah. At least, I think he was crying. I'm pretty sure he was."

"What did you say to him?"

"Nothing."

"Nothing?"

"Nothing. It happened too fast. He said he was sorry about some of the things he'd said to me and he wished me luck and told me to take good pictures, and then he waited for me to say something but I couldn't think of anything to say, and then he hung up. What should I do?"

"Call him back," she said instantly. Oh sure, easy for her. She probably calls him all the time just to touch base and fill him in on her life story. I don't know how she does it, unless Samson encourages her. He's always talking about how important family is and I don't disagree. I just wish it weren't true.

"I can't call him," I told her. "I've never called him."

"Never?" she asked. "Not even on Father's Day?"

"Father's Day is a crock."

"Not even on his birthday?"

"I would have, some years, but I didn't want him thinking it was going to be a habit of mine."

"What's wrong with you?"

"Fuck off, favorite child." Favored after Jacob and Jasmine anyway.

"OK then," she said, taking that in stride, "send him a card."

"No way. Cards are a crock, too. Anyway, I'm still mad at him."

"What the fuck for?"

"What do you think? For never goddamn being there when we needed him, that's what for. The question isn't why am

I mad but why aren't you? What happened to him when we hit junior high anyway?"

"D-I-V-O-R-C-E."

"Big deal. We didn't divorce him, Mom did. He couldn't look me in the face from fourteen on and I'm supposed to have normal relations with men? And where was he when you were busy pretending Uncle Jimmy cared for you like the father you didn't have at home? Where was he when you and I were practically starving to death in college, tell me that? If it weren't for Hank sending us money we would have ended up cashiering at Wal-Mart for the rest of our goddamn lives and you know it. I can't forgive him yet, and if you say you can, you're a liar." And besides, when I was fat I disgusted him, and that I'll never forget.

Sarah said, "Well look, I was just on my way to the grocery store. I'll call you later."

"Right," I said, "you chicken-shit," and we both hung up. She'll call me to discuss an emotional issue the day my tits go flat. This will pass but until it does we'll both brood after peeing at three in the morning and wonder if the other one is right. Divorce sucks. And I know better than to mention Jimmy to her. Any emotional issue is tricky but that one is the worst. It's like bringing up drinking with Pat. A hidden mine field, waiting to blow.

I was surprised to find that Dorothy was right about Kansas. It's boring. Greener than the movie, though, even in winter, and nice enough if you don't mind the politics, hairstyles and ugly clothes. And, not that it's easy to be gay anywhere, but you could really suffer being gay here; the guys are such guys and the girls are such mammas-to-be. There's no room for the deviants, no sliding back and forth on the gender continuum, no freaks allowed. Ick. I can't quite believe Jessica has moved voluntarily to such a place. It's one thing if you're born here, but for a Boston girl to emigrate into the heartland? Even for true love it's a bit much, especially true love with this kind of guy. Meaning, married. Myself, I'd draw the line at married, or at least I always have, and I'd draw the line way before K.C., MO.

"Hey Jess," I said when I got off the train and saw her waiting for me five nights ago.

"Oh Beanie Bean! It's so good to see you! You look wonderful!" She ran over and hugged me hard. That's how I knew she was miserable.

"You look great too, Jess. It's been so long!" She looked great for someone with a hole in her heart but terrible for a pretty Catholic girl who used to live for nachos and beer. Her hair and nails were still perfect, of course, but tense, Lordy Lord she was tense. She held her shoulders like a person with whiplash. I forgot she did that. An hour in her company and my shoulders draw up in sympathy. After a few days I feel like I've caught lockjaw. She still turns heads, though, maybe even more than before. She's gone from solid to shaky, but a lot of men like their women high strung and half nuts.

By descent Jessie's half French and half Italian. She has a combination of olive skin and silver hair like Barbie's, except that her hair has to be touched up with Clairol now but you can't tell. Only persistent acne keeps her from being too good-looking to have any friends. And, thank God, she pretends to look average. But I was shocked by her thinness. She used to have a body kind of like Barbie's as well but that's gone now. She has no tits anymore, no ass, and her torso looked breakable. I was afraid to hug her too enthusiastically in case her sternum splintered.

I didn't mention her protruding joints and kept acting like it was normal to wear size two clothing. As we loaded my things into her car, I told her all the Boston gossip to get her to laugh. It was a relief to be off the train. I wanted us to sit in the warm car, drive around the countryside, share a flask, eat some food, and talk forever, and she wanted anything else. I could tell she was suffering but she resists personal conversation, and there's no hurrying confessions from that secretive, Papist soul. You wouldn't know it to look at her but on the inside Jess is not a girl. I don't mean that she's had transgender surgery or lacks a uterus, I mean that mentally she's like a guy. If you want to discuss feelings, you have to get her drunk first.

Eventually she said, in something like her normal voice, "You have train face." A Barry Manilow song started up on the radio. In Kansas they like Barry Manilow and Chicago and Elton John. It's what they call rock and roll.

"Thanks," I said. My skin tone was sickly, matching my gray fleece pullover; I saw it when I freshened up in the bathroom on board. I splashed water on my cheeks, put on deep red lipstick, hung my head down for a while to get the blood into it, did a few jumping jacks, and all to no avail. I had train face. But at least I got a genuine statement out of her. That was a good sign. "Life in New England," I told her conversationally, "took me away."

She smiled, not widely, and I saw that the song was actually getting to her. A very, very bad sign from the girl who used to worship the Scorpions. I contemplated my next move but we were already home.

"Hey, not bad," I said, as we pulled into the driveway of a two-story suburban dwelling with a semiattached guest house. She was renting the guest house from her old college friend, Trina, now an untenured professor in Lawrence and married. It's Trina's husband who has done to Jessica's physical condition what training for seven Boston marathons never did. Ralph is apparently a nice guy from Indiana who swears he never stepped out on his wife before Jessie started sleeping out back.

I dumped my bags, kicked off my boots, and immediately began snooping around. There was no artwork in the house other than children's drawings, and these were hung on the fridge with the usual assortment of irritating magnets, including a real beaut with *Happy Mother's Day* around the edge of it in Elmer's glue and sparkles. I hate stupid bumper-sticker magnets. *Jesus Loves Me. World's Best Grandma. Is There Life After Golf?* Ugh. *I'm a Born Spinster*. I wonder if they make magnets saying that.

I didn't think much of their interior decorating, either. Strictly Midwestern blah, too much space and no individual stamp, wall-to-wall neutral carpeting, eggshell white on every surface, nondescript furniture, and central television. The ceilings were very high. Ordinarily I like that but it left this particular house feeling unfilled, as though it were too much for the people in it. Only Jessica's little studio and the kitchen felt homey.

"Sleepy?" I asked her.

"No. Tired, but not sleepy."

I nodded. She was stressed. She kept smoothing her hair and fiddling with her nails, and she couldn't sit down. It was one in the morning and there was no place nearby for late-night coffee so we wandered around the house eating pretzels, sharing a beer, being catty about the photographs, getting reacquainted at her speed. Thank God Sam Adams has gone national and we weren't confined to weak American pisswater, which is what I'd been expecting from the middle of the country. Ralph, Trina, and the two boys were in California for Christmas vacation. It was good timing for them because outside the snow was coming wetly down.

Jess has become a half-tamed mink, sometimes warm and soft, sometimes cruel and slashing, and always with this tension about her body. She isn't the kind of person you relax around anymore. She doesn't make you think of chocolate chip cookies and milk. And she's lost her sweetness about men.

This is her idea of the standard male fantasy, told to me over Miller Lite in a Kansas City bar that only played music from the seventies: You're in the living room jacking off and you hear footsteps outside the door, the footsteps of a woman in high heeled shoes. There's a knock. You stop midstroke and say, "Who is it?" A sexy voice answers, "It's a secret, but if you open the door you won't be disappointed." "Come in," you say, hurriedly pulling up your pants. In saunters this knockout drop-dead stop-the-clock looker and the first (and only) thing she says is, "I just want to suck your cock." She walks over to you, kneels down, swishes her long blonde hair and undoes your jeans all in the same fluid motion, sends you a quick look that promises the world from under her eyelashes and then, without further ado, applies her fuck-me-red lipsticked lips to your erect member, expertly and lengthily. She tongues your balls, rims your asshole, and has the staying power of a bionic woman. You come like you've never come and she gets up without her knees popping. Then she smiles at you, secretively but slightly sadly. You both know it's too perfect to last. Just before your buddies come over she walks back out the door. You never see her again and your friends don't believe it ever happened.

Here's my idea of the standard female fantasy, told to Jessica at the same bar but later and over tequila: You walk into the grocery store in the middle of a chocolate frenzy, wild-eyed, horny, and dressed like shit. You overhear a guy telling his buddy in the yogurt section that what would really make him happy is to meet a woman with some meat on her bones, a good brain, and real passion for coffee and talk. He has long hair, is naturally slim but muscular, and looks like the sax player for Morphine, but sunny. Preferably, he says, she wouldn't be high maintenance and—"Oh, hi." He turns and sees you and seems very taken with your eyes. You say, faintly, your cheeks burning, "Um, is there any Dannon Plain?" and wordlessly he hands you his. You walk out to the parking lot together. He drives a truck with a *Kill Your Television* bumper sticker and has boots and skis fighting for space with his guitar case in back. Later you find out that despite his trust fund he did a stint in the Peace Corps and he's crazy for kids and dogs.

"So, how are things?" I started cautiously.

"Oh fine," she said.

"Uh-huh. Does Trina know what's going on?"

She shrugged. "I don't think so. She's been so busy working on her book that we could probably do it on her desk. She wouldn't stop writing long enough to notice."

"Uh-huh." Right. "Don't you think you should at least move out?"

"Yes. But then he'd forget about me."

"And you're not ready to end it, I guess."

She didn't answer except to point out a large, framed photo of a slightly blurred golden retriever. "Butterscotch," she said. "I hated that dog and then she got run over last summer. I keep thinking it's my fault."

"Spare me," I said. "You're just guilty because you're fucking the husband of your friend and mentor. You didn't kill the dog, too."

"Thanks," she said, and took a big drink of cream ale. "Yum. Better than dinner."

"Not better with dinner?"

"No." She wasn't hungry. She hates dinner. She hates being full. All my friends starve themselves when they're stressed and I eat. Is that fair? I decided to force-feed her. "He feels guilty," she went on. "He says he wants to stop. Get a load of this grandmother. Nice dress, huh?"

"Very nice. What color is that anyway? Popsicle blue? And the collar is extremely attractive." We pass the beer back and forth. "So why doesn't he stop?"

"I don't know. I really don't. Maybe he will after this vacation. They're probably walking along the beach at this very moment, holding hands. If she remembers how. Look at this one, B. They were so in love once. This was their honeymoon."

And clearly they were in love, in that shy, intellectual way, standing proudly together in front of Ayres Rock, squinting under the sun in dorky shorts and scruffy T-shirts, her without a bra. "Wow," I said, a little bit shocked at how nice they both looked, and smart as well. They seemed like the kind of people you wouldn't mind having over for dinner and I began feeling guilty by association. "They look so hopeful here. And Australia is a pretty cool honeymoon place. Cooler than expected. How long ago was that, ten years?"

"Thirteen. This month. They got married as undergrads."

"Wow," I said again. "Don't you feel weird, Jess?"

She just looked at me. It was a dumb question. Obviously she felt weird. More than weird. Guilty and confused and lovesick and panicky and out of control and no doubt helpless and horrified and I didn't know how to comfort her. "Well, he probably doesn't mind feeling guilty," I said. "It makes the whole thing bittersweet and acute for him. Are you OK?"

The usual shrug. I assumed that meant either no or so definitely no that it's all gone numb.

I got us another beer and we sat on the living room carpet, drinking in front of the gas fire. "Any chance he'd leave her for you, Jess?"

She didn't answer but her head dropped. Obviously not. I decided to lighten things up. "So. Did you ever do it in their bed?"

"B, that's not funny."

"Oh. So you did." They did. She can glare and scratch all she wants to but they did, and eventually she caught my eye and we started laughing. We finished the beer and got two more, and that set the tone for the visit. We spent it all working out and passing out, sometimes eating out and sometimes talking.

It's after three now and I'm still not sleepy. I haven't woken the squid to chat because I have a feeling that one of the worst memories of my lousy adolescence just boarded the train at the Lawrence stop and is now a few rows ahead of me, reading. Granted, Joe Bloch wasn't always so bad, but that's how it ended up. He was the saving grace of Remie, New Mexico, for quite a few years, but in twelfth grade everything changed. It started with a drunken New Year's Eve and ended when Joe left town that March. Didn't graduate. Disappeared. Rumors filtered back to us, periodically. He was dead. He was in jail. He was at Harvard.

And now there's a guy on the train who looks just like him, with a backpack and hiking boots instead of a longneck and chew. When he walked by me my arms prickled. I'd like desperately to go up there and find out who that really is but I'm frightened. What if it is him? What am I going to do then?

Oh God. He just turned around and stared at me. Right at me. And I think it's him, I do, something about the way he turned his head. Shit! But I look so different now. I am different now. Maybe he won't recognize me. Anyway, why would he be on a train in the middle of Kansas? Remie isn't a town that spawned travelers. And his face didn't change, not that I could tell. Oh please God, I'm just going to close my eyes and pray, God please make it not him, please please please, I can't handle it.

"Hi Bean." It's him.

"Hi Joe." I can't even look further up than the collar of his shirt.

"Aren't you going to get up and hug me?" He's speaking very softly.

"I don't know, Joe. What if it makes me puke?"

"Don't," he says, even more quietly. "I've wanted to talk to you about that for ten years. There's a reason we're on this train together. You have to talk to me. Come have a drink. Please."

My hands are so cold they hurt. And I can't get up. I can't. "No." We're whispering, me fiercely.

"Bean please. I'll stand here all night if I have to. I'll make a scene if I have to. Just come and talk to me. Come on. I'm getting off in a few hours and we owe each other that much at

least. Come into the cafe car with me, we have to talk. Here."
And he holds out his hand.

I sit there for seconds and it feels much longer. Sweat is
starting in my armpits and I haven't looked Joe in the face. I'm
scared to go with him and more scared to stay.

"I mean it," he says again, but louder. "I'll make a scene."

"Fine," I say. So much for overcoming cowardice. My seat
companion doesn't stir but I realize that he's awake and listening and his presence reassures me.

"Thank you," says Joe and steps back a few paces to wait,
braced against the rocking of the train. The squid turns his head
slightly and looks over at me as I stand up. I catch his eye and
tell him, quietly, "It's OK." He nods and closes his eyes and I get
my backpack and camera and follow my personal ghost to the
cafe car.

To make up for the doughnuts and drinking at night, Jessie
and I worked out hard every day of my stay and now, walking
unwillingly behind Joe, who is moving smoothly down the aisle
of the swaying train, I can feel every muscle in the lower half of
my body whimpering. But really I like it when my muscles hurt;
it makes me feel strong. Ha! I'm not afraid of you anymore, Herr
Bloch. Call me a Mexican whore now and I'll fucking throw you
off this train and seduce your brothers, your father, and maybe
your mother too.

"Did you say something, Bean?"

"No. Huh-uh. Just talking to myself." We've paused momentarily in the cold, metal-floored area between two coaches and
the moonlit Kansas snow fields are reflecting whitely through
the windows. I realize that we've left the storm behind.

"It's almost full moon," he says, but I won't look, and he
pushes the door open into the last car before the lounge. Everyone in it is asleep. They look to me so innocent and safe and
I'm quite sure I look neither. I feel neither and never did. The
way I grew up was one long effort to outrun something that

I couldn't outrun and it's made me tired for life. We were always diving, climbing, and jumping things; we took drugs, broke into places, went joyriding and road-tripping and AWOL for days; we had friends we didn't know, sex we didn't want, and families we couldn't change. Sometimes, fucking off or desperate, we nearly died. For the boys where I grew up it was worse than that. Enough of them did die, wrapped around telephone poles or coldcocked in rocky lakes, stabbed in fights or accidentally shot, thrown from horses and trucks and oil rigging and boats. Some of them even killed themselves. If you knew your place in the world it wasn't an easy town to grow up in, and for the rest of us it was hell.

I sent my dad a card from Kansas City after all. It just said, "I love you, too, and I'm sorry. Don't be mad at me." I put my little kidney bean signature at the bottom and sent the damn thing off before I could think better of it. I won't see him for a long time and I don't want that weight over my head. I tried talking to Jessica about it but both her parents are dead and she has no patience with my whining and no patience with my dread about Mom.

Working out one afternoon I said to her, "I'm scared to see my mother. The woman doesn't even like me. Well, she doesn't like anyone, I don't think it's personal, but I can't believe I've arranged to stay there for half the winter. What was I thinking?" Jessica just grunted. I said, "She always makes me feel ugly and fat." Jessica sighed. "And clueless and lazy." Jessica still said nothing. "And scared," I repeated. The Stairmaster was getting to her and she's against talking while training. Without answering she turned around backwards to better work what used to be her quads. "Just once," I said, "I wish I was the skinny one and she was the fat one. Just once, so I could have the upper hand."

"You're not fat, Bean."

"I was. And I still outweigh her by fifty pounds."

"Skinny doesn't give you the upper hand."

"Then why don't you eat?"

Jessica didn't answer.

I dropped my machine briefly to a lower level and got up on my toes, arms above my head. "And what if she's drinking?"

"Do you think she is?"

"No. But if she isn't then she's going to be a lunatic about food. She never eats chocolate, she never eats cheese, no junk food ever, and I think she's gone macrobiotic or something. She's going to watch everything that goes into my mouth and every time I turn around I'm going to catch her staring at my fat ass or frizzy hair, and I know she's going to tell me I should wear more makeup or the men will never look my way."

"So ignore her."

"I can't."

"Wear more makeup then."

"I won't."

"Tell her to fuck off."

"I'd like to, but how? And what if she gets mad at me?"

"Is that the worst case scenario?" No. The worst case scenario is that she's right: I am fat, I am ugly, I should wear more makeup, I'm invertebrate and I'll never do anything with my life or get anyone to love me right. Or, the worst case scenario is that everyone secretly agrees with her and thinks I'm a loser who can't face the real world and will always act the way I act now, like someone from another planet who got dropped to Earth by accident and can't learn the customs.

These fears, however, I can't voice to Jess. "Yeah, that's the worst. I don't want her losing her marbles in my general direction. I don't want her to scream at me."

"Why not? I mean, what can really happen?"

"I don't know. When she gets that tone in her voice I panic."

"Look Bean, you can't make everyone like you all the time. So what if she gets mad at you? So the fuck what? Is she going to spank you? I don't think so. Is she going to run away and leave you? I guess not. What else is there? A little yelling? I think you'll survive that, don't you? For shit's sake, the woman must be all right some of the time. Have some backbone! You're not thirteen anymore. She can kick you out but she can't hurt you. When are you going to realize that you're safe?"

Joe has gotten taller since high school but he's still only my size, and from his body I'd say he's given up weight lifting. Now he looks like your ordinary Seattle-type city boy, flannel shirt and long johns, shaggy long hair, good hiking boots and probably a three-hundred-dollar espresso maker at home. He's not afraid to make eye contact anymore. I'm the one who can't look at him, at the face that kills me still, everything about it intelligent and sensitive and warm; even the hollows under his cheekbones somehow aware. He has the same humorous mouth and long, clear eyes as in my memories of him, the same dark eyebrows, light hair, big nose. He looks like a musician and he used to look like a boxer. He seems quieter. The shitkicker act is gone.

We sit down in the empty cafe car and Joe reaches into his knapsack for a bottle of what turns out to be a very good single-malt Scotch, and I remember how he got me started on the stuff in the first place, somewhere in that summer between eleventh and twelfth grades. When he wasn't around his friends, pretending to like Coors, he wouldn't drink less than Johnnie Walker Black, and always out of the appropriately-shaped container. No leaking Dixie cups when you were boozing with Joe. Age and backpacking hasn't changed that. He's traveling now with matching glasses wrapped for protection in hiking socks.

"They're clean," he says, when I raise my eyebrows.

"I don't care." The cafe car is colder than the rest of the train and he offers me a sweater but I shake my head no.

"You'd rather freeze, huh?" I shrug and we both sip the Scotch. It warms me from my throat out but I could use the sweater. "So you still hate me, then," he says.

"Pretty much," I reply, taking a few idle photographs of the cafe car interior. In some shots I get the edge of his arm and shoulder. "But you must hate me more."

"I don't hate anyone. At least I've learned that."

"Oh please." He doesn't say anything but he doesn't back down, either. He just keeps looking at me square in the face and I keep looking away, playing with my camera.

"I don't blame you, you know," he says, after four minutes have gone slowly by. "In a way you did me a favor."

"Smile." I take his picture, flash on, and then rest the camera on the table "We were good friends, once," I say. "After Sarah went to Texas. When Lily started hanging out with shitkickers you were practically my best buddy."

"Yeah. You were mine."

"Ricky's in Tucson," I tell him from the other side of the camera. I focus in on his hands and the glass of Scotch and slow the shutter speed, leaning on my elbows. "I'm going to see him when I stay with Sarah. She lives there and so does my mom now. Hank died. My dad's in Virginia. Lily's in Chicago. She's a stage actress and goes by Chase. I was in Boston for a long time and nearly got married but now I guess I'm nowhere. What have you been up to?"

"Is that what you want to do? Talk as if nothing happened?"

"Smile," I say, and take a picture with the flash back on, leaning far back in my seat. I look at him through the lens, change the f-stop and take another picture. "Just half your face this time," I say.

"Are you enjoying yourself?"

"Some." I let the camera dangle around my neck. It was Cindy who got me the strap that's holding it there, a beautiful, embroidered thing from an arts and crafts fair in a southwestern motif for my southwestern journey. I still feel like an impostor using it. "Can't we leave it be?"

"No. This ain't the time to pussy around." One of his old expressions and I see that he's trying hard to reach me. He used to say that before the highest dives and the hardest exams.

"I understand playing straight, Joe, but did you have to be so convincing?"

"I didn't know I was." He drinks and I drink too, and he refills both cups. Another five minutes go by. Outside, the sky has changed from black to charcoal and snow lies thinner on the ground.

"You wanted me to be in love with you." The Scotch has begun to work, leaving my mind sharp but softening the world around me to a fuzzy gold version of itself, beautiful and full of meaning. My words reverberate. Everything reverberates and I'm conscious, for a moment, of the fast rhythmic clicking of metal wheels on metal tracks as the train speeds along.

He nods. "Yes, I did."

There had been more to our friendship than simple camaraderie. He liked touching me for no reason, liked giving me neck rubs, and he liked it when I leaned against him stargazing. Sometimes his eyes glowed when he looked my way, and I saw that he noticed my breasts, my movements, enjoyed my hair. But we also danced together a lot and never once did he melt against my body or sink into my eyes like boys in high school do.

"Have you ever been back to Remie?" he asks.

"No. You?"

"Yeah. My whole family's there. I'm spending Christmas with them this year."

"Are they OK with you?"

"No. My mother cries. My father won't speak to me at all. I'm sending him to an early grave. My brothers are all right. They protect me like they always did and the kids love me. Billy doesn't want me to be alone with his son but he acts like it doesn't bother him."

"Hey, at least their wives are safe."

"You're funny."

It's early morning on one of the shortest days of the year and Joe and I sit in the lounge car, quiet, until we hear the clanging of breakfast things from the diner and passengers start filtering in for coffee. That's when he puts his feet around mine under the table and says, "I've missed you from then on. If I'd have known how to find you, I would have done it years ago and now here we are." He reaches his hands out and holds mine between them and says, "Are we going to be friends again?"

"I'm not a fag hag, Joe."

"Don't be an asshole. No one ever thought you were a fag hag." No? "I'm asking for friendship out of you. Real friendship. I want us to know each other when we're old."

"I'm already old."

"Bean, I'm dead serious. Are we friends again? Like we were, but better?"

Dawn is breaking as an overall whitening of the huge, gray sky, and the palest pink spills out from under an edge of the eastern horizon. The train changes tempo and begins the slow ascent of the Rockies. It's 7:21 and the tables around us are full. "Smile," I say, setting the exposure for the sunrise, and this time, when I take the picture, in the shadows of his face I can just make out the smile.

On Labor Day Jimmy got us drunk for the first time. There were a bunch of people over and leftover fireworks and by this point it was late at night. Jimmy was long-married but I don't know where Beth was. Probably home with the kids. I couldn't stand her anyway. For that matter I couldn't stand Jimmy, but he did something for Sarah Jane and it was mutual. As far as they were concerned, that night I was just a warm impediment.

They were talking in code around me and Sarah looked more awake than she had looked in six months. Her eyes were bright. She was wearing a white halter top and cut-off shorts and Jimmy the Pervert kept smiling and handing her beers. Me too, but incidentally. I didn't like beer but I wasn't going to let her grow up faster than me, and then anyway the buzz hit soon enough.

It was so delicious, to stop worrying for once, to not be shy. The air felt silky and beckoning. I left them and wondered around the property smiling and saying hi to people. I wanted to be looked at. I wanted someone to stare into my eyes. I wanted my skin to feel skin. My hair felt beautiful, the heaviness of it swinging over my shoulders. I couldn't wait to see Esteban. I thought that he might kiss me, finally. We'd agreed to meet at midnight, if I was still awake, at one of the small hay sheds on our usual path, but it was only eleven o'clock.

I went back to Sarah and Jim but couldn't find them. Hank and Mom reappeared but I faded away before they could ask me any questions. I had super antennae that night. I was a mind reader, I was hyperaware, and Hank had this way of keeping track of us. It was usually unnerving but with beers in me I was a match for it. From behind the tool shed I could see him looking around and I knew he would sense my presence if I stayed in one place too long. He asked Mom something and she shrugged. He looked worried and started making his way through the crowd but she pulled at his hand and shook her head and then pointed in the direction of the temporary bar. He looked around one more time while I looked away and made myself conjugate French verbs and then he went to get her a drink and I knew I was safe. I got another Bud from an open cooler and headed out into the fields, but I took Horatio with me, not because I was worried about some mugger or rapist but because I was always frightened by the rodents scuttling out of my way when I walked in the corn at night. They sounded sometimes much bigger than they should have.

"You're drunk," Esteban said. I was early to our meeting place. So was he. "I can't believe it. I can't believe your mother let you get drunk."

I giggled. I wanted him to laugh with me but he wasn't amused. "She didn't exactly let me. But then she isn't in the position to preach, is she?" He looked so fine that night, smooth and hard, only a little taller than me but more solid, and dark in the night. He was wearing a white muscle shirt and I thought he would make a good match for Sarah, with her white halter top, and the thought pinched me somewhere deep in by my liver so I said, "Don't you want to kiss me?" He had yet to lay a hand on me and I couldn't stand it anymore.

He shook his head. "It's just the beer talking."

"It is not."

"I wouldn't disrespect your stepfather like that."

"It doesn't have anything to do with him. This is between you and me."

"You're drunk," he said again, but softer this time. He put his arms around me and the smell of him covered me and protected me and I leaned full into him, chest to chest. It wasn't enough, I wanted my whole skin to feel him, so I moved my feet in and felt his erection pressing against my stomach. I moved my feet back out and shifted over so I wouldn't be flat against it. He didn't say anything but his arms tightened around me and he buried his face in my neck. I felt so right, standing with him under the night sky, both of us panting and full of longing but all of it gentle, the air sweet, the smell of the fields rich and warm. Horatio nuzzled between us suddenly, making us laugh and breaking the moment.

"Come on," Esteban said. "I'll walk you home."

"I don't want to go home." I was petulant but he was firm anyway.

"You have to. It's not a good idea for you and me to be out together tonight. You're drunk and it's late and now I've touched you. I have to take you home."

So we walked the long way back but I was mad and wouldn't talk to him until we were nearly at the place where he would go his own way, and then I said, "Sarah and Uncle Jimmy disappeared together."

He made the snapping sound with his tongue and said, "He's not the man your stepfather is. I don't trust him."

"No. Me neither. He makes me sick."

"Your sister is restless. If I had a sister like that I would keep a very close eye on her."

"I can't," I said, but he shook his head. I heard the chain clink softly around his neck, the cross knocking against the ring that no longer fit his finger.

"No, it's not for you to do that. And it's hard for your stepfather. He doesn't want to upset your mother."

"I know. He'd never go against her. He turns into wet spaghetti around her."

I felt him shrug next to me. "That's only natural. Don't be jealous; they're in love." We were talking very quietly and then Horatio growled. We moved in closer together and Esteban put his arm in front of me, cautioning. Jimmy materialized in front of us.

"What's going on here?" he asked. "That you, Eleanor May? Sarah said you might be out here." I hated him to use my middle name. Looking over at Esteban he said, "And aren't you Esther Dominguez's oldest boy? You know better than to be here with her. Beat it, go on, I'll take her home. Eleanor, come with me. Your mother is going to shit gold bullion when she finds out about this."

"Where's Sarah?" I asked, already moving away from Esteban as ordered, and Esteban didn't protest. I was listening for the sound of him walking back to his place but I didn't hear it. For a few moments Horatio was torn between us but I called to him and eventually he came to heel. I couldn't see Esteban in the darkness at all, but Ray kept looking over his shoulder so I knew he was there.

"Where's Sarah? At home, of course, where you should be." He didn't sound guilty at all. You can get away with any goddamn thing if guilt doesn't get in your way. He was speaking very loudly, still drunk, and righteous in his anger. "What the hell were you thinking? You can't run around the fields in the middle of the night with wetbacks, Eleanor. This isn't some goddamn book you're reading, this is life, and you'll end up with a fat belly and a mighty thin wallet before you've got time to whistle Dixie. God Almighty. Your mother is going to have you for breakfast with grits and sausage, you know that, don't you?"

"He's not a wetback," I said.

"Have you two been doing it? Have you? Has he touched you? What have you done together? You'd better tell me, honey, because I'll find out one way or another and it would be better coming from you. What's the story? Huh?" He was leaning over me, breathing hard, half shouting, and I was shrinking back, terrified. I thought he would know my secret thoughts if he looked deeply enough into my eyes but, rabbitlike, I couldn't look away.

"I've never even kissed him," I said, breaking down as usual. "We only ever hugged once and that was tonight." I was crying again. The whole summer Mom had been practically normal but this would send her over the edge, I knew that, knew what I was in for.

"You'd better be telling me the truth." He was talking more quietly, though.

"It's the truth." I didn't even ask him to lie to Mom. It didn't occur to me. All I could think was that I wanted out, I wanted away from this, that I couldn't live with fear hanging over my head anymore. We walked home the rest of the way in silence and I wondered how much Esteban had heard. Probably all. He was making sure I got home safely but the thought didn't reassure me. I knew he couldn't protect me from Jimmy, or Mom, or much of anything.

At Oak Grove, Mom and Hank were nowhere to be seen and the other guests had left. Jimmy said, "Don't think I'm going to forget about this, Eleanor. Your mother needs to know what you're up to." I was numbed by then and just looked at him. "Go on to bed," he said, and left.

By the time I crawled between the sheets that night I'd already resolved to leave the farm and have my custody changed. Dad would take me if I made him, if I kissed his ass enough, if I promised to do school work, if I made friends with Cindy and said I was miserable in Texas. Mom was going to make a scene about the child support but secretly she'd be thrilled to have me back in Remie, out of her way. And even if I did catch it from her this time, it was going to be the last time. I knew that, somehow. I'd had enough.

"Where've you been?" Sarah asked.

"Nowhere. Where did you and Jimmy go?"

"Nowhere."

And we left it like that.

5 It's 7:00 A.M. and raining. I'm alternating between depression and delirium in the usual way and currently depression has the upper hand. Mom hasn't come home yet from her date last night and when she does she'll need to sleep. I was out late myself, and out even later the night before. I could use a morning in bed but I won't get one; from the deepest levels my body tenses as her arrival looms and that's the end of slumber.

At 6:03 this morning, like a veteran warrior trained by years of combat, I snapped out of bed intensely awake, alert, ready for action, perfectly prepared to pretend to a poise that I'm positive I'll never possess. Then I remembered that she's off today and won't, necessarily, be home for hours. I rubbed my face and drank some water. I peed and daydreamed. I went back and sat on the edge of the sofa bed. I waited to get sleepy but it didn't happen. I drank more water, hot, with lemon to cleanse my system. I tried lying down. I got back up. I brushed my teeth and peed again. I looked to see if any pimples were ready. I did neck stretches and extra-slow sit-ups with my feet on the wall. I went back to the bathroom to examine my wrinkles and pluck out gray hairs. Then I gave up, got dressed for the day, made a pot of coffee and started in on *Geek Love*. It looks pretty brutal. I'm in the mood for brutality.

And Mom strolls in at nine o'clock, cheerful and no-nonsense and just as crisp-looking as when she left, not a shadow under the dark Spanish eyes that are like mine but even more so, deeper set, darker, more mysterious. We have the same skin, too, but our noses are different. Mine is just a nose, unremarkable and belonging to some unremembered relative or mailman. Hers is big, sharply curved, and very strong. She can look sometimes like an owl and sometimes more like a sparrow. Today is a sparrow day. "Good morning Eleanor May! Isn't it beautiful outside?"

Oh, gorgeous. I guess it's always beautiful when you're thin and you just got laid. "It's raining, Mom." She doesn't look like someone who was out all night doing it and got no sleep. She looks like someone who spent all week at the Ventana Canyon Resort.

"I know. It's just so lovely. You'd love the rain too, if you stayed here long enough." I'd shoot myself in the soft palate if I stayed here long enough, actually. "Are you going to take pictures today?" she chirps, darting around the living room opening blinds and gathering debris.

I've been here two weeks without doing anything yet but eat, sleep, and drink coffee. And worry about money, and watch the rain, and wish that I could sleep more. Oh, and waste hours getting high with Ricky and hours getting drunk with Ricky and hours watching Sarah and Samson fight. It's been a very productive fortnight, here in the desert. It hasn't rained this much in Tucson since 1983, when bridges were washed out, horse farms flooded, I-10 was closed, and sections of town evacuated completely. I might as well winter in Oregon. I'm sleepy and hungry and lazy and cold and no one did Christmas this year. New Year's Eve was even a bust—stressful dinner with The Dynamic Duo while Ricky did the town and Mom disappeared.

"I don't know how I feel about taking pictures today. I haven't been very motivated. How was work yesterday?"

"Work was excellent, Eleanor." She says this with such vigor, such Bible-thumping fervency that I can sense a moral tale about to take place. Oh God. It's going to be about someone who wanted to be a photographer and just went out there and did it and made a million. Don't, please don't. She says, "One of the customers was a man who specializes in night photography, Brent Harrison, have you heard of him?"

"Uh-uh."

"Well, he's very well-known in his field, quite well respected. And a handsome man, too, if you like those tall, graying blonds." Which she does.

"Is that who you went out with?"

"Heavens no." Heavens no. This from the woman who, drunk, could silence a sailor.

"Coffee?" I ask her.

"Oh no, not for me, baby, I'm going to have some Ovaltine and go to bed." Baby? Ovaltine?

"When did you start drinking Ovaltine?" I know I've got that tone to my voice, that skeptical, accusing, what-fairy-tale-is-this tone that Dad uses on me, but I can't help myself.

"I've always had Ovaltine. Your father and I used to drink it together, don't you remember?" I raise my eyebrows and she gives me one of those sidelong looks, with her jaw pulling forward and her upper lip clamping down. I might doubt, but she won't falter. "Oh, those lovely winter mornings in Santa Fe," she says, putting on the kettle. "Just your dad and me and the powdery snow."

"Oh please," I say, putting down my book, defeated, and idly beginning to flick through a *Scientific American* instead. "I don't think Dad knows what Ovaltine is." Not to mention, any lovely Santa Fe mornings they might have had in the snow were undoubtedly when they were up there with other people.

"Don't be rude, Eleanor. If you have something you want to say, say it." I don't, so she goes on talking as if we're a Stepford family. "Brent Harrison said he'd be happy to show you some

techniques of nighttime photography. Actually," she smoothes
her smooth hair and tosses her head and I brace myself, "what
he said is, 'If she's anything like you, Mrs. Hawthorne, I'd be
happy to teach her everything I know.' He's a flirt, but I assume
you can handle that, can't you?"

"Piece of cake," I say. Not that I have the intention of spending even one minute with Brent Harrison and his no-doubt
stupid pictures of moonlit howling coyotes. "So that's not who
you went out with?"

"Oh no. I'm sure he's married."

"And?" For a while there she specialized in married men.
Got an advanced degree in the field, you could say. In fact, those
diamond earrings she's wearing now came from some sucker a
few years ago. This little condo in the Catalina foothills had the
hefty down payment supplied by another one just last year.
Sarah liked the condo one quite a bit, except for his acid breath,
but Mom booted him out. She said he just got too boring. She
says men her age haven't got a clue about dealing with independent women. "You can't teach an old dog new tricks," she
said, after she ditched him, but she kept the condo and set her
sights on the younger crowd.

"And that gets old," she says. "You don't know. You've never
been in love with a married man, you're far too sensible." She
means I'm too boring.

"You used to like it."

"I was younger. I had more stamina, I didn't mind being
alone on holidays. Now it's different." As she talks she's fussing
around the kitchen, straightening this and wiping down that
and in response I slouch down lower onto the barstool.

"So who takes you to Vegas now?"

"I don't go. Would you like a beer? I really need a beer or
two to wind down after a night like last night."

"What about the Ovaltine?" She just shrugs and turns the
stove off and reaches into the fridge for a Coors. "So, how was

the date?" I ask her. "Who was the date? When am I going to meet him? Is he good in the sack? How long have you been dating? What does he do for a living? How old is he? Is he smart? Can he dance?"

"Why don't you take the day to photograph the desert?" she asks again, her face barely flickering from my questions. "The desert is so beautiful in the rain and I don't have to work. You can take the car and be gone all day." Which she would clearly love, and I don't blame her.

"Actually, Sarah and I were going to go and do something. But maybe I should give her the whole day alone with Elliot." Sarah's doing some sort of research project up at the U for pocket change and prestige, but this is Christmas break for her and Elliot's schedule is totally flex. Maybe they want to cuddle in bed and pretend I don't exist. It's a good day for that but Sarah and I already made plans. In fact, driving out to the desert to take photographs is exactly what the plans were, but just because Mom suggested it, I don't want to do it anymore.

"Yes. Maybe you should. It's probably a strain on their relationship, having you around all the time." Gosh, thanks. "Weren't you over there quite late last night?"

"Yeah." But how do you know? "They fought about the movies she wanted and then they fought about the movies he wanted and then we all sat around fighting about the movies I ended up picking out." I told him he clearly reserved his taste for his girlfriends. "He told me I was an 'unhappy influence' on Sarah." He also had the nerve to tell me that Ricky Serrano is bad news and I'd be better off staying away from him, childhood friend or not. In this, he and Sarah were agreed.

"Well, there you go," says Mom, rummaging through the refrigerator again and this time coming out with cottage cheese and a tomato. "You definitely need to give them some time alone. And that doesn't mean spending all your days with Ricky, either."

"What's wrong with Ricky?"

"Nothing, except that he's not trustworthy, he has a girl-friend, and it's very difficult to be around a man your own age without getting into a situation. That's all. And he's hardly appropriate for anything serious."

"What does that mean?" If one more person tells me to stay away from him I'm going to scream. I'm not fucking him, I don't intend to fuck him, and if I did intend it I sure as shit wouldn't plan on it being anything serious.

She sips her beer. I sip my coffee, less calmly. "Well, for one thing he's a car salesman and on the unscrupulous side," she begins, but she sounds tentative.

"So?" I can tell that's not the real issue. The problem isn't his job and it isn't his married girlfriend. Mom isn't the type to care about connecting emotionally and having similar goals so it's not that, either. She sips more beer but I pour my coffee out. I should eat something. What I wouldn't give right now for a huge and greasy breakfast burrito.

"You know," she finally says, taking the indirect route to answering my question and eating a spoonful of cottage cheese curd by curd in the meantime, "it always seemed that life is easier for white people."

I don't know what to say, so I go back to the magazine. "It is," I tell her, after a minute. What am I going to do? Lie to her? "But if that's your way of telling me that Ricky's unacceptable because he's Mexican . . ." and then I stop talking, because what she's telling me is that she herself is unacceptable because she's half Mexican, and I don't want to say that out loud. I don't even want to think it out loud.

"It wouldn't be an issue if you weren't child-bearing age," she says, not looking at me.

"I think I'll have that beer after all," I say. My head is reeling but one Coors Light on an empty stomach isn't going to make much difference.

For a few minutes we sit together at the counter, drinking the beers and leafing through magazines and carefully not looking at one another. I've got the *Scientific American* and she's got *Smithsonian*. When I was growing up it was all *People* and *Cosmo* but she's gotten to the age now of being able to indulge herself with intellectualism. It's a luxury women have to wait for. See to the family, then see to your brain, unless your brain is so demanding that the family never happens. Then IVF doctors see you instead.

The phone rings. It's Sarah, I already know, but I don't make a move towards it. I don't want Mom to think I'm in a hurry to end this moment, not when she's just shown me, for the first time, the door to the closet where she houses her ghosts.

"You get it," she tells me without looking around. "That has to be Sarah. She never wakes up this early when you're not in town. It's probably driving Samson around the bend." It sounds like it might be driving Mom around the bend as well.

"Hey," I speak into the receiver. It's a relief to have Sarah this close. I know she'll pick up everything from my tone of voice, the tension and its effects, and I wonder if Mom knows also what I'm revealing.

"Uh-oh," she says, in reply. "Do you want me to let you go?"

"Uh-uh." God no. "I'm just reading *Scientific American* with no comprehension whatsoever and drinking beers with Mom."

"Beers."

"I use that term lightly. It's Coors in a can." I hear Mom go "Tch," from the counter, her usual response to what she calls my East Coast snobbery.

"What are you doing today besides drinking?" Sarah asks then.

"Fuck-all, same as every other day. Oh, sorry Mom." Mom, who hit fifty and developed a severe allergy to the word *fuck*, leaves the kitchen. "I wouldn't mind doing something with my hair, figuring out my life, seducing a massage therapist, at least snapping some photos, but in this weather it's hard to motivate for anything but chocolate doughnuts and sleep. Anyway, I thought we were going to do something together. Why? Do you want to hang out with Samson today?"

"Is Mom still in the room?"

"No, she went in the back and the door's shut. I hear the tap running." I'm whispering anyway. "What's up?"

"How many beers?"

"Only one and her eyes aren't puffy. I don't think she's, uh, you know." It's hard to say the word drinking in Mom's house. Sarah understands.

"Do you think it's a good idea to encourage her?" she asks me, with the privilege that comes from being the daughter who's closer.

"I don't know. I'm through worrying about it."

"Yeah, OK." She understands that, too. "So. Wanna drive to El Paso and see Colette?" She has the tone of voice that, if we were standing in front of a slot machine in Vegas with rent money in our hands, would really make me nervous.

"Back to El Paso?"

"Look at it this way," Sarah says. "Seducing a certain massage therapist could be more effectively managed at close range, don't you think?"

El Paso is five hours away; we'd have to take Samson's car and spend the night with Colette and we'd still be gone the better part of tomorrow. I figure that for every hour Sarah spends with me, Samson exacts two hours penance from her, but obviously she knows that, right? Still, it worries me. "With Elliot?"

"He's gone skiing. He left with Eddy ten minutes ago."

"Without you?"

"Fuck him."

"I see. El Paso, huh. I'll take this as a sign from the heavens, then, to get another massage and see Ashur. Not exactly a tragedy. Let's go."

"I'll buy the massage," she says. "Well, Samson will, actually."

"That's not going to endear me to him," I say. But who cares? The first massage was mind-altering. After the second I might proffer marriage, and I'm not sure Ash's answer would be no.

It was sixteen days ago that I disembarked in Albuquerque and saw my beloved mountain town for the first time in years, raw umber for winter and harsh with wind, jagged and proud and changed only in my sense of no longer belonging. Colette was waiting for me, and after I got my bags she drove me around the city until I'd seen enough. She hadn't changed much, either—still a glossy squirrel decked out in redneck clothes— and seeing her instantly brought back my drawl.

Everything on Colette is round and soft. She has round eyes the color of sherry, round arms with lots of freckles, round breasts, a round bottom, a rosebud mouth, and pounds of reddish curls clustered on her round little head. She's the girliest girl Sarah and I know, the only friend with no athletic ability, not a mean streak in her, no leaning to books and arguing, no hawk-like tendencies, no muscles, no competitiveness, no bullying, no baseline irritation to swell suddenly into rage. She temporarily brings out the niceness in me and it was good to see her again. We took a lot of pictures in Old Town and up on the peak, freezing. I reported on my journey thus far and she told me the latest installment of her ongoing affair with her boss. She's particular about her men. She likes them mean, Mexican, and married, and nothing else will do.

The next day we drove to El Paso from Albuquerque, Sarah drove to El Paso from Tucson, and on Sunday night the three of us caught up the years over enormous steaks and tequila shots and promised each other we'd be friends forever and never diet again. "What happened to plump and pretty?" "Who wants to be a dried-up stick girl?" "We don't want to look like teenaged boys!" But none of it meant anything. Of course we'd diet again. On the way home, Colette reminded me about the massage next day, as if I would have forgotten it, even drunk. "You know you have to do it naked," she said. "And Ash is pretty sexy, in a beat-up kind of way." I immediately wished I'd eaten less for dinner.

Ashur Kaddim was not what you'd expect a massage therapist to look like, even one who's part Egyptian and used to be a bouncer, if Colette was telling the truth about him. He's big and has a Brooklyn accent and looks like he's been around the track a few times. His forearms were riveting. I felt immediately warmer in his presence, my skin softer, my body curvier. It was hard to pull my eyes up off the floor. When he talked he looked right at me, but in a very gentle way, the way you would want a good psychiatrist to look at you. He seemed to see all but judge nothing, and his voice was surprising, deep enough but mild. I couldn't decipher his blood line, clearly something pretty mixed, and on his face were lumpy scars from who knew what kind of accident. Glass? A knife? I thought shaving might be difficult for him and then realized I was picturing him in a morning-after scenario. Luckily he had down pat the ability to be strictly professional. After a few minutes I stopped wanting to shift my feet in front of him, and relaxed.

He said, "I'll leave the room while you get undressed. When you're finished lie on your back under this sheet." Colette waggled her eyebrows at me and left too.

I took my clothes off and tried to hang them so the underwear wouldn't show. Why are nice bras so hard to come by when you actually have tits? I stood in the room naked for a minute just to have the quietness seep into me, and then I crawled onto the table, lying down on my back and draping the sheet across me. It was warm in the room and the heavy linen was scratching my nipples slightly. I did my best but it was hard not to feel erotic. I pictured myself with the sheet off when he walked in, a willing sacrifice. Ash had a real presence, and

I had a real surplus of hormones just then. Better not make a fool out of myself, I thought. Colette should have warned me sooner, so I could have been prepared. But then, if she had said, "I have this hot massage therapist friend with a New York accent who isn't gay, would you like to try him out?" I would have said, "And see me naked? No thanks."

In the background was strange, soothing Indian music, and one of those little boxes that makes a whooshing sound was turned on low. When he knocked and walked back in I looked at his shoulders and thought, What am I going to have to do to get this guy to bed?

He puttered about oblivious, adjusting this and that, talking quietly about the weather. Cold, apparently, for El Paso in December. He told me he got the scars ten years ago in a terrible fight that changed his life for the better. He said, "For a long time I walked around with bandages on my head like a freak. Now I look like this. People stare. Sometimes they're afraid. It's good for me." Me too, darling. Yee-ikes.

He came and stood over me and put his hands underneath the sheet, one on my belly and one on my thigh. Slowly he stroked my body, stopping now and then to squeeze, gently. He seemed to be hearing me with his fingers. I wondered what he knew already but didn't ask. He had stopped talking and I said, "Please keep speaking. Tell me anything. I'm going to close my eyes but I need to hear your voice."

He said, "I'm not very good at talking, but I'll see what I can do." So he began the massage and talked about Zen and skiing and how wild he was when he was a kid, and as he stroked and kneaded he moved my limbs about and I listened to his voice and I didn't know whether I wanted to squirm or sleep or dissolve or levitate but didn't do anything. I lay still. I felt. I wanted to hold on to him, I wanted to lie naked next to him, and I wanted just to touch him like a child would, innocent. I wondered if his other clients felt the same current that I felt coursing between my body and his. My eyes were closed, the music was hypnotizing, his voice carried me like the train, like a rocking hot tub, like the warmth of a womb. I've never felt so held.

A long time went by. He was working on my abdomen, gently massaging what was perhaps my pancreas, and then he said, "I'll hold the sheet. Roll over onto your stomach. What is it that you're looking for in this life, Eleanor?"

"Peace of mind, I think."

"Peace is overrated."

"Courage, then."

"You have courage."

"Not enough." He was working on the place where your arms join into your shoulders. I must have been sore from carrying luggage and sleeping on the train; the deep massage was exquisite.

"How much is enough courage?" he asked me.

Enough to stand up to Mom. Enough to have faith in marriage, to have children, to do photography, to tell the truth. I don't have enough, I don't have nearly enough. "I don't know," I answered. "More than what I have now."

"Eleanor, you're a caring, beautiful, sensitive person. That doesn't make you a coward." Maybe not, but can't I just be a skinny blond with perky tits who climbs icy mountains on winter weekends and isn't afraid to ask for a raise?

When he finished he did it by putting one hand on my low back and the other on the top of my head, and he stood still for several moments while my spirit settled back into my body. I was only half glad to feel it in me again.

I got dressed and floated out and Colette said, "Well?"

"Never felt better." I paid him my thirty dollars and we hugged, briefly, before Colette led the way into the sunshine and the chilly El Paso morning. Leaving was odd and difficult and he held my hand longer than he should have. I wanted to never go.

"Wow," said Colette, back in the car. "You had a spiritual experience, didn't you?"

"Yes. Altered states. I'm in love with that guy."

"That was fast," she said, and turned on some Garth Brooks.

When we got back to the house Sarah had clearly called Samson and was ready to go. He must have given her shit about her absence because she blew Colette a quick good-bye kiss, promised to see her soon, tapped her foot while I double-checked my things, and I piled into the car with almond oil dripping down my neck. We didn't loiter returning. In fact, we hardly spoke and she didn't want to talk about it or change off drivers, either. I took the opportunity to finish *Democracy*. We made the five-hour-plus trip in about four, she unceremoniously dropped me off at Mom's with my bags and trepidation and shoved the key in my hand as a good-bye substitute. Mom was at work and to my surprise it was raining. I didn't know if Sarah was racing home to fuck or fight or both but I was glad to have someplace else to stay. And I was glad to unpack my things, and glad to shower off the almond oil, and then so, so glad to eat a little something, to shit in peace, to read in peace, and then to sleep.

That was two weeks ago and I've done nothing since but get rained on, get stoned, and brood. No enlightenment, no epiphany. In a weird way I miss Ash, his house, El Paso. I felt better there, as if I belonged or could easily belong, and here I feel in everybody's way, even Ricky's sometimes.

"Hey Mom?" I call to the back after Sarah hangs up. There's no answer and when I go look she's fallen asleep in her clothes in front of a soap. I didn't realize she still followed them. I watch her for a while, the slackness under her chin, the way her eye sockets are hollowing, the boniness of her wrists. When she shifts in the chair I start walking around, quietly, getting a few things together.

"Eleanor?"

"Sarah and I are going back to El Paso. Why don't you get out of those clothes and go to bed? I'll leave Colette's number but we're coming home tomorrow."

It's her turn to watch me and she does it without lifting her head off the chair, just those black eyes following me around the room. When I lean to kiss her good-bye she gives me her full face instead of her cheek and I kiss her awkwardly on the lips. How does Sarah do this? I can smell her lipstick, and White Shoulders, the beer, and, faintly, something that I think must be from handling pills at the pharmacy. It smells like vitamins.

"You're going to El Paso?" she asks, fuzzily. "Weren't you going to see Ricky tonight?"

"Oh yeah. I'll call him at work and tell him. You don't want to come, do you?" Please say no, please.

"Oh no," she says. "I'm exhausted. Have a good time. Tell Colette I said hi."

"I will." She never could stand Colette. "Nice and boring," she would say about her, pronouncing the death knell.

"I'll call Ricky for you," she says. She sounds more awake. "I have his work number."

We hear a car pull up then and honking outside and I know that Mom knows I'm glad to go. She begins to fuss with her clothing and then she gets up and fusses with the bed and I can see it now for the disguise that it is. She feels left out. She was so hard on us as children that we learned to live without her. Now she doesn't want us to but we haven't learned different. Sarah breezes in and has us laughing in seconds. She gives Mom a kiss but I can see, this time, that her kisses and my lack of kisses are the same thing. Minutes later the two of us breeze out to the old high five as the door shuts behind us and the day opens up. Later days, Mom. On the way to the car she hands me like a war secret a piece of mail.

It's a postcard from Joe Bloch. *Survived Xmas. So did my folks. New fags in town, details later. Reading* The Joy of

Cooking *with much enlightenment. Want to open a restaurant, am considering Portland, OR. Love to Sarah. Stay away from Ricky S.* When I look up to see what Sarah's reaction is she says, "Love to me? I'm touched." And then she hands me another piece of mail. This one is a short letter from Dad on company letterhead. He's crossed out his name on the list of partners down the left side of the page and written in red ink next to it "free agent." He's like e. e. cummings and doesn't use capitals. *dearest elephant, i hope your holidays were rewarding. thank you for your card. perhaps you could be less brief in the future, not for me as much but cindy and the twins request it. go and see buzz in san fran. maybe this will help with the ticket. love to both of you, dad.* There's a check for two hundred dollars and Sarah says, "Looks like you're buying your own massage." Ten minutes later we're on the interstate at 80 MPH.

Oh is there anything in the world better than a sudden road trip when the rain clears and the sky lifts just for you? Sarah and I play Gary Stewart on Elliot's stereo and sip frequently from Elliot's cognac and drive the Beamer very fast. We pull over a few times to take pictures and I get some hopefully good ones by setting up the tripod and directing her, or doing the timer and having both of us pose in different ways. I'd forgotten how unshy Sarah is in front of the camera. Naked, dressed, backwards, forwards, ugly, pretty, she doesn't care. It makes me braver just being around her, makes me try things I wouldn't on my own.

"Mom seems different," I say at one point, adjusting the camera for another shot. "Nicer. Still fake, but better."

"Yeah," she says, and leans back against the car tire, shoulders hunched over, hands between her feet, running sand through her fingers. I get the shot. "But she's the same when she drinks that she always was. It just doesn't happen very often anymore."

I get a few of me and Sarah sitting on someone's gate in the middle of the brush, only our little fingers touching, the wind blowing our hair around, staring at each other, slouched over, no smiling, no trying for anything. In a couple she has her shoes off, or I'm faced the other way, or we're touching more, or less. Sometimes the car's in there too. Once just Sarah and a cow, also looking at each other. Once just the back of me, shirtless, my head bent, hands in my pockets, examining with the toe of my boot a poor dead rabbit we found in the middle of the road.

I like to stand and wait, with my camera in my hands, for the idea of a certain picture to come over me. When I do this Sarah waits patiently with me and I remember that she always did. Even when we hated each other in high school we would still do this together, the waiting and the setting up and the shooting. She never hurried me then and she doesn't now. A few times she points over to something and I consider it, like the gate, and the cow. She knows the kinds of things that get me.

Twenty miles from El Paso she says with no preamble, "I can't leave another man." It's my turn at the wheel, so I keep my eyes on the road and let steering around a big rig occupy me. "You know how it is," she goes on into my silence. "You get involved with some guy when you goddamn know better, right? And you wonder for the first six months what the hell you're doing, and then for the next however long you wonder how you're going to leave. You start out dumping your friends for the guy and end up ditching your favorite furniture to get away from him. And there's always a dog you can hardly leave, or one of his aunts who loves you, or friends of his who have become friends of yours. You're never leaving just the man; there's always something else and leaving that something else is fucking awful."

"Yeah," I say. I still get a pang when I think about coffee with Patrick and the Sunday paper with Bootsie on my lap.

"I can't live through another one of those scenes, B, the furniture truck and the fights and who gets which friends. I don't ever want to do another first year with another person again.

It's too hard. It's not worth it. The freedom of leaving isn't worth the agony of starting over. I can't do it again. I just can't."

"Then marry him," I tell her. "Quit fucking around. Shit or get off the pot. Fish or cut bait. Make a decision, for Christssake."

"So you think I should marry him?"

"Do I look stupid? I'm not going to answer that question for you." And if I were going to answer, it would be to say No! Please, no no no. He's a walking sphincter, that guy. And he hates me. Oh please don't marry him. But of course I can't say anything like that. Besides, he's interesting. Mom's cardinal rule.

Sarah says, like a kid who can't read yet, reciting the alphabet, "If you're more miserable with someone than you are alone, then it's better to be alone."

"Remember what you said to me about Patrick? If you're ready to leave him, leaving will be easier than staying." For a year I thought there was no way I could ever leave him, and somehow that changed to seeing that there was no way I could stay.

"So you're saying I should marry him."

"No, I'm not."

"Then you're saying I shouldn't."

"Sarah, I'm going to deck you one. I can't even decide what to have for lunch; I'm sure as hell not going to decide your marriage plans. Anyway, look at me. What I know about successful romance you could put in a shot glass."

"Good point," says Sarah. "There's always the chance that I'll make him so angry he'll leave me. That would solve all my problems. The end of the relationship and I wouldn't even have to feel guilty."

"Dream on, babe. This is the era of women leaving men, not the other way around. The decision is going to be yours."

"Damn." We drive on through the outskirts of El Paso, starving, having decided an hour ago to not stop again until we get to Colette's. I, for one, am looking forward to seeing Ash as much if not more than I'm looking forward to lunch and massage. I wonder if he remembers me. No, I wonder if he remembers me specially. I think that maybe he does. When I called him this morning to see if he could fit me in, his voice changed timbre. "B," says Sarah. "Do you think it was easier in the good ol' days?"

"Maybe. You just married the first person your parents approved of, or the first person you really wanted to sleep with, or the only other person in town your age. And divorce wasn't an option. Fewer choices."

"Like Russia."

"Exactly," I say.

She sighs wistfully. "I always did think Russia might have its good side."

The next day happens like a dream. I have my massage early, nothing in me but coffee and what passes for a bagel out West. Sarah stays behind to sleep in, a luxury she has to battle Elliot for, and after the massage Ash holds my hands for a moment between his and I can see he remembers me as much as I'd hoped and more. When I leave he says, "Come back anytime. Stay as long as you want." Colette rolls her eyes but I'm soaring.

Next we collect Sarah and head for Juarez. We eat, we shop, I don't care what we do. As we start home, I come millimeters from telling Sarah to leave me in Texas, but don't have the guts. After three hours on the road, mostly quiet, she accuses me of being lousy company but I can't help it. I keep thinking, He likes me! He really likes me!

It's late when she drops me off at Mom's. "Wish me luck," she says, but I don't because all I can think about is Ash and smoothing those scars and I don't care about stupid Samson and his stupid temper tantrums. But, soon enough, I learn to care.

"Eleanor?"

"Yes?" It's the day after El Paso. I'm at Mom's and don't know who's on the phone. A man with a nice, high-pitched voice pronouncing his syllables too precisely.

"It's Elliot Ivers. Or perhaps you know me as Samson. Your sister Sarah's boyfriend."

"I know who you are, Samson." Jesus, what a freak. Elliot is a hawk, curved and watchful and dangerous. He makes you want to cover your jugular. "I've done a lot of drugs, guy, but I haven't done that many. I just didn't recognize your voice on the phone. What's up?" Originally the plan was going to be for me to stay part of the time with Mom and then, when she got sick of me, stay a few weeks with Sarah, but I know before he goes any further that, despite their four bedrooms and two and a half baths in Sam Hughes, staying with Sarah is no longer an option.

"Very well, Eleanor, there's no need to be sarcastic. Why are you so aggressive? Have I done something to offend you? You don't like me, do you? You would prefer it if Sarah and I were not seeing one another, isn't that correct?"

"No, no, of course not." Aside from your being a complete dick, you're a very nice guy and wouldn't offend the nuns. I'd just love to have you in the family.

"Well, you certainly sound combative."

"I'm sorry, you just got me in a grumpy mood." And, as usual, a spineless one. "So, really, what's up?"

"Well, Eleanor, I'm not sure quite how to say this, but ever since you've come to Tucson my relationship with your sister has been strained. I don't, of course, consider this your fault, exactly, but I have noticed the correlation. It seems as if Sarah is much happier with my company when you're not around. I don't for a moment think you're putting ideas into her head. I mean, you wouldn't, would you?"

"No, of course not." I'd love to, you moron, but for one thing my conscience wouldn't let me and for another it wouldn't work anyway.

"I didn't think so." He sounds so satisfied that I lose my temper.

"Look, Elliot, Sarah's got her own mind."

"What are you saying, Eleanor, that your sister wants to leave me and has told you so herself?"

"Did I say that?"

"I think that's what you implied."

"No, I think that's what you inferred." Oh, you go girl. Stopping that paranoia cold, aren't you? "Anyway, shouldn't you be discussing this with Sarah, not me?"

"I don't want to make you angry, Eleanor," he says, changing tactics prudently. "That's the last thing I want. I'm just very worried about my relationship with your sister and this is something I feel I can't discuss with her. She'll think of it as an attack on you and won't listen to what I'm really saying. It's not an attack on you. I like you, Eleanor." He nearly chokes on that but continues gamely on. "It's just that the two of you make a tight circle and I get pushed away. I love her very much, you know. I would marry her tomorrow but she isn't interested." Why is he telling me all this? "I've never known anyone like her. She's just a wonderful girl. Woman. But of course I don't need to tell you that." Then stop, for God's sake, I don't want your confidences. "Eleanor, what would you do about this situation if you were me?"

"What?"

"I'm asking you what to do about the fact that Sarah is very different to me when you're around. It doesn't make things easy, and being in a long-term relationship is difficult under the best of circumstances, although I'm sure you're far too busy being an adventurous spirit to worry about that sort of prosaic problem anymore."

You've got a point there, Elliot, and I wish you'd stop torturing me because of course the virtue of The Relationship wins out no matter what over the unholy state of Being Single, not just in the eyes of all society but in my own head as well. "Elliot," I say, and it's almost sincere, "I'm really sorry to have caused the relationship between you and Sarah any stress at all. It isn't because I've been putting ideas into her head. I haven't and I never would. But maybe you two should be alone more often and I'll see what I can do to facilitate that."

"That's very understanding and mature of you, Eleanor." He's practically purring, the condescending asshole. "Why don't we tell Sarah that you want to be alone for a few days to work on your photography and that you called and told me so? Because she would do anything for you, and anything to help your little project. What do you say?"

"I say fine, Elliot." Actually, I say Uncle. You win, Elliot.

"Bean, please, call me Samson."

I don't say anything.

"One last thing," he says then, and the tone of his voice changes. I wait for the punchline. "I hear you're in love with some knifed-up African who does massage."

"Something like that," I say. Screw him.

"What was your last boyfriend? An alcoholic Irish substitute teacher?"

I just wait.

"I guess this is going to give Ricky some competition. I'm glad to hear it."

"So happy to make you happy, Elliot. See ya."

I hate my life. What does Sarah see in that guy? I can never get one thing right without something else turning to shit.

Jimmy was a dressed-up coyote and you'd have had to be blind or brain-damaged not to see it. He used to say things like this to Sarah: "Danged if you're not the picture of jailbait. How come I don't remember any fourteen-year-olds like you when

I was fourteen?" I always expected her to see right through that line of shit, but you know what? She loved it. She had started working at the feedlot with him early in the summer and was still working for him happily months later. She was showing up at the house with bits of clothing and jewelry that she said she bought with her paychecks. Mom and Hank didn't question it, and when I protested it was feebly and she stared me down easily. In private she said, "I won't push you about your wetback, but don't push me about Jimmy." I capitulated. Esteban was precious to me but he was also a secret shame. I didn't want her telling the town of Remie that the love of my life was a poor Mexican boy who worked at a meat packing plant to support his family.

One day in October I took the little truck out for an afternoon spin. Mom and Hank were off to some exciting place like Abilene, Sarah was in town working at the lot, and I had several hours all to myself before Esteban got off shift and we met at the hayshed. It was Indian summer and beautiful, hot and clear but with a certain bronzed quality to the light that let you know autumn was coming. I thought I'd go out and do some target shooting, read a little, maybe lie out in the sun with no shirt on down a deserted country road. I had a few of Mom's cigarettes, I was reading either *Atlas Shrugged* or *The Fountainhead,* and I was feeling good. I had Horatio in the back of the truck and the .22 in the cab with me. There was only an AM radio but I didn't care. By this point I knew a lot of country music and I sang along at the top of my voice, not thinking about anything, just driving and smoking and squeezing the last bit out of summer.

About a half hour from the house I saw Jimmy's truck stopped under a railroad crossing. Maybe he had just pulled over for engine trouble or to take a piss, but it didn't look like it. There was a shirt hanging from the gun rack. I thought to myself, "Yes, Lord! I'm going to embarrass the holy hell out of him and Beth when I pull up and honk." I even thought that if they didn't hear my truck I'd maybe fire a shot in the air, just to really scare the shit out of her, although, to tell you the truth, I was pretty impressed that she'd even consider having sex in the middle of the afternoon. It was more than I'd given her credit for. Then it occurred to me that of course she would never consider it; that's why he married the silly bitch. Men who fuck around marry women who don't. Ergo, he must be hiding the salami with some other fool, like maybe Mrs. Otterman, whose husband was too busy poisoning dogs and babying sheep to tend to matters at home, and who'd made it plain how she felt about Jimmy after several vodka gimlets at the Fourth of July party.

The thought of catching her out was too much to resist. I turned off the motor and coasted slowly in, hoping they wouldn't notice a sudden silence. "Come on Ray," I said quietly. He was a great dog, and crept at my heels, noiseless except for his panting. Thirty feet off I started whooping like an Indian, and shot the gun into the air. Of course it wasn't Jimmy and Mrs. Otterman at all, but Jimmy and my little sister Sarah, and she was naked as the day she was born and hopping mad.

"What are y'all doing?" I asked, idiotically, the gun still in my hand, Horatio sniffing around excitedly. There was no answer out of either one. "I said, what the fuck are you doing?" I was looking right at Jimmy, and all by itself the gun seemed to start pointing in his direction. "She's fourteen years old. Do you understand that? Sarah, get your goddamn clothes on and let's get out of here."

Sarah walked over to me, naked, barefoot on the plowed earth, and pushed the gun away. She stared right into my face and said, "Fuck off, Bean. Can't you tell when you're not wanted?"

"Sarah," I said, but it sounded so pleading that I wouldn't let myself go on. I swallowed. "You don't want to do this."

"No Bean, you don't want me to do this. Go and live your own life, would you? I mean it now. Fuck off."

I couldn't look at her. I couldn't look at him. "Come on Ray," I said, sharply, and he trotted over. I nearly wrecked the truck on the way home, blinded by tears. She didn't even have to tell me not to tell anyone. She knew I wouldn't. Or maybe she knew that the only person left in my life I could talk to was Esteban, and what could he do? He wasn't even brave enough to have sex with me, much less stop Sarah from having sex with Jim. When I got home I ran out to our meeting place, hoping and praying that Esteban would come early, but that day he was held over at work. I waited and waited and the deep blue sky turned mocking above me. Horatio grew restless but I wouldn't leave. I smoked all the cigarettes I had and tried to read, but Ayn Rand is no comfort in everyday misery. I walked around. I drank out of the irrigation pipe. I talked to myself and got burnt by the Indian sun and still there was no sign of Esteban.

At four o'clock I returned to the farm alone, and that night Sarah didn't bother coming home. At midnight the phone rang. It was Beth the Mouse. She asked for Hank but I said Hank and Mom were in Abilene for a couple of days and she said, "Oh my." Beth was hard to like, and I didn't make it easy on her. I just sat on the phone waiting, and she sat on the phone agonizing. Eventually she said, "Is Sarah there?"

"She's asleep," I said. "Do you want me to wake her up? What's going on?"

"Oh no," she said quickly. And sat there some more. I hated her voice. It was so soft and squeaky and she could never come out and say anything direct. If you asked her had she eaten dinner she couldn't just say yes or no, she had to find out what you wanted her to say, and then say that. I was furious with Sarah but there was no taking anything out on Sarah so I took it out instead on Beth.

I kept on saying nothing. The silence was awkward, and hostile. She was no brain surgeon but she must have known that.

"Actually," she said, "Jim hasn't come home and I'm worried that he had an accident at the plant. Do you mind terribly waking her up and asking her when she saw him last?"

"No problem," I said, thinking to myself, Fuck! I couldn't believe that I was lying for her, I just couldn't. I put the phone down and pretended to walk to the back, then waited, then pretended to walk to the living room again. "I woke her and asked her and she says he left before she did today. Maybe he went out of town."

"Maybe. It's so unlike him not to call me." Yeah, I'll bet. "Well, thank you, Eleanor. Tell your sister I said sorry, OK?"

"Sure thing," I said, and hung up the phone. I promised myself that I would never lie for Sarah again, but I did. I did it often and everyone made it easy to, even Hank.

6 It's wet again and cold. I'm stoned, I'm drunk, I'm miserable, and I'm also still at Mom's place. I thought Elliot would relent but I must have offended the gods. He put his size-eleven extra-narrows down and hasn't picked them up yet. Consequently I haven't seen Sarah since our trip to El Paso and that was twenty-four days ago. At some point she came by with him and left me the scooter, but they did it while I was out. Tucked under the seat strap was Sarah's shorthand status report: an unsmiling smiley face smoking a cigarette. I've tried calling but they won't answer.

So far Mom hasn't said a word about the constancy of my presence, about my crowding her, ruining her alone time, and eating all the food in the house, but sometimes her temper gets short. I don't blame her. I buy groceries but it's not the groceries she misses, it's her life. I spend as much time away as I can, either with Ricky or in the mountains or at the photo lab of the community college—I'm taking a course for darkroom hours— but giving her temporary time is not the same thing as giving her real time in her own place all to herself. I feel bad. If I were fish I'd be stinking to Yuma by now. I keep thinking I should leave Tucson and either go to El Paso or get on with my train trip but I can't do either. I'm paralyzed by supernatural forces and it's going to take an earthquake to move me. Having Ricky around serves only to rob me further of initiative.

When I planned this trip he wasn't even in Tucson. Then I got a call from him late in the summer, over at Monica's. I knew Mom had given him my number. "I hear you're going to Tucson in a few months," he said.

"Hey Rick. How the fuck are you? Where are you? Did Mom give you my number? Are you in Denver still? How's business? How's your love life? Why are you calling me?"

"Slow down," he said. "It turns out that I need a change of locale, sooner not later, and it looks like I'm going to be in Tucson this winter myself. Funny, huh?"

A total riot. "Cops?"

"Husbands."

"Be careful."

"Too late. See you at Christmas. Hope you're not fat."

"Fuck you."

"I'll think about it."

It's 10:45 now and a good thing that Mom is working night shift because the kitchen is a mess and I'm the same. Sometimes when you get high with friends a sense of their inner selves comes flooding into you and you feel open, sharing, warm and tuned in, and it seems perfectly obvious that the only thing that matters in the whole world is the affection you have for other people and the affection they have for you. However, this isn't one of those times. Ricky is not one of those friends.

The rain is easing up. We can hear the hush and whisper of it through the small dark leaves of the straining olive trees outside. I'm really blue tonight and not just stoned, I'm toasted, tenderized, baked, and broiled. I'm way over my quota of hits and the pot is giving me that horrible, exposed feeling, as if my inner self has been left out on a mountainside in winter. I feel as if I might shiver to bits and my hands are frozen. It's not a good night to be getting high.

I'm sitting up on the kitchen counter fretting in my black jeans, black boots, silver jewelry and extra heavy, black silk

shirt. Standing in front of me, immune to the chic and flatter-
ing outfit, is a man I used to know when he was just a boy and
what I can't seem to do, no matter how much beer we drink
together in the evenings, no matter how many joints we cough
our way through on his lunch hours, is find more than a trace
of those childhood days in the face he has now. What's happened to my café au lait baby? I see the skin, but where is the
rest of him?

"Hey," I say suddenly, interrupting his anecdote, which is a
long and wild story that I can't keep track of about having sex
in an airplane over L.A., "do you remember kissing me that
night when we were kids?"

"Not really. Are you ready for another one?" He gestures
with his beer and I nod, or think I nod. I can't take my eyes off
the hand that's holding his empty beer bottle. His fingers are
long, the hands surprisingly graceful, the nail beds flat and
smooth. Then I process what he said.

"What do you mean you don't remember kissing me? How
the fuck can you not remember kissing me?"

"I don't know, Bean, I just don't. Maybe I was drunk."

"Drunk." I think about that. "You were not drunk. You
couldn't have been more than twelve at the most and you hadn't
started drinking yet."

"That's what you think."

"But I remember it clearly. We went to one of those new
houses and then walked back to my place. You sweet-talked me
and then you kissed me. I can't believe you don't remember. It
was my first kiss! You're an asshole, you really are." To my own
ears it sounds as if I'm talking like the grown-ups in a Charlie
Brown movie but he doesn't seem to notice. "Just give me that
beer, would you? Am I talking real slow?"

Ricky starts laughing at me his fake, car salesman laugh. It
hurts my ears. His teeth are white and savage and his eyes look
feral, even with the smile on his face. He's grown up into the

kind of man I wouldn't spend ten minutes on except that, well, I am. When he turns to the fridge I admire his coordination, the ease with which he maneuvers his body. He must not be as stoned as I am.

"Here," he says, "but you better slow down. I don't want your mama yelling at me because I got her daughter too fucked-up to move."

I don't say anything.

"Don't be mad. Tell me more about the train trip," he coaxes me.

"It's my birthday in two days," I tell him instead, and he nods. He knows, I've told him before. He likes younger women is what he said about it. He says women are a pain in the ass when they hit their thirties. I said that was definitely true for me. "I saw Joe Bloch in Kansas," I say next. I haven't told him about the postcards and the talk on the train because he hates Joe Bloch and I didn't want to fight but tonight I need to say the name out loud. What once weakened me will now succor me.

"Joe Bloch? What's he doing these days, besides getting it up the ass on a regular basis? Or is he a top?"

"He can't help being gay, you know." That's not what I want to say. I want to say Look, just leave my house, you're not my kind of person anymore. But I can't. And I can't believe he doesn't remember kissing me. God I'm high. My mouth feels like an actively mined quarry.

"He can help it."

"I have cotton mouth. And don't be stupid, of course he can't help it. You've been living in the sticks too long."

"Yeah right, Miss Mighty East Coast, the tiny town of Denver. The Romans were queer but they had wives and families too. They understood their duty to society." He drinks deep.

"This isn't Rome."

"Whatever. Anyway, I thought you hated him."

"I did, but he's changed. We saw each other on the train and talked for hours between Kansas and Colorado. He's skinnier. More of a city boy. And he's become a human being, not that you'd care. He's turned out so nice. He's just reading and traveling and, I don't know what you call it, being like a monk. Ricky, he's changed. He's on a spiritual quest. He's gentle now."

Ricky puts his beer on the counter and leans towards me. "Oh yeah? You know what's really going on? He's no threat anymore, B, and he's no threat because he's a fag, and because he's a fag he'll never try to take you to bed. Real men scare you and now you feel safe."

"What? Jesus Christ! Where did that come from? I was just trying to say that he's nice. That's all. It has nothing to do with sex. What is your problem?" I'm a lot less stoned, suddenly. He got that from Mom and the thought makes me sick. He always worshipped her, always parroted every statement.

"Listen, Bean, it's a dog-eat-dog world out there, and you don't have to think about it if it scares you so much, but don't tell me about being a human or not being a human, OK? I'm just a working stiff, a nobody, a jerk-off who sells cars and drugs and never had a deep thought? I'm not sitting on a rock somewhere thinking about world peace, I'm busting my ass to pay bills, so now I'm more like an animal than a person to you, is that it? Well I'm an animal that fucking gets those bills paid, and my little sister is in college that I'm paying for, and my mom will never have to worry about money when she's old, and I even have money in the bank for me and Becky one day."

"Becky's married to someone else, Ricky."

"So the fuck what? We have plans! What have you got compared to that? You get up on your high white horse and keep your hands all shiny clean and then lecture to people like me about how dirty we are, but at least I live in the real world. You don't have kids, you don't have a husband, you don't have bills, you're living off your mother and all you have is that dream world between your ears. Now Joe Bloch is part of that world again. Well fucking have a party up there why don't you?"

"Jesus! Stop, all right? I can't believe you! What the fuck did I say? Where did all this come from?"

He walks over and turns up the Pearl Jam he brought over. "I went out into the world when I was sixteen years old and I didn't have time to fucking think about my sorry life and my sorry self because I was too busy trying to find enough food to live on. You think it's a fine thing to turn away from money? That it makes you a better person? That's because you've never been poor."

"Yes I have." I have, too. I lived like an animal in Cincinnati.

"No Bean. You always had help if you needed it and being poor is not having any help, no matter how bad things get. I know that Joe's family had money, that he never went hungry, that in this life he'll never have to worry about keeping a roof over his head. So he might be human to you and all 'gentle' now, but to me he's a rich boy like all rich boys, no different except that he's queer to boot, and if you want to be friends with him again because he meditates under a tree and doesn't need you to act like a person is supposed to act in this world, that's fine, but don't tell me he's human when what you really mean is that I'm not. Goddammit!" He slams his hand against the wall and I jump, slopping my beer. He turns to pace up and down the kitchen floor but after several revolutions he stops and takes a swig from his bottle, staring out the window at the drips of rain.

I take a breath, just in recovery, but he swings back around to finish up. "Oh the Shank girls, so high and mighty and going to college and you know what? You're a fucking bank teller without a job and your sister is an asshole's girlfriend with a fancy degree she can't even use."

"She can too."

"Oh, part-time research. Wow. I'm impressed. She doesn't make enough to pay for her haircuts. Your mom is right, you know that? All you do is whine about her and how mean she was but the bottom line as I see it is that she's making it on her own and doesn't blame anyone for her troubles, and you're drifting around with nothing to show for your easy life but more things to whine about. You're not even working."

"I'm working on photography."

"That doesn't count. Your dad didn't do shit for you. He didn't teach you a thing. You should have stayed with your mom. At least you might have ended up useful."

"Sarah stayed with her," I point out, traitorously.

"Sarah does nothing difficult but at least that skinny prick gives her a good life. You don't have anything! Oh gee, it's so much worse to be selling automobiles and making 50K a year, plus perks and bonuses and what I make on the side." He means selling pot. "What was I worried about? Do you know that I thought you'd make fun of me? I was embarrassed for my life. She kept telling me not to care but I did."

"Who?" As if I didn't know.

"Your mom. But I cared anyway. 'Oh, how can I let Sarah and Bean see me in this sleazy jacket on a car lot,' and 'Oh, Sarah and Bean are going to think I'm slime,' and 'Damn, I should have gone to college.' Whatever. I can't believe I spent one second worried about how I've turned out when all you can do is sit on your ass and moan about your mother and how cruel the world is. And now you think Joe Bloch is a fucking hero! He's traveling around on trains like a hobo and he's a cocksucking faggot who broke his father's heart. Some hero."

"You should watch who you're calling a cocksucker," I say.

"What the hell do you know? What do you know about having a hungry baby sister and no food in the house and wanting to party with the rich boys? Nothing, because you don't know shit about life."

I walk away and clip the yellowing leaves off the philodendron. My hands are shaking. "OK," I say, and tip up my beer. "Are you done yet?" The bottle clinks against my teeth and

I flinch. Ricky doesn't say anything. I turn down the music to think more clearly. Fucking Ricky and his dead father and poor-boy grievances, and his loyalty to Mom and her interpretations of my character. He'd never have come up with that analysis for my behavior on his own, never.

Standing by the fridge, looking out the window into the dark, the way his body is half leaning against the wall, left foot resting on his right, is exactly the way he used to stand when he was thirteen. It takes me back to when we were kids and I never worried about what was going through his mind.

"Goddammit, Ricky," I'm speaking to the back of his head. "I wasn't even talking about my mom. I never said anything against her, I never said anything about my hard life. I know I've got it good, I know I wouldn't be able to take time off without her helping me out. Why are you defending her? And did I ever say anything about your job?"

He doesn't bother answering so I change the music to Morphine, very loud, and stay on the other side of the living room. He's still in the kitchen, leaning against the counter and flipping a quarter through his fingers, rolling it over and under, over and under. I sit on the edge of the sofa and watch him. I never could do that trick.

He's correct though, Ricky is. That I was accusing him of being nonhuman by calling Joe human, and who'd have guessed he'd see right through that? And, of course, I also meant, I could reach Joe Bloch and I can't reach you, Ricky Serrano, and maybe this will open up a chink in your armor. And, even more basic, You can't remember kissing me? Well you'll fucking remember me now, boy.

He looks over at me and I turn the music down. "It's late," he says, "and I'm supposed to call Becky tonight. I need to get going."

"No, Ricky, don't go now. I'm really sorry. It was my first kiss, for God's sake." And I think of Chase, suddenly, furious in her living room at the injustices she suffered at Sarah and my hands, and the picture of her and Ricky together floats into my mind. It was her first kiss too and I bet he remembers kissing her.

As I watch him, obliquely, he seems to come to some sort of decision. He taps out the bone he's smoking, looks down at his shoes for a moment, and then walks over to me, where I'm scrunched up in the corner of the couch. What's scaring me now is that we're not kids anymore and he knows it. We're not in my yard thinking that we'll never be like the grown-ups. We are the grown-ups, this is his world, and once again he's leader.

"Actually, Beanie," he says quietly, staring right at me, "I do remember kissing you. I just wanted to see what you'd do if I pretended not to, and now I know." And he smiles at me. "You sure got pissed off, huh?"

"So that's it? That's all you're going to say?"

"That was just a little fight. What's a little fight between friends?" Then casually he slides his foot in between my two feet and scoots my legs apart. Still looking right at me he steps into the breach and puts his warm hand on the side of my neck. "You're drunk, Eleanor May, and your eyes are shining and you look just like your mama right now."

"Oh great."

Now he's no longer smiling. He puts down his beer and pulls me up to him and I can no more resist him than I could stave off an avalanche, and even as he's leading me back to the bedroom, my mother's bedroom for christssake, I'm thinking to myself, "This is not what I had in mind." Or is it? What have I been doing, spending all my time with him, getting stoned with him, watching movies with him, if not waiting for this moment? What I mean is not that I don't want to be seduced, it's that I don't want to be seduced like this. But I'm not going to be able to stop it, that much I recognize.

Well then, if you can't fight it, you might as well join in whole-heartedly. But I can't do that either. Something's happened to me, the weed or the beer or the shock of his attack, and all I can do is stand there as he undresses me, and continue standing there as he undresses himself, and then a few minutes later lie there as we go to it. Eventually I start moving around and faking interest. My body is functioning adequately but the whole time my mind is somewhere else. It takes him forever and I can't decide if it's because he always has sex like this, or if it's because I'm so uninvolved, or if it's because the pot has me on a time warp. He seems to be one of those nightmare eighty-nine minute and twenty-three position guys but he doesn't go down and he doesn't meet your eyes. At any rate he doesn't meet my eyes and I can't stop thinking about Lily and the things she said about him.

"I was fifteen years old and kind of backwards. It was the year before he ran away from home. He was sweet, Bean, sweet like no one has been since. We would lie together in his uncle's truck and sometimes just look at each other, not do anything else. And other times we talked about everything under the sun. When the rest of you were around we were mean as hell, but alone he would stroke my body over and over and he never had to say anything, I knew he loved it. He made me feel special. If I saw him now I'd do anything for him, and I will for the rest of my life. We had a secret, and the secret was that all of you thought we were a couple of losers, but we had something that you didn't. And you know, we were young, and when you're young you don't usually understand the things you'll think of later as precious. But we did. We knew it at the time. He had the most beautiful skin I've ever seen."

He still has that skin. But I don't think he even sees me. When it's over he says, "Damn," like he just ran a hundred meters, and shakes his head. Then he grins at me, does something to the condom with his right hand while he gives my boob a parting squeeze with his left, then he hops up and heads for the toilet. I sit forward, reach to the floor for my beer, and bury my face in my free hand.

A minute later he sticks his head out the bathroom door and says, "I never in a million years thought when I was a kid that I'd be here one day fucking Eleanor Shank in her mother's bed. It's amazing, isn't it?"

"Yep." Amazing. I get up and change the music to Leonard Cohen. Ricky leaves without kissing me again but he remembers to take his music. He has to call Becky by midnight and it's well after that now. Suddenly it comes to me that in fact he doesn't remember kissing me at all. He was telling the truth the first time around and the second time around was a line. God. How can something be so meaningful to one person and be nothing, just nothing, to the other? It's obscene. And this beer is obscene, and the facility with which he maneuvered me is obscene. Is there no Scotch in this house? Is there no dignity in my soul? I want to run away. I want to go to sleep for months and only wake up when this is all a long way behind me. Actually, I'd better get rid of the Lenny or I'll work myself into a three-week case of the suicide blues. I'll put on something classical instead, Mozart maybe, to remind myself that some things on the planet far outlast a bad fuck. Hey, lookie here, a half bottle of Johnnie Walker tucked in behind the CDs, as well as some gin, vodka, and even a bottle of Campari. Thanks, Mom.

Ah. It's thirty minutes later, I feel much better, and I remember something that I've been forgetting lately: It's snowing in Boston but I'm not in Boston. I hated my job, but I don't have that job. I was miserable with Pat, but Pat's out of my life. I left the bank, I'm in Tucson for the winter, and I'm doing what I love to do. How many people have it that good? How many people get to throw it all away, even it it's only for a while, and live a dream life? Not very many. If absolutely nothing comes out of this at all, and I go back to Boston in the summer dead broke and empty-handed, back to the bank and back to my same shit life with nothing to show for my journey but a tan, I will still have had this time in the sun. And I won't be any worse off than I was before. What was I going to do with my money anyway?

I feel like calling Ricky and telling him to fuck off, that I don't need him anyway and I'll never be stupid enough to sleep with him again. That asshole. I wish I could tell Sarah about this but she would consider me certifiable. She'd lose it. "Ricky Serrano? That slut? What were you thinking? Did you use protection at least? Did you wash Mom's sheets?" Speaking of which, I need to go and change those sheets, but I'm too peaceful right now to move. I do love Mozart's horn concertos. They're exactly what I wish I were; quietly stirring and memorable.

I should get another glass of water or I'll be hungover in the morning, but this couch has gotten so comfortable, and I'm so sleepy, and I don't feel like getting up right now. I'll do it later, really I will.

"Eleanor May Shank, are those hickeys on your neck?"

"What? No. What hickeys?"

It's eight in the morning, suddenly, and Mom's home. I'm balled up on the couch and my neck is cricked and my mouth feels like someone shit in it. I fell asleep on the sofa last night, I guess. Oh Christ. It's hard to stand straight. There are beer bottles everywhere, the Scotch bottle on the floor, and the skinny stubs from two joints in the ashtray. I still have makeup on, and my silk shirt and jeans, and her bed, Dear Lord, I left that bed, I can't believe I left that bed.

"Mom," I start to say, but I don't know how to say Don't go back there. Anyway she's not listening, she's heading for the bedroom and I'm cringing in anticipation.

I hear her gasp, and then, "My God. You had sex in my bed? You and Ricky had sex in my bed? Look at this, Eleanor!" I close my eyes for a moment, wish I had had the extra glass of water last night, and shuffle unwillingly to her doorway, braced for what I am about to see. It's a very attractive picture. The top sheet is kicked down around my underwear, the bottom sheet is pulled off the mattress at two corners and, worse, is lightly stained with what appears to be the last of my period. Ricky's condom is draped over the edge of Mom's glass of water, there on her nightstand, next to her most recent issue of *Harper's*.

I can't help it. I start laughing. "Sex? No, no. No sex here, not us, no sir. What gives you that idea?" She's not laughing, and her stiff jaw strikes me as hilarious. I'm leaning against the doorjamb, weak with laughter, when inexplicably it becomes not funny anymore. I wipe my tears and I look at her. "I'm sorry, Mom. I don't even know why I'm laughing. Let me clean this up, it won't take a minute."

"Just get your things and get out."

"What?"

"You heard me, you little whore."

"Have you been drinking?"

"It's none of your business what I've been doing, this is my house!" That means yes, but she's not slurring. "Get your bags together, get your things, get out of my sight. Call your sister or call the Red Cross. I don't care what you do or where you go but I want you out of my house. Get out, now!"

"Look, settle down. I fucked up, I'm sorry, it was rude of me, but don't you think you're overreacting? Jesus Christ, do you know how many times growing up I walked in on sex scenes of yours the morning after?"

"I said get out and I mean it!" Her famous iron control is iron no longer. "You've crossed the line, Eleanor May. You're always pushing me to the limit and now you know another one. Having sex with Ricky Serrano in my bed is over the limit! Is this what your father raised you to be, a common slut? That boy doesn't love you! Are you stupid as well as loose? You make me sick! Get out of my sight! Go!" She's screaming now, the cords in her neck straining, her eyelids red and swollen and her hands clenched into fists. For a second I wonder if she's going to hit me, and I back up, automatically, but this old cowardice enrages me.

"You're a loony fucking lush!" I yell back at her. "Get a grip! What are you, in love with him or something?"

And then she does it, lets go with her left hand right across my face and I'm way too surprised to duck. Pow. My head snaps back against the doorway and my ear explodes with pain. A loud noise fills my brain and I realize it's me, bellowing. I come at her like an enraged bull, but when I get to her all I can do is grab her raised hands and squeeze them as hard as I can, squeezing as if I could crush her bones, could squeeze reason into that berserk brain of hers, could squeeze sanity back into me, too, and it feels like the top of my head is going to come off. I push her back hard, see her ricochet into the wall and stumble, and I don't know if I should go after her and pound her into the ground or if I should just check myself immediately in to an insane asylum.

Having that thought is like becoming lucid in the middle of a nightmare and I realize that I've regained control. My vision clears slowly of a kind of fog and the room fades from throbbing red back to its natural, clean bright state. It amazes me that the sun is shining. It feels as if minutes pass. I'm still standing at the threshold to her room but now she's sitting on the bed, turned away from me, and she looks so small. We're both panting and gasping and I, for one, have to hold on for balance.

"Mom," I say, but when she turns her face to me, oddly enough, it's triumphant. That sobers me up faster than the slap across my face. For a stunned second I look at her, waiting for the gears to stop turning, to find out in the front of my brain what I already know in the back, and then I realize it. She wanted me to hit her.

I think to myself, That's crazy. But at the same time I know it's true. And she, watching my face, sees my realization and recognizes it for what it is, and sees that I can read that, as well. For long moments the room fades and there is only the channel of our black eyes, one set watching the other. I can hear my heart beating, loud and fast. The sound fills my ears while her eyes fill my eyes and collecting in my body, first my stomach, then my legs, my shoulders, hands, and feet, is the knowledge that I will never be afraid of her again.

"You need to leave," she says.

I shrug and turn away, put my boots on and begin to pack, hands moving efficiently, brain zooming, the tip of my nose icy. Books, camera, equipment, photos, clothes, shampoo, journal, jacket. OK. Walk outside, strap on the luggage like an Eagle Scout and start up Sarah's scooter. As far as I know Mom's still sitting on the bed.

I take Oracle south into town and for once the cars don't scare me so I ride around and marvel at the beautiful morning. In the center of the city I pull into Rincon Market for a coffee and then decide that this is an emergency situation and warrants breaking my agreement with Samson. I'm in their neighborhood anyway. The coffee burns my stomach so I throw it out and head over to their place. Unfortunately, no one's home.

"Are you a friend?" a neighbor asks and I tell her not exactly, that I'm Sarah's sister. "You two don't look a bit alike," she says to me suspiciously and I just look at her. I'm beyond explanations and maybe it shows because she says, with a sniff, "They're gone for the week to Reno. I'm surprised you don't know." That makes one of us. "I'm keeping an eye on the house for them." And she gives me another once-over.

I nod. It figures. And I get back on the scooter and head out before she can ask me any questions. I have a headache. At the next pay phone I pull over and take my Zovies dry, four of them at once. Ugh. Then I scrounge for a quarter.

"Ricky? It's me. My mom just came home and saw the bed and kicked me out of the house and . . ." I don't go on because he's laughing. He's laughing hard and I of course don't think the situation is at all funny. "It's not funny, Ricky. Do you always laugh at shit like this? She popped me one, I pushed her down, and then she kicked me out. What should I do?"

"No kidding? She's just too funny. I love that crazy bitch. She went ballistic, huh?"

"Uh, yep, that pretty much describes it." I stand there for a minute while he snorts and laughs and I think to myself that I really hate him. "Ricky? Excuse me, I hate to interrupt your good time and all, but Ricky I'm standing here like some home-less person at a pay phone and everything I own is strapped to the back of a scooter. Can you help me out, please? Sarah and Samson are out of town for the week."

"Well, why don't you come here," he says reluctantly. "You can stay at my place for now, until you get ahold of Sarah. You know how to find my apartment, right? You've got to hurry, though, I'm going in to work pretty soon."

"OK. Let me get a burrito and I'll be over. Thanks."

I know, I know, I shouldn't do it. I shouldn't stay at his house, I shouldn't even turn to him for help in this situation. There's no question that something is going on between him and Mom, something I don't want to think about but can't exactly clear out of my mind either. I need to talk to Sarah. On the other hand, if I told Sarah Jane that I fucked Ricky Serrano in Mom's bed fifteen minutes after he shredded me like a con-fidential document, I don't think I'd get much sympathy from her. Shit. What should I do? I need to talk to someone. This is too important to figure out on my own, but every person I know who gives a damn about me is long distance and if that isn't a statement of our times I don't know what is.

Should I call Cindy? I could call her collect and she wouldn't mind but then I'd have to explain too much. She has a nose for the truth. In three minutes I'd be spilling over with gory details about Ricky's sexual repertoire or something, and then outlining my mother's drinking habits, how many joints I've smoked in the past month, and probably everything I know about Sarah and Elliot, and she'd tell it all to Dad. I don't want Dad knowing anything about this fuck-up. That's all I need; he never could stand Ricky.

Not Cindy, then, and Lillian is no good. "Uh, hi Chase. Just wondered if you could give me advice on how to proceed in the seduction of your old love, since you clearly did so much better with him than I did." I don't think so. What about Travis? Let's see. It's two hours ahead in Princeton; that makes it nearly noon on Saturday. Hm.

"Collect, operator. Eleanor. Thank you. Hey, it's me, sorry to call you collect but I'm standing like a moron at a pay phone in Tucson and, and . . ." and I start sniffling, readying myself for a big, therapeutic outpour.

"Uh, hi Bean. Good morning, how are you?"

"Oh, hi Trav. Sorry. How are you? How's work?"

"Work is fine. The house is coming along real well, too. And I've met someone."

"You've what? You've met someone?"

"I've met someone," he repeats, patiently. "In fact, she's here now, Bean."

"She?"

"Uh-huh."

"Oh God. Sorry. I'm sorry." My head is just ringing. "But Travis," I start, and then I stop. What am I supposed to say? That I thought he preferred men? That I never once thought he'd meet someone before I did? That he has no business seeing any woman who isn't me?

"Yes, Bean?" He's guessed my next question, and I can hear the answer to it in his voice.

"So she knows," is all I say.

"Yes," he answers. I can't believe it. I can't believe that he's found someone to take my place, someone better than me, someone who can handle the truth. I can't fucking believe it. What kind of a day is this? What are my stars and planets doing to me? I really need to check my horoscope.

"I'm devastated, Trav. I know I don't have any right to be, but I am. How can she not mind? I mean, how can she feel adequate?" Being enough for any one person is a worry, but being enough for a bisexual person is impossible, isn't it?

"She is adequate. More than adequate."

"Travis, don't say what I say!"

"Why not?" There's the noise of him moving the phone to talk to the person next to him and then he says, "The word from the source is, monogamy is monogamy; it's not easy for anyone."

"Oh great. She even has her shit more together than I do. What a horrible day."

"I'm sorry, BB," and he says it with genuine sympathy.

"It's OK, Trav. I'm being a baby. Shit happens, right?" What else am I supposed to say? Gosh, Travis, while you're lying in bed happy I'm kissing good-bye to the end of an era?

"So why'd you call, anyway?" he asks.

"No reason. My mom's hassling me. The same old same old." And I laugh, a little bit.

"Are you hysterical?"

"No. Well, no more than usual. I'll let you get back to your company. What's her name?"

"Laurie."

"Uh-oh." He has the I-think-she's-the-one tone to his voice. "She's that cool, huh?"

"Uh-huh. Looks like your sister, actually." Of course she does. "I met her at a gay bar, if you can believe that. She was there with her brother and he was cruising me. Ow. She has a mean left hook. She wants me to tell people something different, though, about where we first got together." Oh. So she has her hang-ups too. That's reassuring.

"Well, tell her she's got a good thing. If she's mean to you I'll haunt her for three lifetimes."

"Adiós, amiga."

"Bueno bye, babe. See you in the summer, I guess. Congratulations." Betrayer.

The heavens are pissing on me. I shouldn't go to Ricky's. And, of course, I'm going anyway.

It was my day off from the restaurant and I was in my apartment in Cincinnati, watching the sky and waiting for Stuart when I got the phone call from Mom. The Cowboy Junkies say that good news always sleeps till noon, but the phone rang at 5:30 on a purpling spring afternoon while I was home alone and drinking too much of a good Merlot on an empty stomach and I knew, without doubt, that I didn't want to answer that call. I didn't have an answering machine and the phone rang and rang, as if the person on the other end knew I was there, listening and unmoving. Eventually I thought it must be Stuart, who was very good about this sort of thing, calling to tell me he was going to be late, and I forced myself to leave the porch and go inside to where the phone was.

"Hi, Stu?"

"No, Eleanor, it's your mother." Her voice was so calm that only a real tragedy could explain it.

My stomach dropped and I gripped the edge of the occasional table with my right hand. "What happened?"

"It's Hank." Her voice was like the voice of a television lady, perfectly modulated, feminine, controlled. "He was killed today rescuing Guinevere from a telephone pole." Guinevere was their yellow-eyed little tabby. I'd never met her. Sarah's the one who named her. "He was electrocuted. So was she. We're having the funeral in the next day or two and I thought you should be here. Money's tight, unfortunately."

"It's OK. I've got it." I didn't, but Stuart or Travis would. "Have you gotten hold of Sarah?"

"I've tried, but there's been no answer." Of course she called Sarah before she called me. They're closer, that's the way things are. "Somehow I managed to raise two girls who won't answer their telephones," she said, and when she tried to laugh I thought the tears would come but they didn't.

"All right," I said, matching her calm with my own, "let me call the airlines and see what I can do. Amarillo is closer, right?"

"That's right, but Lubbock is fine if the price is better."

"That doesn't matter. I'll call you in a few minutes." The prices were very high, even with a bereavement fare, and I needed to call her back to get specific mortuary details before they'd grant me the discount. Then I phoned Travis and arranged things with him before I called her with final plans. In that time I hadn't cried, even when I told the airline agent why I needed the cheap fare. I imagine Mom hadn't cried either. "I'm leaving tomorrow morning," I said, my voice just as controlled as hers. "I'll be in Amarillo at 1:15 and Travis is going to drive up from Albuquerque. He'll meet me at the airport and bring me to the farm. Is there anything I can do?"

"No, I got hold of Sarah and she's coming in late tonight. She'll help me make phone calls in the morning. He's already at the funeral home. He always wanted to be cremated but I don't think I can do that. I don't know. I need to decide and I can't, isn't that funny? The things your mind gets hung up on. I keep wondering when his birthday is. I can't remember it. Why can't I remember his birthday, Eleanor?"

I didn't say anything. His birthday was September 27. He was going to be fifty.

"Well," and she got brisk. "We all die. At least this was quick. Oh God." Her voice broke, and then she collected it again. "The last thing I said to him was, 'For God's sake, Hank, not again.' Because this is the third time she's gotten trapped up there. He's gotten her down twice before, can you believe it? Twice without incident and this time he dies. Life is cruel, isn't it? Well. Well, all right then. I'll see you tomorrow. I suppose I need to clean the house."

"You don't need to clean the house."

"No, it will give me something to do. I'll see you tomorrow."

"OK. Bye Mom."

But it wasn't until I told Stu what happened that the tears came for me. He held me and rocked me and I tried to tell him about Hank but I couldn't. Talking about him seemed so cheap. Also, I wondered even as I cried in Stuart's arms how this was going to affect our relationship and his opinion of me and whether I was handling grief the way you're supposed to, and I didn't seem sad enough. I cried, but at my core I was locked up, frozen solid, and the freezing was moving outwards.

On the plane the next day I still couldn't warm up. I sat under a blanket with my teeth chattering and didn't have a single coherent thought. I ate the lunch they gave us and was still hungry, and when I got off the plane and saw Travis, the first thing I said was, "Trav, I'm starving," and he got me to a fast food place and let me eat a hamburger and a chicken sandwich and large fries, and I couldn't believe myself that the hollow, hungry feeling inside me was still there after all that but it was.

"I'm sorry about Hank," he said, once we hit the highway, and I looked away, out the passenger side window at the flat countryside, and I didn't say anything. I was furious with him. That morning I had been furious with Stu, and I knew I was being irrational but I couldn't help myself. The way Travis was driving made me crazy. The way he was wearing his hair that year made me sick. He had bleached it blond and this took him straight from handsome to breath-taking. He looked faggy and I hated him.

"Texas is ugly," I said. When we got to Hereford I was crying but I didn't want him to know, so I kept my head turned and let the tears come, silent and hot. After a while he handed me his travel pack of Kleenex. When we got out of the car at Oak Grove I didn't hate him quite so much and he gave me a sympathetic look when he saw me squaring my shoulders for what lay ahead, but when he reached out his hand to touch my arm I pulled away.

I hadn't been there in years and the place looked good. I expected Horatio to come bounding out the front gate, even though I knew he had died three Christmases before, old for a German shepherd. To have the courtyard silent and empty of any food bowls or panting dog was the first real sign to me that things at the farm had changed.

Mom was my second sign. She looked a sick yellow-gray, not her hair but her skin, and there were bags under her eyes. Her nails were jagged, the polish nicked, and her hair was separating in strands, clearly unwashed. When we saw each other we both stood still for a second, and then came forward to hug. I couldn't remember ever hugging her, and her body was unfamiliar to me, tiny and bird-boned and fragile. The hug she gave Travis was deeper, and when she set him away from her there were tears in her eyes.

"I'm glad you're here," she said to him. "I feel as if I know you already. Eleanor, show him the guest room."

"I can't remember the guest room," I said, and she stared at me.

"I don't understand why you never came back here," she said, and her voice was harsh and without inflection, a hostile robot. "Do you know what that did to him? Do you know how that ate away at him? He loved you like a daughter and you let him die without seeing him again. Why did you do that? How could you have done that?" Her eyes were black holes. I was afraid I was going to fall into them and never come out. I didn't answer, and then Sarah appeared.

"Mama," Sarah said, "don't."

"You did the same thing to your parents," I said.

"My parents never thought of anyone but themselves and their own misery," she croaked hoarsely at me. "Hank was good to you! He loved you!"

"Mama," said Sarah again, "please don't," and she started crying. Her tears shifted our focus and I said to her, "I'm sorry, Sare," at the same time that Mom said, "Don't cry, baby." I looked at my mother's small, unbreakable body and I could feel the hatred welling up inside me and it grew cold and hard like steel.

"Come on, Trav," I said, suddenly grateful for his presence, "I think your room might be this way," and we walked with our bags out of the living room, leaving my sister and mother outside together. I stopped for a minute in the hallway to stare out over the porch and the cotton fields and to watch the wind blow, and I couldn't believe that the smell of Hank was still so strong in the house.

7 I'm sitting at my favorite place, the breakfast bar in Ash's kitchen. Three days ago Sarah turned thirty and I'm gathering my mental resources, such as they are, to phone her with apologies and news and belated birthday wishes. I've been in El Paso for nearly two months and this will be our first conversation since I fled Tucson, crying on a Greyhound and suffering with ulcers. I knew it was ulcers or something like ulcers because Monica had an ulcer once and she had the same symptoms I did, pain up high in her chest where the ribs come together, a bad taste in her mouth, and hiccups all the time. Sometimes she'd vomit stomach acid. I hadn't vomited anything but I had a burning that went all the way up my throat. Coffee was murdering me. I still can't drink it. Finally I get to the point of herpes management where, on most days, I can drink a good cup or two of Joe and now I can't anyway. I miss it. Popping speeders from your medicine chest is not the same thing as sitting in the morning over a fragrant cup of Kona, preparing for the day. Nor is it even vaguely similar to hanging with your friends over iced cappuccinos in a summertime cafe. Coffee is a social phenomenon, a grown-up version of getting high but with conversation you remember later, and there's no replacement.

"Another sunny day in El Paso. Don't you just hate it?" Ash calls to me from the other side of the house where he's puttering around happily, getting ready to go food shopping and utterly unaware of the turmoil in my soul.

"Makes me wanna barf," I yell back, automatically, my mind on other things. I hope Sarah's cooled down to conversing temperature because I need desperately to talk to her. I need advice. I need bolstering. I think I need a brain transplant.

"OK, muchacha, I'm outta here, give me a kiss," Ash leans over me and nuzzles my neck. "Are you doing darkroom work today?"

"Yeah. I'm going to call Sarah in a minute though and wish her happy birthday. Will you bring me back something salty?"

"Yes," he says, disapprovingly, gives me another kiss and finally leaves.

Two minutes after his truck rumbles off I'm on the phone. "Sarah, it's me, are you there? Pick up, I know you're home. Oh, hey. Happy birthday."

"It's about time," she says, no hi, bye, or kiss my ass. "It's a good thing I talk to Colette all the time. What would you have done if my birthday was in June? Waited another two months?"

"No, I would have called you sooner."

"You should have called me sooner," she says, unmollified.

"I know. But why couldn't you call? It's OK to phone Colette but not me? What's that all about?"

"Hey, you did the damage, you should make the reparation."

"You're right. I'm sorry, I really am. I feel terrible."

"How was the bus ride?" Sarah asks, her way of reminding me that I left under ignoble circumstances.

"It sucked," I answer, my way of acknowledging my fuck-up. I like trains but I hate buses. They always stink and the toilets are disgusting and you stop at every town on the road and they're only fun if you're twenty-one. I know this is just an illogical manifestation of the human need to feel elite and I prefer Amtrak because I don't have a fancy college to crow about or high-status hair, but I can't help feeling like I'm too good for Greyhound. Snobbishness is embedded in us like impacted teeth.

I was exhausted when I finally reached El Paso and the seedy mess of a bus station which was, like all bus stations, the natural gathering point for every alcoholic, junkie, and runaway in town. I didn't see Colette at first and panicked. Then I stopped panicking and didn't care. I was shuffling down the aisle behind twenty other passengers thinking I could use a manicure when I saw her through a window and saw that Ash was with her. Great. I was ecstatic at being on view after a long crying jag on a long bus ride when I hadn't showered, had just started my period, and had on no makeup at all. I didn't even brush my teeth that day and must have been wearing, at once, every ugly thing I brought down from Boston.

"Hey you guys," I called, stepping off the bus. There were hugs all round and suddenly I got chatty. "You're looking pretty spiffy, Colette. I didn't expect to see you here, Ashur. What lovely weather y'all have. That was some bus trip, let me tell you. I think there were people having sex in the back seats. The driver told us not to do drugs and everybody started laughing, including him. Boy, I could use a shower. And a manicure. No coffee, though. I've been exiled from the caffeine kingdom, can you believe it?" I wanted to stop babbling but couldn't.

"I don't do manicures," said Ash, smiling at me as if he couldn't tell I was coated with grime and sweat and salt streaks. "How about lunch instead? Are you hungry?"

"I think I am, actually." They helped me sort my bags from the cargo hold of the bus. "I can't tell anymore because of my ulcer."

"You were diagnosed with an ulcer?"

"I diagnosed myself with an ulcer. I always feel hungry and then when I eat I want to puke. Sometimes when I don't eat I want to puke."

"Are you pregnant?" This from Colette.

"That's funny. I'm on the rag right now, excuse me Ash, so I believe the answer is no. I have a lot of acid floating around, eating through my stomach lining and wearing holes in my esophagus. Sometimes my food comes back on me."

"How lovely," said Colette. "Could you give us more details? But wait until we're actually eating lunch, OK?"

"Good," says Sarah, mumbling into the receiver and apparently holding the phone with her shoulder. "If you weren't so quick to run away from everything you wouldn't have had to suffer a bus ride at all."

"Yeah, yeah." I start pacing around the tile floor in Ash's kitchen, pulling the phone cord after me umbilically. "What are you fixing?" I ask her.

"Coffee. Raspberry danish. A piece of cheese. Yum."

"Yuck."

"So really. If you were feeling so bad why didn't you call sooner?" I hear the clinking, shirring sound of her spoon stirring cream and a probably unholy amount of sugar into her coffee and my throat tightens with nausea at the same instant that my mouth waters.

"I was afraid you'd hang up on me or something," I say, swallowing down the rush of saliva and my rising gorge. "I couldn't handle it."

"I wouldn't have done that."

"Uh-huh." She might very well have done that and she knows it. I continue, "Then it just got longer and longer from when we spoke last, and things kept happening here, and I didn't know where to begin catching you up, and I didn't know how to start talking again."

"And you hate to have anything be your fault," she points out.

"I don't see why it is totally my fault, you know."

When we got to the Mexican restaurant Ash and Colette asked me irritatingly how my photography was coming along. I said it was coming along fine and they said they wanted details. I ordered a beer before answering and sent up a quick prayer for my stomach lining.

"It isn't coming along, if you really want to know. I mean, I was doing great at the first of the month. I met these two older women at the Desert Museum and took some shots of them that I think are excellent. They weren't shy at all and I was in a real creative space, but then everything fell apart again."

"When you found out that you and Sarah were both sleeping with Ricky?" Colette's amusement was obvious. She met Rick once or twice when we were kids, before he took off for the high adventurous life that ended him up selling new and used cars for Oldsmobile in Tucson, and she doesn't see what all the fuss is about.

"No. God. That was later. In fact, that was only yesterday. What happened is, Becky decided to come to Tucson. She just showed up for a surprise Valentine's Day visit. I was out taking photos and Ricky told her I was staying on the couch for a day or two because I was fighting with my mom. He said that nothing was going on between us. At that point I had been there two weeks and the sofa didn't look slept on. She said Bullshit and nearly turned back for Denver, but he sweet-talked her into staying."

"He sure is something," Colette said and I started in on the chips and salsa. "Now he's been with all the important females of his childhood. Freud would be proud."

The waitress came over and took our orders. She was very cute and tiny and Hispanic and wore a lot of makeup and very tight jeans and gave Ash the eye in a big, shameless way. I was relieved to note that Ash smiled at her nicely enough but didn't check out her ass when she walked away. Or, if he did, he did it subtly enough that I couldn't pick up on it. It continues to amaze me the way women cluster around big men. They get frothy at the mouth when they have to tilt back their heads to make eye contact. I could see it was going to be a pain in my ass, keeping them away from him.

Hey, wait a minute. What? Was I already planning a relationship with a man whose last name I didn't even know how to spell? Oh Christ, let me not get involved again, please no. I can't take it. I need some alone time to sort things out. I'm more screwed-up now than I was at the start of this trip, when the opposite was supposed to happen, and if this month isn't the darkest hour before dawn I'm going to hang myself. Anyway, who said he was even interested? Well, he's obviously interested, but to what extent? A two-week fling? Marriage? Purely perverted sex fantasies? Does he have a girlfriend? Where is his ex-wife? Has he ever hooked up with Colette?

"So you only found out about Sarah and Ricky yesterday?" Colette derailed my train of thought.

"Uh-huh," I said, closing my eyes against the memory. "About an hour before I called you. It seems like a year ago, now. It wasn't a matter of finding it out, anyway. Sarah just came right out and told me on our way to lunch. So then I had to tell her that I was too. Up until then I'd been pretending that Ricky and I hadn't actually done it, just made out a few times, stoned. She was fucking cross-eyed, not because I was sleeping with him, but because I had been lying to her about it. And, even though Samson didn't want me to, I'd been staying at their house for the two weeks since Rebecca had come to town. Sarah went off the charts. You can kind of imagine, right?" Colette nodded but Ash just shrugged. "We never did get lunch. We drove straight back to her house and she wouldn't talk to me again."

"So what did you do?" Colette asked.

"I packed my bags, called a cab, and went to a Motel 6. Called Greyhound and you know the rest of the story."

Sarah had asked me if we'd always used condoms. I said yes, but we hadn't always. Twice we blew it off. She knew I was lying. I guess they hadn't either. Can you imagine the horror of giving herpes to your sister? I never had an actual break out, of course, or I would have been more careful, but still.

"You know it's your fault that we had the fight," says Sarah, "because you wouldn't tell me the truth about Ricky when I asked. Right?" I can hear that she's pacing the floor too.

"He told me specifically to not mention that we were doing it and I promised that I wouldn't. How was I to know that you were going to keep asking me directly and making me lie to your face? You knew I didn't want to talk about it. I even said I didn't want to talk about it. Haven't you ever heard of tact and privacy?"

"You're my sister!"

"So? You don't get to be more rude to people you love than to people you don't give a shit about, you know."

"Yeah, but you shouldn't be more loyal to some outsider than you are to your closest family member."

"What are you, Italian now? A promise is a promise. And besides, I never knew you were sleeping with the asshole."

"You would have, if you had told me the truth about whether or not you were."

"Well, that's true enough." I sigh and wish for coffee or, more accurately, for the comfort of coffee. "I should have known something was up when he specifically said, 'And don't tell your mom or Sarah about this.' But he made me promise. How could I break a promise, even to an asshole?"

"Two months ago he was worth lying to your sister over, and now he's an asshole?"

"He already was one, but now he's an asshole of epic proportions," I say, glad to have things back to normal, and revving up for what I'm about to tell her. But first I have to make sure there aren't hidden mines. "Are you, uh, still seeing him?" I ask, voice as neutral as possible. I'm pretty sure she isn't but need to be 100 percent.

"Christ no. Elliot and I are getting married."

"What? Sarah, don't even joke around about shit like that. That's your whole life you're talking about."

"OK, I won't joke around about it. Elliot and I are getting married."

"Does Elliot know this yet?"

"You're a scream. Here's what happened. OK. You know how we play the dice game, right?"

"Don't even fucking tell me." Whenever decisions have to be made, from who does the dishes tonight to who gets to pick the vacation spot, Elliot says, "I'll roll you for it." He has good luck with dice but Sarah does too, so it turns out to be a fair way to handle things. They even settle fights like that sometimes but the rule is, once the dice are rolled, that's it. The dice are final. For simple yes-no questions, you don't count seven. Two through six is no and eight through twelve is yes. When it's an issue just between the two of them that needs to be settled, the highest roller has the say. The primary rule is that you have to stick with the decision no matter how much it sticks in your throat. I've never seen them back down. They rolled to see if they should move in together and they rolled to see if they should stop doing coke. One night they rolled for an emerald tennis bracelet but, unfortunately, Sarah lost that one.

"Well, he's been trying to get me to marry him for a long time, right, and I've been trying to avoid the issue. The truth is, BB, that after you left I had a lot of explaining to do, to myself I mean. I spent all of March sitting cross-legged under the orange tree and thinking. I had no business sleeping with Ricky either. Even less than you, since I already had a boyfriend, one who never steps out on me, who takes me to the symphony and really wants to be with just me for the rest of his life. Right?"

I don't say anything.

"Well," she goes on, "what I realized is that I'm the biggest coward that ever walked the planet. I was only fucking Ricky, excuse the French, because I was afraid to commit to Elliot. That's it. The only reason. Except that I was also jealous of how close you and Ricky are but I swear that wasn't the deep reason, that was the shallow reason. The deep reason was that I could feel a decision needed to be made about me and Sam, and I think turning thirty had something to do with the pressure building up inside me. You're supposed to be somewhere at thirty, somewhere definite in your life, and I knew that I was heading for the moment of truth. I was afraid to commit, afraid to put all my eggs in one basket in case I dropped the basket, so I wove myself an extra one. Does that make sense?"

"Lots of sense."

"Yeah," she says. "Trust issues."

"So I guess Mom's over it too, huh?" I ask. "I mean, over Rick."

"I don't know. Have you talked to her?"

"No." And I drop bombshell number one. "But I talked to Ricky and he told me."

"You see? That's what I mean."

"What?"

"That he tells you things. He never tells me jack shit. What else did he say?"

"Oh no. I know the rules." And I need to sort out my approach anyway. "You tell me about you and Elliot first."

"OK, I will. Let me get comfortable." She settles back in her chair and I hear her light up a cigarette.

"Are you smoking again?" I ask her, before I can stop myself.

"Uh-uh," she lies, but in a semitransparent way so I'll know it's a lie and know that she just isn't ready to deal with the issue yet and know to drop the subject, which I do. "So," she starts into narrative mode, "I call Ricky two weeks after you leave, middle of March maybe, and the first thing he says to me is, 'Hey, where the hell did Bean go?' So I tell him."

"Oh, thanks." That explains it.

"Sorry. But you have to settle your own shit with him."

"Whatever, group leader. You just felt like stirring things up, admit it."

"I admit it," she says, with unabashed relish. "But any-ways—" Mom would fry her like an egg if she ever heard "anyways" come out of her mouth like that "—I say that you're with Colette and, I'm sorry B, but I gave him the number there, too."

"I know you enjoyed that."

"Yeah, I did." She laughs then, whoops actually like a cow-girl, and says, "Yee-ha! Hold on to your horses, folks, the show's gettin' excitin'."

"You're an asshole."

"Yep." She takes a long, satisfying-sounding drag and I twinge, momentarily, with nicotine lust. She continues the story as she exhales and I picture her face with the smoke curl-ing out through her nose, her eyes narrowed for the narration. "We chitchat a little, you know, and the whole time I'm just waiting for him to say, 'So, when are you free?' like he always does, and when he finally says it I say to him, 'I'm not. I don't want to see you anymore, Ricky Serrano.' He goes, 'I'm not sur-prised. I could see this happening. I guess you're gonna go off and marry Samson now, right?' And you know, B, until he said it, I didn't know that that's what I was going to do, but as soon as I heard the words I could see it was the only way. So I say, 'Yeah. I guess I am. Thank you and good-bye.' And that was that. But I still had to think about Samson some more and think about some other options." She takes a sip of coffee and another drag off the cancer stick. "I wait two more weeks, until April Fool's Day, and that night, when he says 'Let's roll for the dishes,' I say, 'I'll tell you what, Sam. Let's roll for something a little more interesting. Let's roll for marriage. You win, I marry you. I win, I spend three months alone to straighten out my head, and at the end of the three months, we'll roll again.'"

"You didn't." The thought of taking that kind of chance makes my head spin.

"I did. I went and got our special dice."

"You have special dice?" How do people end up with special dice?

"Yeah, the ones he rolled the first time he asked me out. It was at the end of a half marathon in Flagstaff, almost four years ago exactly."

"I remember, vaguely."

"I hadn't done that well and I just wanted to get home but he wanted to take me to dinner and wouldn't move out of my way. Finally I looked right at him and he smiled at me and I thought he had a beautiful smile, like the sun breaking through clouds. He said, 'Hang on a second,' and he reached into his car and pulled out these beautiful dice. 'How 'bout I roll you for it?' he said to me. I liked that. It was interesting. Men are so rarely interesting. And he made good time on that run, I remember seeing his neon green shorts sailing past. I couldn't believe it later when he told me that he used to be huge and slow, lifting weights and taking steroids. Anyway, they're ivory I think, antique maybe. Very valuable."

Naturally.

"So there we are, April Fools' Night and I've turned it into this perfect romantic dinner. The lights are low, we're drinking wine, and I'm dressed in black silk and pearls. I put on "Bolero" and ceremoniously place the dice on the table. And as he's jiggling them around in his hand I'm thinking, 'It's in the hands of fate. The rest of my life will be affected by this roll.' And then he looks at me, and hands me the dice."

"What did you get?"

"Ten."

"Jesus, Sarah."

"Yeah." She takes a long drag to relive the moment and I can almost see her shaking her head in disbelief. "He looked at the ten and then he looked at me and his eyes got that gambling look in them that turns me on so much. He picked up the dice, kissed me, and rolled."

"And?"

"Got an eleven. The funny thing is, he kept waiting for me to say April Fools', and I never said it. After a while he got tired of pretending it didn't matter to him, but it took me a half hour to convince him that I meant it."

"What if he hadn't won?"

"You know the rules. I could stand to straighten my head out some, but you know what I'm going to do? I'm going to do it with him. I'm going to be there for him like I never was before."

I start humming "Stand by Your Man."

"Shut up. Everybody thinks they can sort out their issues all alone and then carry that information into the relationship, but the problem is that a different behavior comes out of you depending on who you're with, right? Each person has an effect on you, and you on them, so how can you figure everything out ahead of time, all alone? It's apples and oranges is what it is."

"Or at least apple cider and apple pie." I'm a fan of sorting the shit out alone, so her analysis doesn't thrill me.

"You handle it however you want. I'm going to be old-fashioned and sort it out while I'm actually married to the person, what do you think of that?"

"I hate you."

"For what?"

"Oh, you know. For doing things so sensibly."

"Yeah, Ricky Serrano was sensible."

"Still. It's less drastic than me. You don't have to go off like a loose cannon the way I always have to, and figure things out halfway across the country from where you were the week before, always by yourself, always dead broke, always scared, always doing something really extra stupid before you learn the lesson. Elliot never knew about Ricky and now he'll never have to. I think you did good."

"Maybe you'd better tell me about Ricky now," she says. "And don't even think about saying to me that your tone of voice is because you're stupid enough to be hooking up with him again."

"Well, goddammit," I say, releasing the hatch cover to bombshell number two, "you're the one who sent him out here! And he was so sad, and lonely, and every person he counts on has dumped him. You weren't seeing him and I wasn't seeing him and Mama stopped, of course, and Rebecca went back to her husband in Denver. She sent him a Dear John letter for a birthday present. He got it like the day he talked to you. He thought it was going to be a let's-think-it-over letter and then he saw what it really was and freaked. Her husband had written at the bottom of it, 'If I see you I'll do my best to kill you.'"

"Impressive."

"Yeah. Anyway, less than a month later—"

"—getting desperate for lack of sex—"

"—pining plaintively for poontang, he drives up here, rents a hotel room and finds me at Colette's. I was having an insecure day. He talked me into going drinking and one thing led to another and before you can say rabbit-down-a-hole he's telling me his sob story and we're back in the sack at a Super 8."

"You fucking retard. That's all it takes? You screw every guy you feel sorry for?"

"Well, actually, it's not the first time. It's like dispensing the ultimate comfort. Florence Nightingale and all that." And besides, he was desperate for me. Finally I had him where I wanted him, pleading with me, looking into my eyes, hoping against hope that I wouldn't turn him down. How could I say no to that? And that's not all.

"Sex is sex, Eleanor May. It's not chicken soup. Jesus!"

"Well, before you really get disgusted, wait a minute. That's not the worst of it."

"You didn't agree to marry him, did you?"

"No no. I sent him on his way. I haven't seen him since or wanted to. Mission accomplished, whatever the mission was.

It's something else." Bombshell number three. "You see, there's this other guy that I'm kind of seeing. In fact, I'm seeing him, not kind of."

"Ashur, of course," she says. "Colette told me."

"I'm crazy about the guy, Sare, like I always wanted to feel this way about someone and now I finally am. I only realized it fully the day before Ricky got up here, though. I mean, I knew I liked him and I thought he was fine and I wanted to touch the line of his collarbone all the time, but I didn't realize it was bigger than that until we saw a fat girl on the street and he was nice. You know how it is for me, to see the morbidly obese and have people be mean about it."

Sarah, her whole life, has been mean to fat people. She hates them. She won't be friends with them. Before I got so fat she used to say, "If a person's messed up enough to be that fat, then they're messed up in all kinds of other ways too." She's right, of course, but a lot of skinny people are fucked up as well and the world excuses them a hell of a lot faster. However, it's beyond me to confront her on the issue; I'm just grateful every day to have my eating back under reasonable control, but even I'm not as grateful as she and Dad are. I think they suffered my weight more than I did, and even now I can sense her skepticism over the wires.

"Listen to me and try to sympathize, would you?" I ask. "We were in his truck on the way to a movie and there was a really fat woman in tiny little pumps walking down the sidewalk, rocking from side to side, ponderous, slow, agonizing to look at. I was watching her with one eye and Ash with the other. I saw him shake his head and I said, 'What?' just bracing myself for the worst, some comment about the psi on the soles of her feet or that joke about rolling her in flour. All he said was, 'Poor woman. Her feet must be killing her.' And I was so relieved. I looked over at him and I thought to myself, Holy shit. I'm in love with this guy."

Sarah makes a noise right then, a slight exhalation that tells me she's impatient with this. Big deal, she wants to say, so he was nice about some fat chick. You fell in love for that? But she won't say it out loud, she's on good behavior.

"He asked me what it was like for me when I was fat. He said he could tell when he massaged me that I used to weigh quite a bit more."

"How did he know? Stretch marks?"

"Maybe. He asked me all about getting fat, what triggered it, how I handled it, everything. Sarah, I've never been able to talk about that with anyone. It's even worse than the herps."

"Bullshit."

"No, it's true. Herpes just happens to you, it can happen to anyone, especially when you're young and ignorant. But fatness is like character weakness, like being a coward in the war. Everyone despises you for it."

"Like being a lush?"

"No, much worse. Alcoholics are charming, dangerously charming, right? Like half the Irishmen in the world."

"Amen," Sarah says. She's had her Irish experience too.

"Well, that isn't true for fatties. You could come up with the cure for AIDS and still be nothing but a fat pig to people. Jane Doe, Jane Doe, hm. Wasn't she that heifer from Helsinki? Well, actually she cured AIDS. Whatever, she was fucking *fat*. Maybe it's different if you're Chicana, or black, living in that culture, I don't know, but fat white chicks suffer."

"Yeah, you're right," Sarah says guiltily, suddenly extra-grateful for being whip-thin. "So have you told him about the herpes?"

"No."

"Hm."

"Don't *hm* me. I'll get around to it." Maybe. "So I fell in love with him, or realized how much I loved him, right then and there. And of course, being me, I immediately freaked out.

I wasn't sure he really felt the same way back, I was all insecure, I was afraid suddenly that the blinders would come off and he'd realize that I'm this untrusting, demanding, neurotic mess who couldn't get her shit together to save her life. I felt vulnerable, endangered, all that crap, and then for two days afterwards I didn't hear from him. He flat-out disappeared. It was unprecedented. It turns out that he'd gotten a call from his ex-wife, who wanted them to get back together, and it took him a while to realize that he didn't want to anymore, that he was over her and in love with me. But I didn't know! I just thought he hated me suddenly. So when I had Ricky show up treating me like gold and being so grateful, well, I fell for it."

"It's understandable, B," she said, sympathetically, which didn't help.

"That's still not the worst of it." There's still bombshell number four, the monster.

"Well?" she prompted me, because I'd stopped talking.

"Well, I had sex with Ricky, and then I had sex for the first time with Ash the very next goddamn day! It was April 10th." As if remembering the exact date will help something. "I don't know what my problem was. I wasn't thinking on my feet and Ash wouldn't take no for an answer. I couldn't believe that such a nice guy would be so adamant. I couldn't hold him off, Sare."

"Well, you didn't want to."

"Right. I've never done anything quite like this before. I've been talked into having sex before I wanted it, but never in these circumstances. I knew it was getting to that point between us, between me and Ash, and then I panic and give up on him and go sleep with Ricky first. Why did I do such a thing?"

"Big deal," she says, still trying to help. "It was a mistake and it won't happen again. Ash doesn't need to know. You glitched, last second, but now you're fine."

"Not exactly," I say. I don't say anything else and I hear her get another cigarette and light it before she speaks again.

"Bean," she says, on the inhale, and her voice has gone very careful on me, "are you pregnant?"

"I don't know. Maybe."

"What do you mean, 'maybe?'"

"I mean yes."

"Jesus Christ. And you don't know which one is the father."

"Exactly."

"But you think it's probably Ricky."

"Exactly. He pulled out and Ashur didn't so that complicates things but, let's face it, redneck birth control has knocked up a lot of girls."

"Yes it has. You're talking to one." We're both quiet for a few moments with the weight of my mistake, and then she says, "Wow. I just don't know what else to say. I thought you always used condoms."

"I do. I almost always do, I swear. That's what I can't understand. Obviously I wanted to be pregnant. It doesn't take a psych degree to figure that out. But Sarah. Two men in two days two weeks from my period? Was I crazy? Was I possessed? Was I just bored? I was so happy with the way things were developing with Ash, and then he gets a little distant and I fuck it all up."

"Maybe you had more doubts than you're admitting."

"Maybe I can't handle a normal relationship, maybe I don't think it's love unless I'm miserable."

"Maybe. Or maybe your biological clock is ticking more strongly than your brain."

"Hm. I did feel possessed by something, something stronger and greater than just my rational mind. I was like Michael Caine in *The Hand*, only it wasn't my hand."

"Nice. And you're sure you're pregnant? Never mind, of course you're sure." She remembers how it was with me before.

"I'm sure. I feel the same way. Sick as a dog. But anyway I should have started my period by now so I did a pregnancy test this morning and it's a big 10-4, good buddy."

"Abortion's out?"

"Abortion's out."

"Does Colette know?"

"No. I want to tell her but I had to tell you first."

"Damn right. Does Ash know?"

"Christ no. I mean really, do you think someone who would sleep with two men in two days without protection when she actually loves one and hates the other is well adjusted enough to tell the one she loves the truth? Be logical."

"Maybe you should have moved in with Ash when he asked you back in February."

On the way to Colette's, after lunch my first day in El Paso, the three of us stopped at one of the giant supermarkets out West that covers acres of scrub and I picked up a week's worth of groceries, a coffee cone, and some Pepto Bismol. Ash got herbal tea and beans and Colette bought fruit and vegetables. I always forget about fruit and vegetables.

Standing in line, swigging from the bottle of Pepto, I decided to tackle Colette about accommodations. "This isn't the polite way to do this," I began, "but I was wondering if you minded my staying with you for a while?" And then we all cracked up because obviously I was going to be staying with her for a while and it was a little late to be asking, especially since I'd already inquired about whether her stove was electric or gas (gas, thank God) and if she already had olive oil and garlic (yes to both) and a coffee maker (no). "I was thinking of a month or two and let me pay you some rent."

"How's your financial situation anyway?" Colette asked me.

"Oh fine," I said, but my eyes dropped. Precisely why I'm such a bad poker player. "Well, actually, I guess it's lower than it should be." Especially with ninety Zovirax costing me a hundred dollars and the scorn of the pharmacists each month. "But I'm fine for now and my taxes are due back. I could pay you good rent, if you'd like."

"Thanks, Donald Trump. I'll manage."

"You could stay at my place too," Ash said. "There's an empty bedroom that gets sun in the mornings, and two full bathrooms, and even space for a darkroom, maybe. You can stay rent-free and have all the privacy you want." Which I figured to mean that he wouldn't try to be my boyfriend.

Colette and I exchanged microlooks and I didn't say anything. I paid for my groceries, they paid for theirs, and on the way out I wiped my sweaty palms on my jeans and said, "I'll stay at Colette's for now, Ash, but thank you." Then Colette bumped me right into him as we got to the truck. My whole body heated up.

"Jesus," I whine at Sarah on the phone, "Colette even told you about the grocery store? What didn't she tell you?"

"She didn't tell me about Ricky. Listen, B, Sam and I are going to San Diego for two weeks. We have to go, it's a family thing with his parents, but when I get back I'm coming to visit. Don't tell Colette 'til I get there, OK? I want to see her face."

"I'll try, but if I puke on her shoes one morning she'll probably figure it out."

Ten minutes after I hang up the phone Ash stomps back through the door with his arms full of grocery bags and a new hair clip for me stuck in the top of his own shaggy mop, looking ridiculous. "Hey little bear," he says, using my favorite pet name of all time and kissing me a dozen times on my face and neck. "Hunting and gathering isn't what it used to be, but I'm adaptable. I got you potato chips, tomato juice, Chinese food and feta cheese. Is that enough salt for today?"

I grab the food greedily and then the smell of Szechuan eggplant sends me on a pretext straight to the toilet, where I puke and then sit, sweating and despairing.

A few years ago I got sick for weeks with a bad summer flu. I lost weight, down to 170, the thinnest I'd been since Hank died. I looked at myself in the mirror the day I got out of bed and the very first emotion that hit me when I saw my sagging skin and thinner self wasn't pleasure and it wasn't hope. It was fear. "Oh my God," I thought, or something like that, "I'm too thin, way too thin, I'll never be safe like this!" And I ran to the fridge and ate, standing in front of it, half a dish of leftover lasagna and I can't remember what else, maybe the frosted Oreos that we kept in the freezer and Stu made sure I was never out of. Whatever, it didn't really matter, it was just to fill the chasm and I ate and ate but it wasn't the same. I sat there, at the end of that rampage, on the bed, and I looked at myself in the mirror for a long time. I looked then the way I look now, pale and still and with old, old eyes.

"Everything OK in there?" asks Ash.

"Peachy," I answer, through the door, but I don't get up. I can't get up. I'd kill to nap. Why don't people warn you that when you get pregnant you'd sell your soul for sleep? I'd do anything to lie down right here on the bathroom tile, a roll of Charmin for my pillow and a towel for warmth and wake up in nine months with everything settled.

The silence is the worst. I want to tell Ash the truth and have him coddle me and tell me that things will be fine. But things won't be fine and I can't say a word, and I can't figure out how I screwed things up so thoroughly in such a short space of time when I was so determined that this time I was going to be smart.

When I was in school, I used to look at sensible girls as if they were Martians. They would tell you that they liked a guy, and when you asked if the guy liked them back they would say, "Why would I like someone who didn't like me back?" A month later they were still just going to movies together, and two months later kissing goodnight, no groping. It was a mystery to me, the way they'd help each other with their homework, drive each other to the airport, wait a year to have sex. A year! Travis always says the longer it takes you to sleep with a guy, the longer he'll stay in love with you. As suspected, I'm doomed.

"I got us a movie for tonight," Ash calls in to me. "If you hurry up and get to work on your photographs, then we have all night to be together. Doesn't that sound good?"

"It sounds good," I say, and drag myself to my feet. "I hope you got something long and romantic, with a nice, happy ending. I'm in the mood for that."

The last time I saw Hank alive he was helping me in much the same way he had helped Colette about a year previous. He was paying for me to get an abortion. It was the year after high school and I knew I needed to get the hell out of Remie for good, so I did the only things I knew how to do. I got a boyfriend and a job. The boyfriend's name was Dolly and the job was actually three jobs that I hated. I spent my time in a deep, gray fog, dreaming of the day I'd be ready to go, moving through my life on remote.

I was working at a pizza place, an insurance office, and a drive-in restaurant. Carhopping at the drive-in was particularly bad. The customers I didn't know were mean because I wasn't pretty then and also sucked at the job, and the customers I did know wouldn't shut up about college and why wasn't I there and what was I still doing in town and what were my parents thinking and on and on. Sometimes I wanted to print up a T-shirt saying "My dad's partner ran off with our money, OK?" so that when I got asked about it I could just point to my chest.

One terrible, dark, windy day in December my old photography teacher swung his car and family into my station and cheerily beeped for service. My stomach dropped. I went miserably out to their Wagoneer with my order pad and dirty apron and, to judge by the look on his face, his stomach dropped too. He said, "Eleanor," gasping like he'd seen me walking Central Avenue in Albuquerque, and then he didn't say anything more.

I wanted to explain everything but obviously I couldn't so instead I said, "Hi, Mr. Morse. Are you guys ready to order?"

That same night Dolly got me pregnant. We'd been together five or six months by then. I had often flirted with him drunk during high school and liked being known as his girlfriend afterwards. He tipped me extra for two months at the drive-in before he asked me out seriously. Dolly was a good guy, several years older than me and nice looking. Bowlegged. I admired how he wore his boots and jeans and he had the kind of hair Mom would have approved of, thick and straight and dirty blond. He worked out of town at the meat-packing plant and he had known Esteban. They were both shift supervisors at a very young age in a very tough place and he would tell me stories about a hard side of life that I didn't know at all.

It was still summer and we were on a road trip to the lake when he asked if I had ever dated Esteban in earnest and I hesitated a long time before I said, "Not really. We hung around together when I was at the farm. We never did anything." And Dolly nodded and changed the subject and that evening, drunk, we pulled over off a dirt road and, in the pickup truck on the way back to town, officially started our relationship by sleeping together.

Dolly, whose real name was Donovan Madison, was the kind of big fish in a small town who's rebellious as all get-out in his youth and then becomes a pillar of society in his middle age. At twenty-five he wasn't quite at his pillar of society stage yet but he was heading there and he had marrying plans. I was relieved to know that someone respectable wanted me in an honorable way and in one part of my brain I even wanted to marry him and just give up the impossible struggle to become something I wasn't, a city girl, educated and sophisticated and unafraid, all the things I would have been if I had grown up somewhere else and had had the right kind of life.

The December night I saw Mr. Morse I found Dolly easily after work, dragging Main in an uncommitted kind of way. I got in with him and began kissing him up. An hour later we were in bed and for once I really liked it. He knew there was something different going on with me because he kept looking into my eyes and saying my name, not Bean but Eleanor, oh Eleanor, and our bodies worked together just right, the way they were supposed to. We were rednecks but we knew better than to have sex without protection. Still, that's exactly what we had.

Dolly had real feelings for me, perhaps even love, but I couldn't feel anything back then except the dual weight of my sadness and rage. And the reason I think now that he loved me isn't that he told me so. He didn't say it and neither did I. But sometimes, when we had sex, he would cry afterwards. Not a lot, just a little embarrassed sniffling that left me puzzled, and embarrassed also. He would eventually laugh into my shoulder and roll me around the bed and that would be my signal to relax.

"That wasn't very smart of us," he said after sex on this particular night. Not only had we skipped the condoms, he hadn't pulled out and I hadn't made him. I could have, I'd done it before and, in fact, he seemed to think that it was only right, that it was the job of my female brain to keep rational when his male brain was obviously not.

I didn't say anything. I often didn't, around Dolly, and he never seemed to mind.

"Oh well," he said, burying his hands in my hair, "we'll just get married if I knock you up. What do you say?"

I shrugged, and he could feel the movement under his forearms. He shook me a little by pushing me into the mattress under him.

"I said don't worry, we'll get married if you're pregnant." Clearly he wanted something from me.

"OK," I finally said. I couldn't see it. Married to a squinty-eyed shitkicker who would come home nightly smelling either of blood or of booze and hadn't been further from home than

Dallas, Texas. Of course, he also made decent money and was learning computers at night to prepare himself for the future and was admired by everyone in town between the ages of fifteen and forty. I could do worse and I knew it. I was about to.

In one week flat I knew I was pregnant. My period didn't come and didn't come. I avoided Dolly for a few days and pretended I'd menstruated. I lost five pounds, then another five, and I was exhausted. Cindy thought I had mono. I pretended that maybe I did. I said that Dolly had it but I kissed him anyway because it wasn't a bad case and I didn't believe in being able to catch it that way but it looked like I was wrong. She said she hoped he wasn't handling meat while he was infected with something. I said he had taken time off work precisely because of that, and then I disappeared for a walk outside before she could pin me down further. Later that day I phoned Sarah. We put our enmity aside for real emergencies and any good parties and a week or so afterwards I called Hank.

"Hi," I said. "It's me, Bean." It had been Sarah's idea to call him and I phoned when I knew Mom would be in class. She and I hardly ever spoke but I knew from Sarah that pharmacy training ended at Christmas and she would be fully licensed by the new year. It was weird to think of Mom working.

"Hi baby," he said, happily. "How's my girl?"

"Oh, fine."

"Hm. Handling all those jobs OK?" He must have known it was serious by my voice because his own voice stopped sounding happy and started sounding cautious.

"No problem," I said. I didn't know how to go on, so he filled in for me.

"Your mom finishes school pretty soon, but you probably know that. Have you been getting my letters?"

"Oh yes. I get them on Saturdays." I wanted to say how much I needed them, how sometimes they were the only things that felt real in all the world, but I was quiet.

"Why don't you come visit us sometime, honey? We miss you, not only me and Sarah but your mama too. She just doesn't know how to say it." Right. "It's pretty out here this time of year, you know we get snow sometimes when you don't. I always expect to see you up here taking pictures on the weekends but I guess you're too busy for that nowadays, huh?"

"I'm pretty busy," I said, and then I was silent again.

"What's up, darling?" he finally asked. "Are you in some kind of trouble?"

"Yes I am, Hank." And I cried for the first time in a year, hard, into the phone, knowing that he was on the other end and cared about me. It's not the money, I finally told him. I'd been saving mine for college but I could use some of it. It's just that I had no idea where to go or what to do and I didn't want anyone in town knowing about it.

"Are you sure you don't want to marry him?" he asked me.

"I'm sure."

"He seems like a good person, honey."

"Oh Hank, I can't get married now, I'm not even nineteen! And I don't want to live here my whole life."

"Does he know about this?"

"No sir. I haven't told him."

"Well, perhaps you should talk it over with him?" He didn't have much hope of me actually doing that, and he was right. I'd never tell Dolly. I wouldn't tell him I was pregnant and I wouldn't tell him I aborted. I just needed to get it done and then leave, and fast. It was horrible being pregnant but at least it had given me a sense of direction, which is more than I'd had before. I knew what to do.

"I know what I want to do," I told him. "I mean after the abortion. I want to go to Albuquerque. UNM is an OK school and maybe I'll like it there. I can't get financial aid this year but next year I think I can. I have to be independent for tax purposes and then they'll consider me." I was learning some of the ins and outs of paying for college, things I should have learned before. "I just need a little help at the moment. I'm sorry to trouble you like this."

"Oh now," he said. "I'd do anything to help and you know that. I just wish I had the money to pay for your college."

"It's OK, Hank. You've done a lot already."

I'm glad I said that to him because when he drove me to Lubbock for the abortion I didn't say much. He paid for it. He only asked me once if I wouldn't reconsider and put the baby up for adoption but nine months of my life seemed like forever then and I said no. I would have had to tell people and there was no way that I could ever tell Dad my situation, and no way I could live with Dolly looking over my shoulder for the next seven or eight months either.

After I moved to Albuquerque, tried school for a while, and then moved to quite a few other places, I stopped talking to Hank at all. I didn't know how to stay in touch with him without telling him the truth about my life and I didn't see any way to tell him about my crazy, fucked-up life, so I ended up somehow never seeing him again. He found me through the mail pretty regularly, thanks to Sarah, and he would write me a good letter always and send me photos when he had them and money when he could. He saved my ass multitudinous times, in Virginia Beach, Cincinnati, New York, Memphis. It was like he had ESP about when I was desperate. I always used the money fast and read the letters slow, but I never wrote him back and I don't know why. Sometimes I think I could have saved myself years of unhappiness by writing him a simple letter, just to say thank you, to say that I loved him and I missed him and one day I'd make him proud, but I couldn't write it. All those years I thought about him and talked to him in my head and not once, not one time, did I ever write him back. I just couldn't.

8 I'm being sorry for myself and sick to my stomach on the wrong side of the Coast Starlight, winding up the edge of the Pacific to Oakland and then on to San Francisco. It's 6:00 P.M. and everyone else on board has shifted over to the left side of the cars for a better view of the sunset and the sea, but I don't care about the sunset or the sea or anything else except getting to the end of this trip. I'm almost three months pregnant and I've lost twelve pounds since conception. If this continues I'm going to recommend getting knocked-up as a diet aid to everyone I know who can stand vomiting. I doubt my symptoms will improve much once I get to Auntie Buzz, but at least I'll be stationary. Morning sickness is bad, but morning sickness on a moving object is awful.

When I spoke to Beatrice back in May and told her my situation she said I could stay with her as long as I liked, but the truth is I can't really. Her budget is small, her apartment smaller still, and living with no money in no space is the best antidote there is to a nice relationship. I'll stay about a week, two if I'm lucky, then head north for Oregon. If I were braver, I'd have gone straight up to Joe's and plunged headlong into my new, Pacific Northwestern life. Instead, I'm taking the slow way there. San Francisco was on my ticket from the beginning and it seemed stupid to pass up on Aunt Buzz, even as sick with pregnancy and regret as I am.

I hope she doesn't bug me too much about this kid. As soon as people know you're carrying a baby they all turn into obstetricians. She was never the finger-pointing type and I doubt she's changed, but who knows? I don't even remember what she looks like. Writing letters back and forth keeps us current but it's been years since visual contact. Does she still come across like a hybrid of *Mother Earth News* and *Vogue?* I'll soon find out. Oakland is only two hours away if we remain on schedule, and in Oakland we disembark, take a bus across the bay to the Ferry Building in San Francisco, then sanctuary I hope by 10:00 P.M.

My aunt has written to me five times since Memorial Day. Her routine was to send someone a handwritten note each night; with me in crisis she simply added my name extra times to the roster. She must like her penmanship. In addition to the nightly letters, she also keeps, religiously, three separate journals. One is to log activities, bowel movements, diet, moods, and weather; one to record dreams, fantasies, and spontaneous ideas; and one to aid her creativity with three pages each morning of no-editing-allowed, stream-of-consciousness, mind-clearing scribble à la *The Artist's Way.* She has time for all this because she doesn't have a job. She's also learning Russian at the moment and considering a martial art. She's the kind of person who is constantly acquiring knowledge and skills, but is never driven to apply them. "There are enough practical people already," she says. Her last interest was stained glass. Drawing before that. Rock climbing was short-lived. She subsists on Uncle Charlie's life insurance and occasional publication of erotica. Dad says she's a woman who would always choose scrimping to working, a character flaw nearly as deadly as lesbianism, apparently.

I wonder what happened between her and Isabel. I considered them a sure thing, a hypermodern, sexually smoking, intellectually stimulating, long-term item, but my second June letter said they'd broken off the romantic end of the stick. Beatrice didn't sound devastated. The letter said that they still go to the same meditation center; they still have breakfast once a week; they still intend to see Spain this winter together. I don't get it.

Damn. We've gotten delayed by traffic on the bridge and the shuttle is just now pulling in, late by over an hour. There are times I wish I could afford airplane tickets. I'm sick of the train. I'm sick of people smiling at me. Most of all I'm sick of feeling the way I do, sluggish and ugly and pukey. I thought having a baby would be more fun.

"Hi Auntie Buzz. Sorry we're late. You look terrific."

"Don't worry, I called for your arrival time before I left the house. You look terrific, too. I used to think I was going to have to worry about your looks, you know, but now I see that isn't true at all. You've really grown up well."

"Gosh. Thanks. I'm overwhelmed."

"Have you been eating?"

"Yeah. Some."

"Sit," she says, pointing over to a bench.

"My luggage."

"It'll wait. Here." She reaches into her bag and hands me a sandwich of avocado and sprouts and egg salad on the blackest bread I've ever seen.

"Interesting combination."

"You need protein and I'm not good at meat."

"I'm not hungry, but thanks anyway." In fact I can smell mayonnaise through the plastic and it's making my stomach roil.

"When did you eat last?"

"I can't remember. What does it matter? Everything makes me throw up."

"Hm." Beatrice gives me a look that I won't return and she puts the sandwich away, then links her arm through mine and we go back to sort through my things. I don't feel like talking and she's not forcing me. An air of patience follows her around, more marked than in her letters. She turned fifty-something last month and looks like one of those steel blue monkeys from a wildlife calendar, the ones with long ruffs of ice-tipped fur and wrinkled, wise faces. Her face isn't that wrinkled but there's some look to it of ancient knowledge. I don't want to fake happiness in front of it.

She talks me into sorting and repacking and then leaving almost everything I have in storage at the station, and we walk out to hail a cab carrying only my backpack and camera. Beatrice doesn't have a car. Outside, the air feels nothing like the desert. It's cold and foggy and I can smell salt water, and suddenly it seems that El Paso really is gone for good.

"Let's get a drink," I tell her.

"You mean alcohol?"

"I could stand a beer."

She just looks at me, eyebrows raised.

"How about half a beer, then? You can't get fetal alcohol whatever from half a beer. I need to get my mind in the same zone as my body."

"Drinking doesn't seem like a great idea. I'll take you to yoga tomorrow," she says, and flags down a taxi. "I think you'll find it very grounding. Valencia and 16th, please."

I don't answer. I don't want to go to yoga. I want to sit still someplace dark and be left the hell alone with nothing but a pint of Guinness for company and good tunes in my ear.

"Definitely yoga," she goes on. "It'll do you the world of good. Deep breathing can change your life, you know. And regular food couldn't hurt. How is your protein intake?"

"How much protein is in banana pudding and Sun Chips?"

"Why aren't you taking care of yourself?"

"I am."

"You're not."

"Because I hate being pregnant, OK?"

"You said it was solving the mysteries of the universe for you."

Fuck the mysteries of the universe. I can't believe I ever thought that. "It was, for a while. Now it's just a pain in my ass. I'm sick all the time and I'm so ugly."

"You're not ugly."

"My whole life has been torn apart by this, and there's six months left of dragging around and feeling like shit. Then a baby to feed and change and pay for when I can hardly feed and pay for myself. I don't think I can do it, Auntie Buzz." My eyes are burning, I want to cry so badly, but I will not let myself go.

"You'll be fine," says Beatrice calmly, and leans forward to stop the cabbie.

Before April ended I already felt very pregnant; pale, nauseous, wiped out, and sweaty, like having a mild case of malaria. It was hard keeping the news from Colette. She dropped me off at Ash's one day and told me to ingest iron if I wouldn't ingest liver. "And you haven't been eating breakfast," she said. "Are you taking diet pills to impress Ash? Are you Bean?" The one thing about having a history like mine is that everybody thinks it's OK to question me about what I'm *really* doing. I summoned enough energy from God knows where to lie about a flu bug, then scurried off with a smile pasted to my face, grateful that Sarah was coming soon and the truth would out.

The end of May limped into sight. Sarah was due around lunchtime, sans fiancé. Colette was dropping by after work and Ash was doing two massages first, then joining the three of us for a picnic in the park. I wasn't looking forward to games of Frisbee and wedges of Brie but there didn't seem a graceful way out. It was my job to pack food for the party and I couldn't make myself do it. El Paso by then was well into summer; I was suffering. The Southwest goes from a brief, cold winter almost directly into real heat, none of the slow warming and greening of Boston. When I was young I loved that schism between the seasons. This time I missed the gentler gradations of temperature, the silent, secret budding of trees, the way you wake up one morning to find February gray losing the war.

"Hey, aren't you getting stuff together for the shindig this afternoon? You know where everything is, right?" Ash strode in and surveyed the kitchen, so beautiful in shorts and a T-shirt it made me want to cry. Oh please God, please have made him the father.

"I'm unmotivated," I replied, not looking his way. He's perceptive and I felt the truth leaking without permission from my eyeballs and armpits.

"How come, baby? Are you worried about seeing your sister? It'll be fine. What did you get her for her birthday?"

"Get her?" I echoed blankly.

"Yeah, you know, that tradition of buying people something for their birthdays? No? This is news to you? So I shouldn't expect anything in October, huh?" October? If we're together in October, Ash, I'll bankrupt myself for your birthday present. "So I guess you're not a gift giver. Huh. Maybe I'd better rethink this whole situation." He was teasing me.

"Yeah, maybe you'd better," I answered. It came out wrong, though, and he stopped going through the cabinets to give me a look.

"OK," he said. "What's all this about? Are you afraid I'll fall in love with her?"

"No." In the old days, perhaps, but I had real fears now.

"Are you feeling sick?"

"A little bit. Maybe I'm premenstrual. I get off schedule when I'm stressed."

"Do you want some herbal tea that'll make you feel better?"

"No. I feel like being miserable."

"Hey," he said gently, and came over to rub my neck. "You're so tense. Relax a little. Whatever it is, it ain't that bad, believe me." I didn't believe him, but the neck rub was starting to help when the doorbell rang. Ashur kissed me and pulled me by the hand to the front door, where together we greeted Sarah smiling, the image of connubial-like bliss. She seemed taken in. After a few minutes Ash excused himself to go to the office side and greet his next client, but on the way out he kissed me in front of her possessively, then left me standing, red-faced, in the entry hall. Sarah shook her head as we headed to the kitchen for iced tea and fruit. "Boy, do you have it bad."

"I know, I know."

"I hope he's the father."

"I know. Oh God, I know."

"You don't like the smooth path, do you?" she asked, rhetorically. I handed her a glass of ginger peach tea and she handed me a postcard in return. It was from Joe Bloch and it said, *I'm getting bad vibes from your direction. What's up? Tell me everything. How's the weather? How's the love life? Send me some pictures.* He included his phone number and new address.

I stuck the card in my pocket and led Sarah on a tour of the house. Before we made it half the way through I had to stop at the back toilet to puke. She paled but I took my tea back and said it was no big deal. "That'll hold me for hours. Now I think I'm OK for the picnic." She was mildly reassured. "Well, this is the darkroom. What do you think?" When Ash bought the house it came with a fully plumbed workroom that, until me, he had never used for anything but laundry and storage. Together we had transformed the space into the best little darkroom in Texas.

"It's so professional!"

"I am professional. Colette got me a job doing some promotional photography for her radio station, just little things, pocket money to them, but it's all I need to live on."

"I didn't know you could do color."

"It's not what spins the planet for me. I had to go to a workshop to relearn it but the station paid, thank God for employee-boss sex."

She looked my way, eyebrow cocked.

"Not me," I answered. "Colette."

"Oh that. Yeah, your timing was good. They're ending that affair, aren't they?"

"They're trying. She wants to keep her job."

"You really do have the gift, you know." She was looking through the usual assortment of advertising crap and some portraits of radio personalities that I'd taken on the job. Not exactly an undiscovered cache of photographic art, but better than a lot of things I'd seen.

"Thanks," I said, considerably cheered. We went through some of the other photos. "Here's the picture I'm going to give you for a birthday present." I showed her the one from when we posed together half naked on the wooden gate in the middle of the desert. Her front was toward the camera but her face was turned to me, and my back was to the camera but my face was turned to her. "It's probably the only picture where both of us look good at the same time," I said, and she nodded.

"I love it. It's not just beautiful, it's really art." And then, "So what's it like being pregnant? You look pretty calm for a brain-damaged lunatic."

"I thought of what it's like, but you won't get it 'til you do it."

"Tell me anyway, know-it-all."

"When I was maybe seven or eight Dad made me go look something up in the dictionary. I'd done it before, but this time when I got to the right letter and asked, 'Where's the word?' he just said, 'What's the alphabet?' And I looked at him and looked at him and then suddenly I saw that the dictionary wasn't just alphabetized in the big chunks, it was alphabetized all the way down. Everything lit up and the world became super-connected. It was amazing. I felt like Einstein."

"Diós mío," said Sarah.

"Yeah well, that's what it's like being pregnant. Suddenly my whole body makes sense. I see what everything's for. I've been initiated into the deep mystery and it's so amazing to me that everywhere you go are all these other pregnant women who have been initiated in as well. I see the big picture, I'm part of the big picture, and Sarah, the little things, like fucking up in high school and taking forever to graduate college, they suddenly seem inconsequential. When you think that a man can never know this feeling it makes up for a lot of shit."

"Gross," marveled Sarah. "I never thought you'd sound so disgustingly maternal."

"That's me. You can call me Mama Bean if you want. Can you believe that Ash heard about a guy who was selling his entire darkroom, everything in it, and bought the whole setup for me? He says it was an incredible deal, but still. He's something, isn't he?"

"Don't get all mushy on me, chica. I never did that with Samson and you owe me."

"Fine. How are things with him anyway?"

"You don't like him because of his feet, admit it."

"I like him fine," I lied as convincingly as possible. Moral or not, some lies are necessary. "We've just been defensive around each other over you but I guess that'll stop, now that he's got you for sure."

"Well, interestingly enough," said Sarah, turning her back on me tellingly, "now that he's got me for sure, he doesn't seem to want me anymore." She was facing the wall and staring somewhere in the direction of the phosphorescent clock-timer, her way of saying that this was important.

"Oh Sarah, it's just a guy thing, no big deal. They always freak out when it's really time for the commitment, they can't help it, they're wired that way, like girls thinking baby clothes are cute. Don't worry about it for another second."

"Really?"

"Really. Just back off, tell him he's right, that maybe you'd better think about it, and don't bring it up again. He'll bring it up."

"Are you sure?"

"In this case, Sarah, I'm sure. He loves you, he really does. The guy can be a prick but he loves you from the bottom of his heart. Relax. You're just doing that girl thing. Now that the idea of marriage is in your head, admit it, you've been thinking about nothing but."

"You're so right," she admitted. "And I've been talking about the wedding nonstop. Where to have it, who to invite, how much to spend, everything I thought I'd never do. Mom calls three times a day, his mother calls four times a day. No wonder the guy is backing off."

"It could be worse," I told her. "You could be twenty-four and talk nothing for eleven months but wedding dress."

"I don't suppose you and Ash have ever talked about marriage, huh?"

"Not exactly." And the topic made me miserable again. I kept swinging from elation at being pregnant to absolute despair about being pregnant in such ridiculous circumstances.

"When you tell him that you're pregnant, is he going to want to marry you?"

"Um. Hi," said Ash, who had materialized without warning outside the darkroom door. "I didn't mean to sneak up on you, but now that I'm here I guess I should tell you that I overheard that last part. Hi again, Sarah. I guess you already know what I just officially found out."

"I think I'll go and see if Colette's here yet," said Sarah and scooted off, looking horrified.

"Thanks," I tried to say, but my heart was filling my mouth and it came out all mumbled.

Ash was smiling at me but his eyes were tight and worried. He waited for Sarah to be out of range and then took my hand, which was ice cold, and said to me, softly, "Do you want to talk about it?"

"Not really, but I guess we need to. Give me a second to put this stuff away." And I fumbled around the darkroom, sorting things as if it would be my last time in there. "Don't you have another client?"

"No show," he said. "We don't have to talk if you don't want to. I just thought it was maybe my business too, but it's up to you."

"Of course it's your business. I should have been talking to you already, but I was afraid. Let's go to the kitchen."

"What about Sarah?"

"Colette will be here in a minute and I'm sure they have a lot to discuss. Don't worry about them. You wouldn't believe all the times I had to tactfully disappear when she and Elliot were fighting."

"Maybe some of that fighting is going to stop, now that they're getting married," Ash said, and we looked quickly away from one another. The air was heavy between us and I felt dread in my stomach worse than any morning sickness so far.

When I walk into Beatrice's apartment my resolve crumples and I start crying, the first tears in a month or more, and she just puts me in the armchair silently and brings me the box of Kleenex. After a while I stop and she says, "Do you feel better?"

"Uh-huh." I don't feel any better. It isn't that kind of crying.

"Do you want to tell me the story now?"

"No. I want to forget the story. I want to pretend that I'm not pregnant, I want to stop worrying, I want my life back the way it used to be."

"You're worn out, child. It's not a good time to think about things. Why don't you eat some food and then go to bed?"

"I'm not hungry."

"Have a little something. It'll make me happy." She goes to the kitchen and comes back with a cucumber-yogurt concoction and a piece of bread. I eat two spoons of yogurt and one bite of bread and can't eat more. But it doesn't make me nauseous.

"How did you leave things with Ash?"

"Who?"

"You don't want to talk about this yet?"

"No." I pour myself a glass of Cabernet from the open bottle on the table and she doesn't try to stop me. It doesn't taste good, even with pieces of bread as a buffer, but something makes me keep drinking. Eventually Beatrice has a glass as well, her pale eyes watchful, but not unkind. She puts on something classical, Rachmaninoff maybe, and we don't talk anymore. Then the wine on my nearly empty stomach hits my head. More specifically it hits my eyes and I feel, suddenly, as if there are weights attached to my eyelids, forcing them shut. "Screw it," I tell her. "I can't think anymore. I'm sorry to be so horrible but I've got to sleep."

She takes me down the short hallway and I find what passes for a second bedroom, just bigger than a closet but with a daybed already made up and cozily waiting for me. In three minutes I'm out flat, teeth unbrushed, face unwashed, dreaming of Ash and, Beatrice tells me later, whimpering.

When I finished in the darkroom Ash and I headed together to the kitchen, sitting on the barstools where we always sat, facing the window that we always faced, leaning our elbows on the counter and waiting. I thought about our weeks of sunny mornings and easy talk, the cups of tea and coffee shared together on those same barstools and for a moment I thought, I can't bear it, I can't bear the next thirty minutes, I can't do what I need to do to get us from here to there.

"If it helps," he said, "I already knew that you were pregnant. I massage a lot of women's bodies and I can tell some things. You're, uh, you're changing already. Your breasts. Your belly, just a little. And I haven't seen any sign of a period. You taste different, too. And your appetite is low."

"My appetite?"

"Both of them." We almost laughed, but remembered just in time that we couldn't, and gravity settled itself solidly around our shoulders. "I thought I'd better leave it to you to bring up," he said. "But maybe I should have asked you. I didn't know how far along you might be or what you wanted to do." In other words, he didn't want to presume too much, and if I got an abortion he wouldn't stop me.

"Ashur," I started, but at the sound of my voice, or maybe the tone of it, he suddenly got up off the barstool.

"We don't have to talk about it," he said, and I realized that he was scared. He walked around the kitchen for a minute and then stopped and I saw from his back that he was taking deep breaths to calm himself, trying to do what he calls centering. I waited for him to gather himself and sit back beside me and then I told him about Ricky. He started out looking intently at me, but by the time I finished he was staring at the counter and his head was in his hands.

"But I thought you liked me," he said. "I thought it was obvious that there was something special going on between us. Was I wrong? Did I push you into this relationship?"

"Oh God. Ash, I don't know how to say this now so that you'll believe me but I've never felt about anyone the way I feel about you. If anything, that's what scared me so much at the beginning that I even ended up sleeping with Ricky again."

"That doesn't make sense."

"Not to you. I was afraid, don't you see that? I wasn't sure you felt the same way about me. When you disappeared for those two days I didn't know Yvette was trying to get you back. I thought you were coming up with ways to put distance between us. That's when Ricky came to town and by then I had stopped thinking clearly at all. My head was a mess."

"Finding you made my head clear," he said. "Since I met you I've been like a different person. I'm not lonely anymore. I knew you were the one. But for two years I wanted Yvette and my marriage back, and when she called it took time to tell her the truth, and even to tell myself the truth, I guess. As soon as it was settled, I came looking for you."

"And that was the first day we were together." One day after the not-so-Super 8.

"I knew it was meant to be, with us. That's why I was so pushy, remember? I didn't want you to say no because you'd been burned by Patrick and didn't have faith anymore in love. I wanted my faith to be enough for both of us. I guess I had it wrong."

"No, Ash, it was the same for me. Only different," I said, lamely. I was going to lose him, I could see it like I could see the clear blue sky outside his kitchen window, the edge of adobe outlined against it. The contrast of that deep blue and the sweet, curving white made me want to weep. "Listen, Ash, I'm crazy about you. Right from the beginning I knew things were special with us, but I don't have the best record with men. I'm not that good at sticking around. I was afraid to trust things with you and me, that's why I hooked up with Ricky. I thought, if things didn't work out with you and me I could say they went bad because of Ricky, and not because there's something wrong inside me that makes a person not love me right and makes me not love back. It *was* a lack of faith, being with him. It was fear. I realized it at the time but I wasn't strong enough to walk away until after. I left him that night and I haven't seen him since. I would never be with him again, or anyone else. There's no one for me but you. I mean it. I really mean it."

"I know you mean it, I can tell by the look on your face, but how am I supposed to believe in you now?"

"I don't know."

"What if something comes up between us again, something hard, some bad times? Are you going to take refuge in another man every time you have doubts?"

"No, I never would. But I don't know how I can convince you."

"I don't know how you can either. And what about the baby?"

"What do you mean?"

"If it's his are you going to be with him?"

"I'll never be with him."

"What if the baby's his?"

"I don't know. I don't even know if I should tell him. There's nothing between us."

"But girl, if the baby's his you have to tell him."

"Why?"

"It's only right."

"Maybe he should have thought of that before we had unprotected sex. Why should I feel obligated to tell him anything?"

"You and I had unprotected sex."

"That was different."

"That's what I thought, at the time. Now I don't know." He was looking out the window too, his fingers drumming on the counter. Then his fingers got still and he turned to look at me. I steeled myself instinctively and he said, his voice remote, "What if you need money?"

I didn't say anything. Across the blue sky I could see the trail from a jet slowly dissolving. What if I need money? The question swirled around in my head lazily and, lazily, I looked at it. His eyes were magnets but I forced mine to stay fixed on the sky. There was no question that I'd need money; did I have the right to ask for it? And who would I ask and what would it mean? If the baby were Ricky's, he expected me to ask Ricky. If the baby were his, he expected me to ask him. Either way, he wasn't thinking anymore of us as a couple, that was obvious. He was thinking of obligation and duty, and whose obligation and duty would be determined strictly by whose seed took root.

My daydreams had been different. I never really believed that I'd be alone, struggling with money and not knowing where to live, wondering how to sign up for food stamps and not having a birthing partner. It never actually occurred to me that I would have to do it solo. And that's just the pregnancy. What about after? How could I have been so stupid? I thought love would conquer all. I thought it would even conquer the question of parentage, but apparently it doesn't, not for men. I could love any little baby eventually. I guess Ash can't.

When I woke up this morning, my first in San Francisco, I was puffy and aching and stiff, my mind blooming with images of dead crocodiles and rendering plants. I thought for a minute that I was back in Cincinnati, getting evicted for not making rent. Then I remembered that I'm pregnant, broke, and in San Francisco, that I'd be throwing up a lot in the next eight hours, that I felt pretty bad and it was the best I'd feel all day. Now I'm lying in bed discouraged, trying to imagine what Ash is doing. Of course, he's probably doing exactly what he'd be doing if I were still there: seeing clients, making breakfast, listening to music, straightening up.

I get out of bed to find the apartment empty except for me, the fish, and the furniture. Buzz must be out taking her constitutional. I put on Lou Reed and start looking over the list she has on the fridge. It's called *Evils To Be Avoided* and taking the top position, underlined three times, is television. Second is credit cards, third the plastics industry, and then it goes on with fat-free cookies and call waiting and catalog shopping and thinking too much and mindless hurrying and cheap utensils and bad coffee and so on and so on. It's a long list, several pages, and at the end I see that it's been updated quite recently. I get a pencil and write in at the bottom, very lightly, *morning sickness*.

My mouth is dry so I pour a glass of water, crack open the phone book and look what's listed under Pregnancy, Abortion, and Adoption. There are lots of numbers. Lots of options. At this point my aunt comes in with an armful of flowers and a pint of half-and-half. She sees the lists I'm making and doesn't say anything except, "Coffee or espresso?"

"Coffee, please," I answer automatically. Espresso is for after lunch, in my opinion. Then I think about my stomach. "Wait, let me see how I feel." I feel all right. All right enough to risk it. "Yes, coffee. Just half a cup, though."

"Is that adoption or abortion?"

"Both. And La Leche League as well."

Beatrice starts banging around in the kitchen and swearing at her espresso maker and after a minute brings me a plate with a sourdough loaf and butter, and a pot of strawberry jam.

"No thanks," I say, but she leaves it there and I start eating. So far no puke.

She comes in with our coffees and opens the patio door. A breeze pours damply in and my hair, which has gotten even wirier in pregnancy, immediately starts frizzing around my face. "You ready to talk? It's decaf."

"I don't have anything to say. Do you have a hair clip?"

"Do you want to end the pregnancy and put yourself out of this misery?"

"I don't want to think about it." I take a sip of coffee. "I'm sorry," I say, after a minute, and put my cup down. "I guess I can't drink coffee anymore."

"The body knows best."

"I need some Tums."

"I'll get you candied ginger. Tell me the truth, Eleanor. Do you want to abort?"

"Not really. I can't, Buzz. Not another one."

She drinks her coffee and we sit there, watching the clouds scud across the sky. "So you're feeling all right?"

"Actually, yeah." And I've eaten all the bread she put out.

"Let's go to yoga, then. We'll walk. You haven't even seen the city."

San Francisco turns out to be something like Boston, only looser, friendlier, with a lot more Asians. There are bookstores everywhere. Coffee shops thrive, eating establishments pop up every few feet, people walk around dressed every which way, and I can see from their signs that bars serve espresso as well as beer, which I appreciate but would appreciate more if

I could stand either one right now. It's a beautiful, washed clean morning, breezy and chilly until we start walking, then humid enough to make us sweat. The particular smell of the city is strong, roasting coffee beans and the taqueria grills, bread baking and maybe even chocolate chips. It isn't making me sick at all. In fact, I'm kind of hungry.

"Nice place, don't you think?"

"It's like Cambridge," I answer, "but sexy."

"Yes indeed. Even intellectuals do it in Berkeley."

"So what did happen to Isabel?"

"Her husband. He's very tolerant, but he's not that tolerant. She made him promises and began to feel bad and I don't blame her. I wouldn't have stepped out on Charlie for either sex, and Charlie and I had our differences. He was a difficult man, did you know that?" I shake my head no. "Oh yes. I started meditation because it was either that or murder him. And now I miss him every day."

"I'm sorry."

"Don't be. I'm also happy, every day, that he's not around anymore. Life is so much easier now. Don't look so shocked, honey, you're making me feel bad. Well, here we are. Prepare to stretch."

That first yoga session was humbling. Beatrice is like cooked spaghetti and by comparison I'm raw. I'm not flexible, I can't relax, I'm not adept at deep breathing. I thought I'd be good at it because I'm good at sports, but I was wrong. It doesn't seem to matter, though. I've been three times since and, even though I'm terrible, all that stretching of the body and emptying of the mind is calming my gestation anyway. Or something is, because I haven't thrown up in five days now. I wake up and feel all right. I walk around and feel all right. I go to bed at night and sleep for ten hours at once, which I've never done without drugs.

During the days, Beatrice and I do a lot of people watching. She gives me natural pregnancy tidbits from the Bradley book and I practice squatting, do Kegels, and eat. We do a fair bit of grocery shopping. The first days of appetite I polished off her cashew stash. Then the pasta went, the cheese, the olives, the goat milk, the bread. This situation has caused her to unveil a previously hidden Betty Crocker side to her personality and she can't walk past her kitchen anymore without making me food. I eat whatever I'm handed. Hummous, pesto, Greek salad, cake. And cottage cheese for protein every time I turn my head.

"Here," said Ash. "Drink this." He was standing over me with a glass of something dark and vile-looking and the unexpectedness of his voice, gentle as ever in the midst of my thoughts, made me jump. "You're pale," he said, and smoothed his hand over my forehead. I could feel him wipe the sweat away.

"Yuck," I said, drinking the stuff down and feeling better.

"It's good for you. I just saw Colette and your sister drive off. Are you hungry?"

"No. I can't eat. I need to know what we're going to do now."

"I don't know, girl." He sighed and looked so sad that I hated myself. But I hated him too, for not loving me enough. If he loved me enough we could have overcome this. "I want to be able to say that I love you so much it doesn't matter," he said, mind reading as usual. "But the truth is, it matters. You know my marriage was a mess, right?" I nodded my head. I'd heard all about it from Colette. "She wasn't true to me, Eleanor, and I can't live like that again. I wish I could tell you I was stronger, that I still had enough faith to overcome this, but I don't. And I don't know if I want to raise another man's child, watching it grow up to look like someone else, wondering the whole time if my wife is going to run off with the guy the next time he asks, or we have a fight, or she gets insecure."

I nodded again. It made sense. I pushed myself back from the counter and walked around the room, touching the tabletop and the windowsill, playing with the curtains and staring out into the blue El Paso day. After a few minutes I realized that my shoulders had loosened a little. "I'm hungry now," I said.

"That was fast. Does it mean you've decided something?"

"No," I said, lying. He turned his back to me and looked out the window. "Ash?"

He tilted his head but didn't turn around and I knew that he was crying. Scared, I walked slowly over to him but when he felt my hand on his shoulder he shrugged it off and said, "Don't, Eleanor. Please don't touch me. I can't stand it."

"Ashur, no." I pressed my body against his back and wrapped my arms around his chest. With my face against his spine I said, "I'm sorry, I'm so sorry. Please forgive me. We can work through this. I'll have faith for both of us. Turn around, give me a kiss. Put your arms around me, please."

He stood, rigid as a statue, and then pulled my arms off him. "I don't want you to touch me anymore," he said, and when he turned to face me his eyes were like rocks in his head. I watched my reaction from far off and saw that, mixed in with the shock and the pain, was a strange feeling of relief.

I stepped away from him then and sat back down at the counter. I felt tired, but better than I had before. The weight that had been pushing down on my stomach was gone. It was over. I betrayed the man I loved and he stopped loving me. End of story. Another jet crossed the sky and I watched as it left a long, pale curve in the blue, turning from takeoff sharply north and west.

Keeping his back to me, Ash walked out of the kitchen and towards his room, where I knew he would sit in meditation, cross-legged on the square mat. I watched him go and then made myself a sandwich. It was clear what I had to do. I had to stop hurting him and I had to find a safe place to live. I looked over Joe Bloch's postcard again and I thought that in a day or two, when I was ready, I'd call Buzz. Now, though, a sandwich and a cup of tea would do. The truth is, I knew where I was going.

Today is already my last in San Francisco; at 8:30 tonight I go back to Oakland and the Coast Starlight takes me the rest of the way to Portland. Joe says he'll be at the station tomorrow afternoon with bells on and it's a good thing I didn't chicken out. Beatrice and I are supposed to have breakfast someplace fancy this morning, her treat, but she's procrastinating. It's ten o'clock and while she's been futzing around I've already had carrot juice, cottage cheese, avocado on rye, and a piece of leftover pizza that she made from scratch. A couple weeks ago that amount of food would have held me for days. Now it'll hold me for two hours max.

"What's taking you so long?" I ask her.

"Want to try some decaf?"

"Sure, if you're still farting around. Maybe I'll get lucky and start to like it again." She makes me coffee the way they do for sissy Americans in cappuccino cafes, watered-down espresso, single, with a shot of cream.

"I can't believe I let myself purchase this ridiculously expensive behemoth," she says in my general direction about the rococo Italian espresso maker in her kitchen. She says it two or three times a day, whenever she makes a coffee or the florid tones of it catch her eye, but I overheard her once calling it Luigi, darling, so as usual I ignore the lamentation.

She's still busy with the steam and I'm working on pelvic tilts when the phone rings, an unusual occurrence, and I realize that this is why she's been dawdling. However, she makes no move to leave the kitchen so I pick up the phone.

"Shank residence. Or, Silverman residence." I can't remember which name she uses.

"Hi honey. It's Dad. She goes by Shank."

"Oh. Hi Dad." I give Beatrice a look but her face is perfectly neutral.

She mouths at me, "Tell him I said hello."

"How did you know I was here? I mean, did you know I was here? Buzz says hello."

"I just figured I might find you with your aunt. Tell her I said to come visit. The twins miss her. They miss you, too."

"Mmh." I'm waiting for the real reason he called.

"How are you?" he asks. Something about his tone of voice tells me that he knows my secret.

"Fine."

"How's the baby?"

"When did she tell you?"

"What do you mean?"

I look again over at my aunt and this time her face is more revealing. "When did Auntie Buzz call you with the good news?"

"Oh, I can't remember."

"Bullshit, Dad."

"Memorial Day."

The same day I called her from Colette's house, fragmented and hysterical. "She didn't even wait twenty-four hours to tell on me?" I tilt the phone away from my mouth as Beatrice walks in with my coffee. "You didn't even wait twenty-four hours to tell on me?"

"Nope," she says, unrepentant.

"Did you tell him everything?"

"Everything."

"Were you going to tell me yourself?" Dad asks.

"I felt stupid enough without you reinforcing it. And I didn't have the energy to fight."

"Who says we would have fought?"

"Oh please. Would you have told your parents if you were me?"

"It's not the same."

"It's not that different, Dad."

"Beatrice tells me you look great," he says. "That means it's a boy. Your mother used to say that girls steal your looks."

"I'm happy with whatever it is," I say. "Don't get your hopes up."

"I'd love you to have a little girl," he says. "With a whole mess of dark hair just like her mother. What are you talking about?"

"I know you like boys better. You wanted me to be a boy." Beatrice is looking at me like I just forgot my last name or started speaking Mandarin but I ignore her. "You did and you might as well admit it."

"What kind of a fool put that idea into your head?"

"You."

"You're wrong, Elephant. You're just plain wrong."

"Sure I am. You liked Sarah better than me and you like Jacob best of all. You're always talking about owning up to things. Why don't you own up to this?"

"Because those aren't the facts. I love all of you the same."

"Yeah yeah, just in different ways, right?"

"Right."

"So you love Jacob nice and me mean. Gee, what's wrong with that?"

"I treated you kids the same."

"Yeah? How come you wouldn't let me do any girl things when I was growing up, but you let Sarah and Jazz? How come you played sports with me and Sarah got ballet?"

"What's wrong with sports?"

"Nothing! But I wanted piano lessons and you said no. I wanted art and you said no. If I wasn't throwing you a baseball you were nowhere to be found. I always had to be a hundred percent tough. Remember saying that to me? No sissies allowed."

"I don't know what you're talking about."

"Yeah, when you're ready to face the facts let's talk again. In the meantime, here's your sister. I'll go outside so you two can plot behind my back." And I hand the phone to Beatrice, grab my coffee, and step out onto the patio. The worst of it is that even I hope it's a boy. God! You think you can bypass all the shit you were force-fed just because you know it's shit, but those old ideas sneak past you every time. I put my coffee on the railing, lay my hands on my stomach, and keep them there until my shoulders relax. Then I pick up my cup and drink, looking out over the traffic below. The coffee sucks. Another bummer in the larger scale of stupid and wrong things. And I'm getting hungry again.

I go back inside. Beatrice hands me the phone looking not one bit worked up about any of this.

"Hey, it's me again," I say. "Sorry about that. I really did think you wanted a boy."

"What else?"

"What else what?"

"What else are you mad about?"

"Nothing. Well, you weren't there very much."

"No, I wasn't. But everything I did, I did for you kids."

"So I hear. You could have spent some time with us."

He doesn't say anything. What is there to say?

"All I'm asking for is acknowledgment, Dad. You've never in your life said you were sorry about the way we were raised."

"It could have been worse."

This time I won't break the silence. Beatrice appears with a bowl of cut fruit and a fork. I sit down and start in on a piece of excellent cantaloupe, still holding the phone to my ear. We can sit here all day if he wants. It's not my dime.

"What are you eating?

"Fruit."

More silence. I've gone through all the cantaloupe and half the peach when he says, "I'm sorry, Elephant. I thought it would be enough to just love you. And I do, you know. Very much."

When I swallow, the peach is salty with tears. "Thanks," I tell him.

He lets me blow my nose and settle down and then he says, "Honey, there is one more thing."

"What is it?"

"How do you feel about the name Baylor? It's got such a ring. Cindy would be thrilled and the gender won't matter."

When I hang up the phone and turn on Beatrice, all she says is, "You're probably ready for breakfast. We should walk, don't you think?"

"That's all you're going to say?"

She shrugs. "Your hair looks good. I think the fog will lift soon. Have you finished packing?"

"You know what I mean."

"Oh Eleanor. Happiness is nothing but a habit. Can we go eat now?"

Joe was having the wildest New Year's Eve party on record while his parents were out of town for the holidays. Everyone around our age who had ever tasted beer was scheduled to be on the scene, and two of his brothers would be there as well. And Ricky was in town. Sarah kept saying, "Big deal, so Ricky's in town," but rumor had it that he was tall and fine, and she was as carefully dressed and made up as we were. That night was just like it used to be, me and Sarah with Lily in her father's Monte Carlo, all dolled up and dragging Main, smoking cigarettes and pulling over occasionally to drink beer and talk to people. We stalled for an hour or so. We didn't want to show up too early.

Joe lived in a huge ranch house north of town with dogs, horses and, not too far away, the cattle. Everyone knew the property, which was demarcated by miles of barbed wire and white rail fencing. Everyone was also familiar with their livestock. Joe was a good rider but he just wasn't interested in the land, the Angus, or the horses. His dad gave him grief about it.

We got out there at nearly eleven and had to park way down on the dirt road for all the cars already there. We were halfway holding hands and laughing, pushing each other and all worked up, talking about who was going to hook up with who and checking out the boys on our way inside. The house was a sprawling mess, added onto every year for a decade by a different contractor, and it showed. However, it was huge and solid, had two living rooms and several bathrooms, and even with three of the boys still living at home there was always a hush when you went inside. I looked first for Joe and went to say hi but he was in a mood and barely nodded in my direction. Embarrassed, I went back for Lily and Sarah and the three of us stood around until nearly midnight, drinking and talking to people and being cool. There was no sign of Ricky. Then, as the countdown began, he showed up behind us.

The rumors were true. He was close to full grown and damn good-looking. We made a big fuss over him and he preened and strutted. "I guess you all have to kiss me now," he said, and we obliged, happy to have him with us again and getting into the fun of sandwiching him in public. I looked up and saw Joe watching us with an inscrutable expression on his face. I waved at him but he didn't wave back.

"What the fuck is up with Joe tonight?" I asked, but they didn't know and didn't care, so we stayed where we were, in the circle of Ricky's long arms, and asked him about Las Cruces and school and his family. He didn't want to talk about any of it, he just wanted to take turns making out with us in front of the whole room, looking like a hotshot, and we were drunk enough to do it. Even Sarah was enjoying herself.

"Hey man, there's people want to say hi to you, come on." It was Joe, tired of the spectacle we were making of ourselves, pulling Ricky away from us and giving him drinks from the bottle of Jim Beam. Ricky went easily, so we drifted over into the other, high-ceilinged living room to dance. After a while I said, "I'm going to find Joe. I want to ask him what's up."

"Don't do it," Sarah told me. "He's acting like an asshole. Maybe he's trying to move in on someone and you're cramping his style."

"Bullshit," I said, worried. "Anyway, what do I care? I'm just gonna make sure he's doing all right, that's all."

Sarah shrugged and I started a systematic search of the house. Eventually I found him near the back of the east wing in a small spare bedroom that his dad used as an office. We did our homework there, sometimes, because the room had a full set of *Encyclopedia Britannica,* anatomy and zoology books, and a big oak desk. The door wasn't even all the way closed. Ricky was leaning back against the desk with the Jim Beam in one hand, and Joe was kneeling on the ground in front of him, sucking his dick.

"Holy shit," I said.

Ricky jumped and opened his eyes and Joe howled. There's no other word for the noise he made, and it scared me. Ricky pushed him away and pulled up his pants, not quickly, and Joe stayed crouched on the ground. When he stood up, his face was unrecognizable.

"Bad timing," said Ricky. "I guess we should've locked that door. Bean, what the fuck are you doing in here? Can't you see me and Joe are conducting a little business?" Ricky didn't say it mean. He wasn't even embarrassed.

I was just staring at Joe Bloch. "You guys do this?"

"What's it to you?" asked Joe. His face was flushed, his breathing ragged.

"Hey, I'm no faggot," said Ricky. "Twenty bucks is twenty bucks, right amigo?" He swirled the fifth of Jim Beam and drank down the last swallow.

Joe turned on him and knocked the bottle out of his hands. "Get the fuck out of here."

"Mellow out," said Ricky. "Who cares? It's just Bean."

"I care," said Joe.

"Me too," I said. I thought I was going to faint but then my head filled with blood and I could feel my lips burning and tight. I put my hands on my cheeks to cool them down. I couldn't take my eyes off Joe. "I can't believe it," I said, and started to cry. "I can't believe you let me go around, all this time—"

"You dumb-ass Mexican whore," Joe said, gripping my arms and pulling me the rest of the way inside the room. "How much more obvious did I have to make it?"

"Why didn't you just tell me?" I was pulsing with shame and suddenly my whole body felt huge. I nearly threw up. I thought about the clothes I had worn for him, the tight shirts, the different hair styles, all the moments of leaning against him and taking pleasure in it. "You fucking jerk," I said, still crying and unable to stop myself. "Does everyone know except me?"

"No one knows, and if you ever tell anyone about this I'll kill you." He was pushing me back against the door, emphasizing every word with another little shove.

"Get your hands off me! What's wrong with you? This is me, Eleanor, remember? I'm your best friend! Why are you being like this?" Now I was yelling, outraged.

Joe shouted in my face, "You're not my friend! You moron! How could you not know? How blind can you be?"

"You stupid faggot," said Ricky. His face was hard. "Leave her alone. Bean, why don't we get out of here and leave this maricón white boy to himself?"

"You get out of here," I said. "I hope that twenty dollars comes in handy."

"You know what? It will." He walked out and left me and Joe just looking at each other with no words to fit the situation.

After a while Joe said, "Are you happy now? Did you really think you and I were ever going to get together? You make me sick. You make me want to puke, OK?"

Then I did throw up, right there in front of him, all the beers and bourbon of the night rushing out of me in one burning fountain. When I was finished, he was gone. I left the vomit on the floor, went to the bathroom and cleaned myself up, then walked out into the main living room, where Lily and Sarah and a bunch of other people were standing around.

"Joe Bloch's a fag," I said to Sarah. I didn't care who heard me. "I just walked in on him giving a blow job to some guy and he admitted it. He's gay. Joe Bloch is gay." And then I started crying, and she and Lily came over and took me by the arms and led me outside. After I threw up one more time they wiped off my face, put me in the car, and drove us all to the truck stop for breakfast. We didn't mention the incident. It was our last outing together.

Joe Bloch never went back to school. He left town in March without talking to me again, but in the mail I got a box with all the tapes and books I'd ever lent him, all the notes I'd ever sent him, the bottle of Scotch I managed to get him for Christmas, and his favorite book of constellations. I looked at the stuff for a while, played one of the tapes, drank enough of the Scotch to get solidly drunk, then went out to the dumpster and threw it all away.

9 I'm gazing lazily up at Mount Hood and drinking a cup of disgusting green tea at Joe Bloch's coffee shop, waiting for him to finish with a customer and come out to look at my newest photographs. I've been here for nine weeks and still can't get used to that mountain, floating above the city like a cloud. It makes me feel almost spiritual, like fasting without the misery. If listening to classical music as an infant enlarges your mind, I wonder what growing up in a beautiful landscape does for you. I wonder how your brain would be different growing up in Machu Picchu as opposed to Midland-Odessa or Newark, New Jersey.

"Are these the new ones?" Joe asks, appearing at my table in his hetero-looking uniform of beat-up jeans, torn T-shirt, boots, and an apron, and I nod my head without talking. The most pleasant thing about an old friend is that you don't have to always say something interesting. We were only close for six years, strangers for double that, but the years in between seem to count, I think because the friendships you have when you're young are different than the ones you get later. You haven't yet learned to cover your real self in acceptable behavior; you haven't yet learned to stick with your own kind; you're more genuine than you will be when you're old and know better.

When I was seventeen I had a hundred ideas a week, and Joe remembers a lot of them. He remembers my sexual escapades and social embarrassments and brilliant monologues on acid, and I remember his. I can burp in front of him and fart in front of him. I can be inconsistent of mood, of reason, of motive; I can be ugly, impractical, hard, or sweet. Best of all I can be silent, and that's a good thing.

"Customers?" I ask.

"Dead for now. I'm sick of making iced coffees anyway."

While I was busy getting knocked up he was busy getting money and a business plan together for a coffee shop in Portland. He says his shop is different from the rest and I think it is. In addition to the standard coffees, he offers live music on several nights, great movies on Tuesdays that I get to pick out, and real food, simple main courses and no-frills snacks, plus fresh salads and slow-cooked soups. Uncomplicated combinations of superior quality. That's his private motto. There's limited seating and a limited menu but it's high-quality, cheap, vegetarian food that's not too weird, and very good breads and desserts that, so far, he makes himself. Business is generally good. In fact, if he gets much busier he'll have to farm the work out and he knows I'm no cook. I can make excellent brownies, though, a mean espresso, and about a B+ cappuccino. Occasionally gays come in here looking for fancy drinks and they say, "We'll wait for Joe to make ours," because I don't get the foam stiff enough. This leads to all sorts of sophomoric humor, exacerbated by my belly and Joe's good looks. My acknowledged inferiority in the matter bends me all out of shape but they're right, I don't get the foam stiff enough.

Joe has abandoned his drifter life of leisure and now works his ass off, the quintessential small-business owner, in bed at eleven or twelve and up at five, but he says he's never been happier and he sure looks like someone happy. Probably I do too. We don't have time to be miserable. Since I've gotten here we haven't had a day off, although on Sundays we close at three and don't offer hot meals at all. I nap when we're slow and do photography at all hours but I'd be lying if I said the summer was one long walk in the park.

Of course, when Sarah called two weeks ago she said she didn't care how much I worked or how pregnant I was, my summer was easier than her summer. Uh-huh, I said. She was in Reno at the end of a Labor Day weekend spent water skiing. Joe and I had just closed and cleaned the entire shop and gotten ready for the next morning. He was making a midnight supply run and I was working in the darkroom when she called so I questioned her premise, but she said Reno sucked, she'd lost the ability to slalom, and she wished she had never rolled the dice the way she did that night.

"You used to love Reno." I didn't believe her about the water skiing or about the dice.

"I don't love anything anymore." Tucson was apparently approaching a hundred days of temperatures over a hundred, she and Elliot were still playing tug-o'-war over the actual date, and his parents were coming down from Rochester to stay with them for an entire month to "help" with the wedding and pester her about real employment. He was currently out gambling and she was moping in the hotel room alone pretending to have a headache. All the years of their relationship he had wanted her to be more domestic and, now that she was, he was running around like a chicken with its head cut off. She was miserable but wouldn't say so. She didn't want to antagonize him while wedding plans were underway and he was footing the bill. Which is the drawback to other people footing the bill, I guess.

I did my sororal duty and told her to rediscover her good sense and her backbone and to do it fast. I said, "I'm horrified to see my erstwhile spunky sister losing her famous independence under the pressure of approaching nuptials. Snap out of it! You owe it to NOW to keep a grip on your natural tendency to wilt in the face of a wedding dress."

"You'll do it too," she said.

"The opportunity won't arise," I answered.

"It's contagious. Colette is already dating a guy kind of seriously who isn't married and isn't an asshole. His name is Stan."

"Stan? A white guy?"

"Very white. Extremely white. Strictly Land's End and subdivisions. He comes from, I don't know, Iowa or something. She says he's a lot like her dad."

"Uh-oh."

"Uh-huh. The coupling up has begun. In a year, everyone we know will be married."

"I think my morning sickness is suddenly back," I said. "Travis and Laurie have been asking me very pointed questions about pregnancy too. I'll bet they end up living the perfect life together, having the perfect kids, and still being in love when they're eighty. It's enough to make a grown goat vomit."

"That's lovely," said Sarah.

"I still haven't heard from Ash." I turned the subject to what I really wanted to talk about.

"Gosh," she said, "I wonder why not. How big is your stomach now?" She left my bait lying untouched on the floor.

"Big," I told her, clinking around in the fridge for bottled water. "I think I'm fat but I don't even care. You wouldn't believe how many food items I know how to prepare now. Brownies. Soup. Killer salads. It's a crying shame I'm not marrying someone; I could almost pull my weight in the kitchen." Sarah lit a cigarette and started mimicking Elvis singing "That'll Be The Day," which I ignored. "So, did Colette or did Colette not mention Ash when you talked to her last?"

"For someone who left someone else, you sure are interested," said Sarah.

"Don't give me any shit, Sare, just tell me."

"She said he's not doing so well. There, does that make you happy?"

"Yes. Give me details."

"I don't have any, B. Just that he's blue and moping around and she can't cheer him up and he's been talking about maybe leaving El Paso and starting over somewhere else. He says he's doomed in romance. He says maybe he's not meant to be happy. He says his life is over and it doesn't matter to him what he does now."

"Shit." The news gets me out of the fridge and onto a chair. "That's more than I want. I want him to miss me and I want him to be sorry, but I don't want him going off the deep end. He never struck me as that kind of a guy."

"I was making it up anyway."

"You suck."

The last time I talked to Ash where any real content was exchanged was at the end of June, a week before I left El Paso. We were still pretending to be friendly, and I was still doing some photography work at his house, but he knew I was going and I think he knew where. By my standards he didn't try hard enough to stop me.

"I just don't understand why it's happened like this," he said to me that day, for what felt like the hundredth time. He looked awful. I felt awful but the glow of pregnancy seemed to be a real phenomenon in my case. I spent half my new life bent over or thinking about bending over the toilet but gosh my hair was glorious, my skin dewy, the whites of my eyes remarkably white, the darks a lustrous dark.

"I don't know," I answered, the same answer I always had. I was tired to the bone and sick of the whole situation. I suddenly thought that I just wanted to go, to be free of the inquisition, to put my mistakes behind me and march on. "Why did you have to push me into having sex so soon anyway?" I asked him, fed up with apologizing and moody in the bargain.

He closed his eyes. "I feel bad about that," he said. "I rushed you because I was afraid to lose you. Ironic, huh?"

I just shrugged. I was nauseous again. "I should have socked you in the jaw or something, but I thought you knew better than me. And I was afraid to lose you, too. *Pues aquí estamos.*"

"If we'd been able to wait a month, or even a week, things would be so different," he said.

"Even three days," I contributed, not helpfully, "Maybe one day. But it's irrelevant." We were at the breakfast bar again, trying to have an amicable discussion and talk things out properly, but his eyes were bloodshot and there were shadows under his cheekbones. He has the kind of body that loses weight under stress and I could see the muscles in his arms getting ropy. He hadn't shaved. As the hot spring days passed tensely for us I was watching him change from a dark Irish wolfhound to a half-starved winter wolf, my fault and I knew it.

"Yeah," he said heavily, and got up to walk back and forth, restless, "that's a useless line of thought."

"Things happen for a reason," I said, expressing one of his philosophies.

"Or so we hope," he answered bitterly. "So we hope."

I watched him pace off the Spanish tile in the kitchen for a while and then I went to the bathroom on the other side of the house to throw up. When I was finished he was nowhere to be found and I knew, then, that if he didn't want to continue the discussion he was as ready for me to go as I was to leave. So I called Joe Bloch, right there from the kitchen phone, and I didn't care that it would show up on Ash's account or that Ash might walk in and hear. In fact, I wanted Joe's telephone number to show up on the bill so he could track me down and call me in Oregon in case he changed his mind. Which apparently he hasn't.

It's now two and a half months later and I live, conveniently, with Joe Bloch in the pine-floored apartment above Mean Joe Beans, where I have another darkroom of my own, or do now since Joe did a little redecorating. We have to share the other bathroom and it isn't very big but neither one of us cares. In

Albuquerque I lived with eight people, in Cincinnati six. I can easily handle sharing a bathroom with one person, even Joe, who spends twice as long in there as I do so that he can come out looking like a guy who hasn't seen a mirror since 1979. I tell him all the time that the purpose of dressing down is to stop primping, not to force primping underground. He says that all style takes a serious time commitment. Uh-huh, I say. I wear ugly clothes too, but at least I only spend five minutes a day putting them on. Pregnancy has destroyed any fashion sense I might have had. I'm not spending money on clothes I'll only wear a couple of months. In this way my expenses are kept to constantly dwindling photography supplies, the poor girl's version of maternity wear, the poor girl's version of baby wear, and visiting the birthing center, which is wonderful.

Travis told me he'd pay for me to see a proper doctor and have the baby in a proper hospital but I don't want to. I said, "Don't you want to pay for the midwife instead? She's an absolute bargain." And Travis replied, "Over my dead body."

I said, "When I have this baby I might just do it at home, you know, squatting on the floor like an African. It's more natural and I won't break my tailbone."

Travis said, "I'll break your tailbone for you if you don't get a doctor's opinion on this. You'll be nearly thirty-two and having your first kid. You're not in the prime age for gestation, face it."

"Thanks." Everyone wants you to bow down to the gods of the medical establishment but I'm not going to. I'm fine, my baby's fine, and I don't need ultrasounds and lectures and cold examining rooms with bright lights, big bills, and condescending people to tell me what the midwife and I already figured out, that everything is silky smooth and natural is better.

"They're good, B," says Joe, going through the photographs. "I like these two especially," and I nod, wiping the sweat off my upper lip with the bottom of my T-shirt. Absentmindedly he starts fanning me with the other photos while he looks at the shots of the neighbor kids. In the first photograph the girls are both staring, transfixed, at an adolescent boy who's jogging slowly past their yard dribbling a soccer ball. He's completely oblivious to the small girls, absorbed in his own skill, full of grace and energy and beautiful enough for them to stop in the middle of playing school and look after him with bewildered, tragic faces. The next shot is after the boy is gone and the two girls come back to earth, signaling their experience with a small, mutual look of acknowledgment. The look is a serious, almost grown-up one; he represents what they're going to spend a huge chunk of their next decades agonizing over and on some level they seem to know and dread it.

"So much for the women's movement, huh?" Joe says, and again I nod, this time smiling, because the problem with woman's lib is that we keep forgetting how deeply susceptible to men we are. It's no biological accident, either. If men weren't irresistible to us on a level far more powerful than rational thought, we'd banish them at the onset of puberty to little islands lacking iron ore and visit them for occasional sperm donations only. "And the darkroom seems to be working out pretty well, right?" he asks me, and I know it's only because he wants me to tell him again what a terrific job he did putting it together. I oblige and he puffs a little bit, gratified.

When I left El Paso Ash told me to take the developing equipment with me. I struggled with that decision but the pragmatic view, that I would use the stuff and he wouldn't, won out over the honorable view, that he had bought it and he should dispose of it. Once I got to Portland it only took Joe a day to set up my bathroom for developing, and he did it with the kind of skill that made me stand by watching like a mute, open-mouthed in admiration, handing him the occasional tool like a nurse in the OR. I wonder if men ever stand around awestruck like that, knocked out by the way women manage to do some kind of impossible-to-them-seeming task. If so, I wish they'd tell us about it.

"Joe," I say suddenly, "I'm going to have to find a legitimate job pretty soon, you know that don't you?"

"No way," he says, predictably. "Look Bean, if you find work, I'll have to pay someone to work here with me. You know there's too much for one person to do, and I'd rather give you money than give it to some snot-nosed sixteen-year-old with rich parents and a bad attitude."

"Someone like you were, you mean?"

"Exactly. What is it you need that you don't want to ask me for?"

"Nothing, Joe. You get all the necessities and more than that, and don't think I'm not grateful because you know I am, more than I'll ever be able to say. It's just that sometimes I want to be able to buy little frivolous doodads that aren't sensible or necessary or aren't, maybe, even for me, and I can't get that kind of cash from you, I just can't. It's like getting an allowance from your folks and I'm too old. I have to earn my own money and probably would even if I were married to the father of this carbon module."

"There's no way you can think of my money as our money?"

"No."

"Fascinating," he says in the voice of Spock, eyebrow raised. "Humans are so illogical." And back to his own voice, still twangy with New Mexico, "I thought you were against both parents working."

"Full-time, Joe. I'm against the television-as-nanny concept."

"Don't women like being taken care of? I'd like it."

"For how long?"

"For as long as it would take me to get bored or guilty."

"Uh-huh."

"But you're having a baby; isn't that the perfect time to let a man help you out?"

"Even if the man didn't father it?" I ask him, chin on the steeple of my hands, elbows on the table.

"Hey Bean, we're all here to keep the human race going. This might be the only contribution I get to make."

"I don't know, Joe. It's awfully nice of you, but those guilt-free days might be over for women, unless their husbands are super rich. I have to contribute."

"You *do* contribute."

"Financially, Joe."

"You contribute financially, you idiot. Do you think I could do this without you?"

"No. I mean tangible amounts of green stuff with my name attached to it, OK? It doesn't have to be much, but it has to be mine. Intellectually I agree with you, but emotionally I'm not there. If I don't have my own money I'm going to feel subservient to you and no amount of reasoning is going to exorcise that demon. Period!"

Joe smiles at me then and says, "It's a beautiful day, isn't it?" And I realize that I've gotten flushed and worked up and my voice has even risen. I lean back and put my feet on the other chair and make myself relax.

"Sorry."

He just shrugs. It takes more than that to upset Joe.

"Yeah, it's pretty. Prettier even than Texas," I tell him, looking around at the dark greenery and pale blue sky, touching Mount Hood with my eyes like a rosary.

"I have an idea," Joe says, after checking inside to make sure everything's all right. The few customers of the hour are taken care of. The movie I picked for tomorrow night is *The Decline of the American Empire* and I've already got it posted and reviewed on the board, four beans, dark roast. Joe's started the sauce for tomorrow's pasta. I prepped flats full of strawberries this morning for the Italian custard that will be poured on them and found a company to make us travel mugs at a reasonable price. For the moment, everything's set. He sits down on a backwards chair and picks up one of my hot, damp hands. "Bean, why don't we turn this place into a studio for your photographs? We could mount them ourselves, use simple frames, and if you wanted to sell them we could and if not we wouldn't have to, but we could make this officially your exhibition center. I need to do something about the decor anyway and maybe you could put up occasional pictures of us or the clients. People love that. What do you think?"

"I think you're a fucking genius, you big fairy."

"Aw shucks," he says. Then he grips my hand harder and leans forward. "Just don't leave me to manage this place alone. It's not as much fun without you here."

"Never fear, dear, I only run away from boyfriends and family."

"OK then," he says, and lets my hand go.

I drink down the last, now cold bit of my tea. "Just think, Joe. We get such a mix of people in here, some of them even with discretionary income. I won't have to sell that many photographs to justify my existence, you know."

"Just think," he says. "All existences are justified, but some existences are more easily justified than others."

"Hey," I ask him, before business takes him away again, "am I preventing you from having a love life?"

"No," he says, squinting off into the distance like a ship's captain. "I have a love life." It's true that he goes without sleep entirely on the occasional Saturday night, and lets me bake the cinnamon rolls and open shop on Sunday mornings solo. But he's never brought anyone home and doesn't talk about anyone permanent so I worry.

"A satisfactory one?" I ask.

"Do you mean are you preventing me from having a boyfriend?"

"Yes."

"No." That's all he says, and he's still looking at Mount Hood. "Do you mind elaborating a little?" I ask him.

"I would but I see customers approaching so you'll have to just take me at my word," he says, and disappears inside, leaving me outside with my prints and my plans. My own personal photography gallery, wow. After a few minutes I hear the phone, and then I hear Joe calling my name. "Eleanor, for you!"

I know it can't be good news because I talked to Sarah just the other day and no one else is due to call me, so I sit for a minute gathering my photos and my thoughts and then I go inside. I always think it's going to be a bill collector or a death in the family when the phone rings. I could live very happily on letters alone.

It's Ash, calling five minutes after the rates get cheap in Texas. "Hi girl," he says, and the sound of his soft, scratchy voice is an amazing thing, powerfully evocative and stirring. My mouth gets immediately dry and my heart starts pounding. I put my hand on my stomach, just in case the baby needs reassurance about the adrenaline that's no doubt surging secondarily through its system.

"Oh, hi Ash," I say, as casually as I can manage it. "Let me change phones." And I hand the receiver to Joe Bloch, who's in the middle of an iced latte but sends me a reassuring wink anyway, and I run, not lightly, upstairs. "OK," I say, and Joe hangs up his end. "Hi," I say again to Ash, and then I just sit on the edge of my bed, staring down at the worn wood floor.

"Hi," he says, and then we both just sit there. Faintly, from downstairs, I can hear U2 on the CD player. "So, how are things?" he asks.

"Oh, fine."

"How's the baby?"

"Seems to be fine."

"Have you seen a doctor?"

"The midwife gave me the big thumbs up." He doesn't say anything and the silence worries me so I start babbling. "I feel great. I really like being pregnant, should have done it long ago. You're in a state of grace when you're expecting, you really are. People are so nice. In a way I dread going back to normal. Everyone smiles at you. I never realized before how hostile the default setting is for regular interaction. Now I'm getting spoiled."

"I'll pay for paternity testing," he says.

"You can keep your money," I say back. "I don't care anymore who the father is. I don't need your money and I don't need Ricky's money so you can forget it. Move on."

"I'm not moving on," he says. "Don't be dumb. You could be carrying my baby."

"Probably not," I answer.

"So suddenly you think that Ricky pulling out got you pregnant, when you weren't sure before. Why is that? What's changed? Were you lying about it, Eleanor?" I don't say anything but there's a huge pressure at the back of my head and I get a mental picture of me smacking him with a telephone right across the temple. "Well, were you lying?" he asks me again, and he's struggling to keep his voice reasonable.

"No," I tell him, quietly. What I want to say is "Fuck off, and don't ever call me again," but I know that I can't. My whole body seems clenched around the telephone. My palms get even more sweaty and I wonder, distantly, how this might be affecting things *in utero*, but I can't move to put my hand back on my belly.

"I don't know what to believe anymore," he says.

"Believe what you want," I say, and expel my breath. Holding the phone with my shoulder I wipe my hands on my shorts and touch my stomach.

"I can sue you for the test," he says then.

"Suit yourself," I answer. I kick off my Keds and my toes look very far away from the rest of my body, miniature red-tipped sausages at the end of my brown, swollen feet. Joe painted my toenails for me last week and the polish still looks good.

"I don't want us to fight," Ash says.

"Don't lie. You think that by fighting with me you'll break me down."

"Goddammit, Bean! I'm losing it here! I love you, I wanted you to have our baby, I wanted to be with you for the rest of my life, why did you fuck everything up?"

"You sure lose your enlightenment under pressure. I thought I could count on you through everything, but I guess this is too much, huh?"

Now it's his turn to sit in silence, and when he talks again his voice has changed. "No. This isn't too much. I'm sorry I attacked you. This is hard on me."

"Yeah." I lift my feet to stick them into the air from the fan and wish, futilely, that it was a little less humid in Portland. Or that we had a huge, powerful air conditioner that I didn't have to pay the electricity for. And Joe says it's been a dry summer! Just then the baby stirs, and I look into the mirror over my bed to see that I'm smiling.

"I still want us to be friends," Ash says.

"Yeah." But I have enough friends.

"Don't," he says then. "Don't push me away. Please don't."

"Oh God." I swing around and lie down on the bed, with my head at the wrong end and my feet resting up on the wall. Soon I won't be able to lie on my back but, for now, relief. "You know, Ash, my life would be much easier without you."

"Eleanor, listen to yourself. It would also be easier to get on welfare."

"Not anymore."

"It would be easier to watch TV all day. It would be easier to drink, it would be easier to lie, it would be easier to give up totally. Is that what you want, for everything to be easy?"

"Yes, that is what I want. That's exactly what I want. What's it to you?"

"Is that what you're going to do?"

Downstairs Joe Bloch must be DJ-ing his own U2 special because the music has just switched from the heartbreaking end of *Achtung Baby* to the rousing beginning of *War*. "No, goddammit," I answer him. "Of course that isn't what I'm going to do. But Ash, I like my life as it is now. Why would I want to fuck with that?"

"I'm not asking you to fuck with that. I'm just asking you to do the right thing and keep me in it. That's all."

"That's the right thing? How do you know that?" He doesn't say anything. "In what capacity do I keep you involved?" He could, I know, easily sue me for paternity testing and then, if he's the father, sue me afterwards for custody. Lawyers would slobber over this case. Would he go to that extreme?

"How about as a friend of the family?" he says, and I can tell by his tone of voice that he's rehearsed the phrase.

"A friend of the family. Uh-huh. Sort of like a godfather?" No answer from Ash. "I can't see myself calling you up when I've had a hard day minding the cafe and the photos aren't working and my feet are puffy to chitchat and commiserate, Ashur, I'm sorry."

"What exactly do you want out of me, Eleanor? First it was completely accepting the baby, no matter who the father is. Now it's nothing at all, no matter who the father is. I don't get it. I was so happy with you. What happened?"

"I was happy with you too." At least, I think I was.

"Then why did you leave?" he asks me, and my heart cracks in the very foundation of it. "Why don't you come back? You can stay at Colette's house. We can figure stuff out." The old daydreams resurface instantly, me and Ash and the little bambino, taking baths and traveling the world together, the three of us happy and safe and strong, a small and perfect family.

"If I'm such a terrible person who has done such an incomprehensible thing and betrayed you so badly, why do you want me around at all?"

"Because, Eleanor, you might be carrying my child."

"I see." I see so much that I don't want to open my eyes. "So if you could have access to my uterus, fully functioning on auxiliary equipment for the next four months, you wouldn't have to bother with me at all. Unless, of course, the baby turns out not to be yours, at which time you could phone me so that I could get it and my uterus back. Well, that puts everything into perspective for me."

He doesn't say anything. I take turns reaching down with one hand and then the other, rubbing my legs from ankle to thigh, squeezing blood back into the rest of my body. He still doesn't say anything. He knows me well enough to just wait.

"OK," I say finally. "I'll find out about paternity testing and I'll get it done when the baby's born and I'll send you the bill with the results, how's that?"

"I found out about it already."

"Yeah, so did I, actually." In San Francisco I looked it up in the phone book under Paternity and asked a million questions and the lady on the phone was so nice. She was trying to make me feel better. She said this kind of thing happens all the time.

"So you need my blood and Ricky's blood and the baby's blood," says Ash.

"Yeah." And about five hundred dollars.

"That means you have to tell him."

"Yeah. But I should anyway. It's only right. Goddammit." What a fun scene that'll be. I would love to call his house and just leave a message on the machine, "Hi, I'm pregnant, might be yours, bye." He's going to stroke out. He'll ask me why I didn't abort, why I didn't say anything sooner, what kind of compensation I'd be willing to sue him for. He'll probably accuse me of doing it on purpose.

"I'll come up there in January," says Ash, decisively. "January, right?"

"Right. But you can just send the DNA report, can't you, or have one lab send the blood express?"

"I don't know if two labs can do it. Anyway, I'll come up there," he repeats.

"Why? You think I'd lie about the results?"

"No, darn it, I just want to go with you. And I want to see the baby."

"Darn it? Dang it? Aw shucks? Where'd that come from?"

"Eleanor, you know, I love you."

"Yeah. It's oozing out your pores and making a puddle on the floor as we speak."

"You like being bitter," he tells me then. "It makes you feel good."

"So?"

"So nothing. Whatever works, girl. I'll keep in touch. And listen, call me if you need money, I mean it."

Buddy, I'd rather sell serum. "And what would I do, Ash, pay you back if the baby turns out to be Ricky's?" I ask this in a civil tone of voice but he's not fooled.

"Don't be such a bitch," he says, and hangs up. Ah true love.

I feel like drowning in music so I get up, feeling old again, and put Faure's Requiem loud on the little box in my room. Half-heartedly I call down from the staircase to see if Joe needs help, which he might but says he doesn't so I lie thankfully on the bed, put my feet back up on the wall, and try to cry. I can't, though, so I get some cream and rub it into my stomach. I should be swimming. Being suspended in water is supposed to be very good for a pregnant mother and the baby, but I guess I'll have to save that for my next child.

I'm lying on the bed, half-asleep, when the phone rings again near the end of the Requiem. "Mean Joe's," I answer it, getting up reluctantly to turn down the music, and I hear Mom on the other end hesitating. I don't know how I know it's her but I recognize the way she breathes in. "It's me, Mom," I tell her. "That's the name of the coffee shop. Hi."

"So my oldest daughter is finally pregnant."

"Yes, she is."

"Congratulations."

"Thank you."

"I'm sorry about Ash."

"Thanks. It wasn't very bright of me, was it?"

"No, not too clever. You're definitely my daughter. I haven't gone about my life in the most sensible way either, especially when I was young. But not only then, obviously." She pauses a moment but I don't interrupt. "There are so many things I regret," she says.

"Are there?"

"Yes, baby." There she goes with the endearments again. "If you asked me to explain myself, you know, I wouldn't know where to begin." And I know that she means the men and the drinking and all the rest of it, and particularly she means the confrontation over Ricky just before my birthday. I don't know what to say next and it seems as if she doesn't know what to say next, so we wait and the fan whirs and the Requiem ends on its painful, poignant, fading note.

"I'm sorry too, Mom."

"You have nothing to be sorry for," she says, which is funny because I have billions and billions of things. Then the conversation turns easily enough to my photography, and she actually seems interested in what's going on, so I keep talking and before long I've told her all sorts of things, including a short form of the conversation with Ash, and she's still acting just like a normal person, listening and being nice. She asks me about the pregnancy and we compare notes and I realize that this baby has given us something in common, finally, safe ground, Switzerland, a neutral place to talk.

Eventually she says, as the conversation winds down, "Well, don't misjudge Ricky. He might be thrilled about the baby and it's only right to tell him," and her voice isn't accusing.

"I'm going to," I say, "as soon as I'm finished with this call."

"All right." She takes that as her signal to get off the phone. "I'll arrange work to keep January flexible. I can come up and help you with the first few weeks. I know you think you won't need it but believe me you will. I would have given anything for my mother to be around when you were born and she was nowhere to be found, of course. I won't let the same thing happen to you and that's a promise. Even if you want me to." And she laughs.

"OK," I say, and just before she hangs up the phone I squeeze in, "Thanks, Mom."

I go to the bathroom, then check to see if Joe needs help. Again he says he doesn't but I do some dishes and make a few specialty coffees for the after-work espresso crowd and then, before the early diners come in, I make the salad dressing, wash and cut some greens, and write up the board for tonight's menu. Joe has the custard setting creamy in the fridge so I prepare a few strawberry cups ahead of time, cross my fingers for luck, and go call Ricky before I lose my nerve.

I left San Francisco with money in my pocket, food from Beatrice, a bun in the oven, serenity in my soul. It was eighteen hours to Portland and every hour was good. I thought I'd never be frantic again. Beatrice had packed me sweet oranges and dates and oatmeal cookies and I ate them, one after another as the train sped along, thinking that I had found the perfect foods and would never need anything else as long as I lived. I got diarrhea. I slept perfectly. I sat, dreaming for hours with my hands on my stomach, just like those women do who used to annoy me so much with their smug motherhood and inner absorption, and I actually thought I would always feel like that. I was wrong.

"Hi, it's Bean," I say, when he answers the phone. "I didn't expect you to be home."

"Then why did you call?"

"I was going to leave a message."

"Do you want me to hang up so you don't have to talk to me in person?"

"No. Well, yes, but don't."

"OK, I won't. What's the message? You made it pretty plain that you were in love, the real McCoy this time, and you didn't want anything to do with me again in this whole lifetime, and don't pretend you didn't. Now you're on the phone. My, how things do change."

"I'm five months pregnant," I say, ungently, "and you might be the father. I don't know. The day after I was with you at the hotel I was with Ash. You pulled out, do you remember?"

"I remember."

"He didn't. So I don't know. I can't find out until the baby's born and I'm due in January and I'll need a blood sample from you then to do paternity testing."

"You sure know how to wake a fellow up," he says. "Where are you? Are you all right? Is the baby all right? Do you need money?"

"This isn't what I expected," I say to him.

"You don't know as much as you think you know," he replies.

"I'm living with Joe Bloch in Portland, Oregon, and we're running a coffee shop," I tell him, with more than a little satisfaction. "His coffee shop, in fact. He's not sitting under a tree anymore but I still like him. I know how to cook a little bit now."

"Joe Bloch," he repeats, in wonderment. "Joe fucking Bloch, in Portland fucking Oregon. What happened to the massage guy?"

"He dumped me when he found out about you," I say. There's something about Ricky that makes the soft touch superfluous. He cracks up.

"I can't blame him, Bean. I'd have done the same thing."

"Yeah, but Ricky you're an asshole and he's not. I didn't think he'd do it."

"What, you thought he wouldn't mind?"

"No, I knew he'd mind, but I thought he'd forgive me. I thought he loved me enough to overcome the fatherhood question but I guess not."

"Welcome to the real world, dreamer," says Ricky, but not unsympathetically.

"I guess."

"What's that shit you're listening to?" he asks then.

"Schubert. One of the masses." I'm in that kind of mood.

"You're a freak," he says.

"So you'll help me out with the paternity thing come January?"

"Bean, I believe we have some things to discuss here. Don't be trying to squirm off the phone yet, you hear me? I'd be psyched if you had my baby, we'd have an awesome kid together, and maybe it would be a boy. Can't you find out the father before the baby's born?"

"No one'll do it," I say, "And even if they would, I wouldn't. It's dangerous. But maybe a fortune teller could tell us."

"Yeah, or some tea leaves or cat's blood or peacock feathers."

"Fuck off," I say, cheerily. I guess things are back with me and Ricky the way they used to be.

"Maybe you and I should get married, no matter who the father is."

"Maybe not," I say, utterly untempted. "I'm stupid but I'm not that goddamn stupid."

"I could provide a good life for you," he says.

"Nah. I'm through with guys who step out on me. One of them was enough for a lifetime. Thanks for the offer, though."

"Why don't you let me send you some money, then? Business has been good."

"Cars?'

"That too," he says, cagey because of the telephone, and because guys who sell drugs love being cagey.

"No babe," I tell him. "I'm doing all right. I'll call you if I get desperate, and I'll call you when I have the kid."

"Looking forward to it. Hasta lumbago."

"Bueno bye," I say, and go to the bathroom again. Then downstairs to help Joe with dinners and desserts. In between customers I tell him about the Twilight Zone that's taken over the small universe of my friends and family, further evidence that biology is stronger than modernity. "My theory is that being pregnant gives people a chance to rally round a good cause and be nice. It's built-in protection for the continuation of the species," I tell him.

"Or maybe it's you, letting people be nice to you for the first time," he says, putting together a hummous plate with quarters of organic tomato and thick slices of his own best rye, plenty for two people and only five bucks, typical of the way Joe does business.

"Maybe," I say, cutting a piece of three-layer carrot cake with cream cheese frosting for someone else. "In which case I should have taken money from the both of them."

"Yes, you should have," he says. "You don't have to make everything so hard."

After our small dinner rush is over Joe brings me a cup of Darjeeling, decaf, to where I'm sitting behind the register with my feet up on the telephone table. "Listen," he says, "I have another idea. I want you to think about it before you say no."

"OK," I say, and look thoughtfully at the deep-dish apple pie. There was a time when I wouldn't have been able to work in a place like this without gaining twenty pounds from grazing or losing ten from overcompensating. Now food is just food to me, something I have to have in small doses several times a day to be able to keep going. It's still nourishing, comforting, fun, all that, but it's not protection anymore from the world. What a relief.

"I think we should get married," he says, and my feet drop to the floor.

"You and me?" I ask.

"You and me," he says. "A friendly marriage of convenience, practical instead of romantic. I think we can really make it work. It'll be better for me, as far as insurance goes, to be married. Nobody wants to insure fags anymore. It'll also be better for the baby, and easier for you to get on a health plan. We won't have to clarify our situation for everyone who walks in. You know I've always wanted a family and I won't be able to have one in the normal way."

"But thirty-one is so young for a man! What if you fall in love? What if I meet someone I want to marry, or Ash changes his mind?"

"We'll cross that bridge then, won't we? Anyway, are you saying that you'd marry Ashur now if he wanted you to?" Joe asks, putting on the Chopin, our end-of-work music.

I sip my tea and think about it. "No."

"Is there anyone you'd tie the knot with?"

"Dolly Madison, if he weren't already married with about eighteen children and probably happy. Daniel Day Lewis, Nicolas Cage, the sax player for Morphine. Tom Waits, kind of. A doctor I once went to for the veins in my legs. I can think of more."

"So it's a yes, then?" asks Joe.

"I'll tell you what," I say, and take my time adding a packet of sugar to the last half of my tea. Joe waits while I put my cup down, reach into my pocket for a quarter, and smile at him. "Cut me a piece of chocolate cake and pour yourself a little Scotch. If you're brave enough, cowboy, I'll flip you for it."

The fortune-teller turned my hand up, ran her fingers over my palm, and began to laugh. It was August and I was in New York City with Travis and sweating in the back of a tiny apartment in Greenwich Village. Meeting in New York was my idea but I didn't know my way around the city well enough to be an effective guide so we ended up doing the usual touristy things and suffering in the heat. I said Boston was cooler and he said so was Albuquerque. I was very fat and Travis had to work hard not to look shocked when he saw me. I'd warned him over the phone but he wasn't prepared. Always my weight was going up and down, depending on my substance intake, but I'd never been two hundred and plus before. I knew it was ugly and I knew I was ugly, but I didn't care.

"I thought Stuart was going to come," said Travis. Travis didn't mind Stuart. Nobody minded Stuart. This was before the abortion and I didn't even mind him yet.

"His mom got sick," I explained. "He's back in Cincinnati visiting her, and when he comes home to Boston he's going to try and talk me into moving back there. I'm going to say no and we're going to fight, and then as soon as she feels better his mother is going to call and ask him to move home and the same thing will happen again."

"Sounds like you guys have it figured out," said Travis. "Are you happy with him?" He looked at me sideways, an invitation to talk about being so heavy, but I wasn't ready for that.

"Oh yeah," I said, without conviction. There was nothing wrong with Stuart, but I had other things on my mind altogether in those days.

"Let's find a nice cool place to sit and have a cup of coffee," suggested Travis. We were in the Village, a place I usually liked, but that weekend I had the feeling something bad was waiting for me around every corner and I was constantly braced against all possible situations. "You seem tense," he said.

"I'm sorry. I have this feeling of foreboding. It's probably the weather." There was some sort of storm brewing; the air was heavy and oppressive, and the heat was the malevolent kind. My sinuses hurt, like they do before the rain, and even my joints were stiff. I was irritable and hungry. I was always hungry but I had to hide it around people, even Travis.

"I could stand to get something to eat," he said, shameless the way thin people are about their appetites. We'd been nibbling all day. "You?"

"Yeah. Let's find some little place that can give us a good cup of coffee, decent cognac, and maybe some kind of sandwich that won't turn our stomachs." Instead we went to three separate places, one for each thing. At the coffee shop I had a piece of chocolate cake. At the bar I had onion rings, at the restaurant I ate lasagna, and for dessert more coffee and cheesecake.

Eating usually made me feel better but it wasn't working that night and Travis could tell. My stomach was full, but something else in the region of my solar plexus still felt empty and scared. He suggested that we just walk around and I acquiesced. He did most of the talking but I was loosening up slightly after an hour or so. At around 11:30 we came across a sign advertising palm reading and Travis wanted to do it.

Anna didn't look like a fortune teller to me. She looked like somebody's mother who was having problems putting healthy food on the table. She glanced at the two of us and seemed to see a lot. "You first," she said to Travis in a bored voice, and barely looked at his hand. "You'll end up married to a nice girl," she said, and Travis laughed.

"I don't think so."

"Yes," she said. "I know why you don't think so, but you will. Your mother will live for a long, long time. You're very close to your mother, yes?"

"Yes." Travis didn't like talking about his mother to this stranger but he answered truthfully.

"Your father loves you more than you know," she said. "You should name your first daughter after your grandmother on his side. You'll make a lot of money but you won't realize your artistic side. You'll be happy. Now you," and she pointed at me.

"That's all?" asked Travis.

"For fifteen dollars that's all."

Travis looked at me and I looked at him and then I shrugged, very small. We didn't like her and didn't think she was very good so he got up and let me go next.

When she laughed at my hand I said, belligerently, "What?"

"You're going to have a baby with a man like him," she said, pointing her shoulder at Travis.

"What do you mean like him?"

"You're going to have a baby with a man who likes men," she said, and for the first time looked directly at me. "And the baby will have many fathers." Her eyes were the same kind of eyes as mine, deep-set and dark, and there was intelligence shining there clearly, and experience also. She didn't look so much like the mother of six yelping children anymore, she looked like a fortune teller is supposed to look. I realized that she was beautiful, the kind of beauty that creeps up on you and when you finally see it you wonder how you could possibly have missed it the first time around.

"Am I ever going to be an artist?" I asked her.

"Yes. You will go on many journeys. You just lost your father?"

"No. Oh. My stepfather, last year." And, the thing that always happened, my eyes filling at the mention of Hank. I was fine until I talked about him.

"You and your mother and your sister are close?"

"No."

"You will be very close," she promised. "As close as you want. Closer," and she started laughing again. "Two abortions," she said, then stopped laughing.

"No, one," I corrected her, but she shook her head.

"Two," she said. "The hand doesn't lie. Your dark blood is drawn to dark blood. You will be torn always between men and pictures. Thirty dollars."

Travis and I each gave her fifteen dollars and I left feeling as if I'd been genuinely touched by the supernatural.

"What a waste of money," said Travis.

"You're kidding."

"Oh come on, Bean. They're just very good at reading people and saying things that are going to apply to most of us."

"Uh-huh."

Travis went on, pointing out all the ways she could have known what she knew, and all the different ways her statements could have been interpreted as being meaningful by any person walking through the door, and he wound up by saying we should open up our own fortune telling enterprise, that thirty dollars for ten minutes wasn't bad. What I noticed is that when we left she looked even more exhausted than when we came, but I didn't say so.

"Did you think she was beautiful?" I asked him.

"That old hag? I'm not letting you go to any more of them," he said. My feeling of imminent disaster was gone, so I just shrugged. I didn't care what we did.

"Two abortions?" I asked, after a while. "I fucking hope not."

"God it's hot," he said.

"Is it? I feel all right. Want another drink?"

We went back to the hotel with a bottle of Scotch and got room service to bring us a cheese plate. Then we turned off the lights and sat, drinking quietly, looking out over the city. Travis said, "Sometimes I feel as if everything's going to be fine."

"Me too," I answered. We could hear the traffic filtering into the room even as high up as we were and I liked it. It was a nice night.